OXFO

THE SAUP
M.

THE SAUPTIKAPARVAN is the tenth book of the great Indian epic, the *Mahābhārata*; it provides a conflux of the entire work's narrative and mythic streams in an account of the cataclysmic events that mark the end of the war.

Attributed to the mythical seer Vyāsa, the Sanskrit *Mahābhārata* acquired its present encyclopaedic form over a period of perhaps 900 years (*c*.500 BCE to 400 CE) as part of a fluid tradition of oral composition on the Indian subcontinent. Even in its present form, however, the epic undoubtedly contains and reflects much earlier material, some of it perhaps Indo-European in origin. Over the centuries it has been widely recast in Indian vernacular languages, and retold in countless dramatic performances, visual representations, and music. In this way it has come to have culturally talismanic significance—a status which is reflected in its assessment of itself: 'What is here may be found elsewhere, what is not here is nowhere at all.'

W. J. JOHNSON was educated at the University of Sussex and Wolfson College, Oxford. He is now Senior Lecturer in Religious Studies at the University of Wales, Cardiff. His publications include a new translation of *The Bhagavad Gita* (Oxford, 1994) for Oxford World's Classics, and *Harmless Souls* (Delhi, 1995), a study of karma and religious change in early Jainism.

OXFORD WORLD'S CLASSICS

For over 100 years Oxford World's Classics have brought readers closer to the world's great literature. Now with over 700 titles—from the 4,000-year-old myths of Mesopotamia to the twentieth century's greatest novels—the series makes available lesser-known as well as celebrated writing.

The pocket-sized hardbacks of the early years contained introductions by Virginia Woolf, T. S. Eliot, Graham Greene, and other literary figures which enriched the experience of reading. Today the series is recognized for its fine scholarship and reliability in texts that span world literature, drama and poetry, religion, philosophy and politics. Each edition includes perceptive commentary and essential background information to meet the changing needs of readers.

OXFORD WORLD'S CLASSICS

The Sauptikaparvan of the Mahābhārata

The Massacre at Night

Translated with an Introduction and Notes by
W. J. JOHNSON

Oxford New York
OXFORD UNIVERSITY PRESS
1998

Oxford University Press, Great Clarendon Street, Oxford OX2 6DP
Oxford New York
Athens Auckland Bangkok Bogotá Buenos Aires Calcutta
Cape Town Chennai Dar es Salaam Delhi Florence Hong Kong Istanbul
Karachi Kuala Lumpur Madrid Melbourne Mexico City Mumbai
Nairobi Paris São Paulo Singapore Taipei Tokyo Toronto Warsaw
and associated companies in Berlin Ibadan

Oxford is a registered trade mark of Oxford University Press

First published as an Oxford World's Classics paperback 1998

British Library Cataloguing in Publication Data
Data available

Library of Congress Cataloging in Publication Data
Mahābhārata. Sauptikaparvan. English
The Sauptikaparvan of the Mahābhārata : the massacre at night/ translated with an introduction and notes by W. J. Johnson.
(Oxford world's classics)
I. Johnson, W. J. II. Title. III. Series : Oxford world's classics (Oxford University Press)
BL1138.242.S28E5 1998 294.5'92304521—dc21 98-15912
ISBN 0-19-282361-2

3

Typeset by Pure Tech India Ltd., Pondicherry
Printed in Great Britain by
Clays Ltd, St Ives plc

For my mother
and her grandsons Jonathan and Patrick

CONTENTS

INTRODUCTION

The *Mahābhārata*

For the non-specialist western reader the *Mahābhārata* can resemble a vast but distant mountain range obscured by clouds. Just as many people are able to identify only Everest among the Himalayan peaks, so, in the *Mahābhārata* range, perhaps only the *Bhagavadgītā* stands out, usually with little recognition that it is rooted in something much larger, more demanding, and yet no less rewarding to explore. For even the most tentative approach uncovers in the text many, if not all, of those key assumptions, tensions, and questions—mythological, theological, and soteriological—that converged, precisely during the period of the *Mahābhārata*'s crystallization, to form the great and variegated religious culture subsequently labelled 'Hinduism'. Beneath and beyond this, according to some, the *Mahābhārata* represents one particular expression of a common Indo-European way of viewing and shaping human experience. Common, that is, to those who express and have expressed themselves in the languages, past and present, of the Indo-European family—languages as globally scattered as ancient Sanskrit and its descendants, modern English and its predecessors, and the large majority of contemporary European languages. Again, perhaps, the mountain simile applies: from some perspectives the *Mahābhārata* seems distant, from others very close.

Once properly aware of the *Mahābhārata*, however, it would be an act of cultural and historical astigmatism to continue to ignore it, for it is a 'world's classic' in an even wider sense than those suggested above, an epic, and a body of mythological material as significant for our self-understanding as the works of Homer and the Greek dramatists (with which it is often compared), the Bible, the Qur'ān, or, more recently, the plays of Shakespeare. It is this universal quality that prompted a recent western theatrical adaptation to characterize it as 'the poetical history of mankind'.[1] Indeed, like Shakespeare, but with an even wider compass, the *Mahābhārata* has acquired, in India and beyond, an iconic and culturally talismanic significance that is

[1] Jean-Claude Carrière, *The Mahabharata: A Play Based upon the Indian Classical Epic*, trans. Peter Brook (London: Methuen, 1987), 3.

reflected in its assessment of itself: 'What is here may be found elsewhere, what is not here is nowhere at all.'

It would, nevertheless, be naive to assume that what *is* there is immediately understandable without some orientation in the *Mahābhārata*'s very specific religious and cultural context, and the circumstances of its composition. What follows, therefore, serves first as a general introduction to the formation, nature, and significance of the *Mahābhārata* as a whole, and second as a more specific consideration of its short but, in narrative terms, crucial tenth book, the *Sauptikaparvan*, translated here as 'The Massacre at Night'.

The significance of the *Mahābhārata* in Indian religious culture

The *Mahābhārata* is often called an 'epic' or 'epic poem' by western scholars. What they are usually referring to is a text of approximately 100,000 verses in the sacred classical language of India, Sanskrit.[2] This is divided into eighteen 'books' of unequal length (each with various subsections), of which the *Sauptikaparvan* is Book 10 (*parvan* means 'section', 'division', or 'book'). According to a traditional Indian scheme of classifying texts, the *Mahābhārata* is *itihāsa*, a term that suggests 'history' while making no distinction between such 'history' and what many educated modern readers would regard as 'myth', or 'legend'. The other great Indian 'epic', the slightly later and more self-consciously structured and poetic *Rāmāyaṇa*, is sometimes similarly classified, and similarly 'mythological' in content. While the texts of both these 'epics' have always been, and continue to be, interpreted on a number of different levels, it would be idle to pretend that the historical genuineness of the events they depict is not taken for granted by many Hindus.[3] Most

[2] On the verse forms, see 'A Note on the Sanskrit Text, its Translation, and its Metre', below. One hundred thousand verses produces 400,000 lines of text, making the *Mahābhārata* more than eight times the length of the *Iliad* and *Odyssey* together.

[3] It is tempting to make a comparison in this respect with the literalism with which some Christians regard biblical events such as the flood, and the consequent anxiety of the more self-conscious, in both cases, to provide archaeological proof for such claims. The comparison would be misleading, however. Claims about the historicity of the contents of the *Mahābhārata* have more to do with national identity, and even nationalism, than the theological need for an authoritative text to be accurate about the way things were (and will be). Indeed, the *Mahābhārata* is often characterized as 'India's national epic', or, more conservatively, 'Hindu India's national epic'—see, for instance, Alf Hiltebeitel's entry on 'Mahābhārata' in *The Encyclopedia of Religions* (New York: Macmillan, 1987).

scholars, however, would probably agree that we actually know little or nothing about the historicity of these stories (i.e. have no evidence for it), and pass on—some more regretfully than others—to different forms of analysis.

Technically, the *itihāsa* texts are not classed as revelation, for according to Brahminical orthodoxy[4] it is only Vedic recitation and commentary (the Veda itself) that is uncreated, beginningless, and self-authenticating. Nevertheless, because the Vedic material is the private religious and ritual property of the brahmins, and comes to be used and interpreted within an essentially ritual framework (although much of it is broadly mythological), the authority of the epics is not necessarily perceived as subsidiary or subordinate to it in practice. The effectively autonomous authority of the best-known part of the *Mahābhārata*, the *Bhagavadgītā*, is merely the most obvious example of the gap between theoretical and actual status. Indeed, the *Mahābhārata* calls itself the 'fifth Veda',[5] despite being 'authored' by Vyāsa, and despite the fact that technically it belongs to (indeed, effectively inaugurates) that 'tradition', or *smṛti*,[6] which is both distinguished from Vedic *śruti*,[7] and ultimately dependent upon it for its authority. In other words, while the Veda constitutes a notional absolute authority, its actual, line-by-line contents have never been known to more than a few highly trained brahmins. Nests of stories concerning heroes and heroines, the exemplary tales of devotional Hinduism, and 'mythic' events involving gods and anti-gods (including the great classical deities Viṣṇu and Śiva), on the other hand, have always been accessible to all classes in a wide variety of forms, and have the authority of tradition in the widest sense. This does not mean, of course, that much of this material has not itself been derived and developed from broadly Vedic sources.

It is important at this point to realize that, while the Sanskrit *Mahābhārata* (part of which is translated and commented upon here)

[4] The brahmins are the hereditary priestly class who are the arbiters of correct religious and therefore social behaviour (see below). Their authority is derived from their knowledge of and access to the Veda, an orally transmitted collection of hymns, ritual instructions, and religious teachings in Sanskrit. This material was first assembled in three Vedas, with a fourth added subsequently. The term 'Veda', however, is also applied to a wider range of material, including the *Upaniṣads*.

[5] See, for instance, *Mahābhārata* 1. 57. 74 f.

[6] Literally, 'what has been remembered'.

[7] Literally, 'what has been heard' by the Vedic seers.

represents the earliest available version of the text, the story it tells has been widely recast in Indian vernacular languages, and retold in countless dramatic performances, visual representations, and music. Perhaps the greatest work of Sanskrit dramatic literature, Kālidāsa's *The Recognition of Śakuntalā* (*Abhijñānaśākuntalam*), is based on a short episode in the *Mahābhārata*, while, at the other end of the cultural spectrum, Indian children's comics feature Arjuna and Kṛṣṇa as readily as their western equivalents reproduce football heroes and Batman. The celebrated Indian television serialization of the *Mahābhārata* in Hindi, and Peter Brook's international stage and video versions, are merely the most recent manifestations of this process. As a noted scholar of the epic, Alf Hiltebeitel, remarks, the *Mahābhārata* is 'an ongoing fluid tradition, one sustained in both Sanskritic and vernacular forms, and—in what does not always amount to the same thing—in classical and folk forms as well'.[8] Indeed, its popularity, in a variety of guises and levels, and the force with which many of its episodes and characters have retained their dramatic, religious, and cultural vitality over 2,000 years or more, are hard to overestimate.

The origins, composition, and transmission of the Sanskrit *Mahābhārata*

The *Mahābhārata* derives its name from the fact that its central narrative deals with the conflict between the descendants of a probably mythical, and certainly prototypical, ruler, Bharata. It is 'the great (*mahā*) [story] of the descendants of Bharata (*bhārata*)'. The name, however, is more than simply descriptive: modern India, as any postage stamp attests, calls itself 'Bhārata' ('[the land of] the descendants of Bharata'), and this reflects an ancient perception that Bharata was, as one scholar puts it, 'somehow the forerunner of all Indian culture'.[9] Its name therefore conveys to its audience the idea that the *Mahābhārata* is a text that tells them about their origins and significant past. Moreover, in dramatizing the inherent tension between the efforts and aspirations of individuals, and the wider concerns of universal order, it provides a variety of models for

[8] Alf Hiltebeitel, *The Cult of Draupadī. Mythologies: From Gingee to Kurukṣetra*, i (Chicago: University of Chicago Press, 1988), pp. xx–xxi.

[9] Ruth C. Katz, *Arjuna in the Mahabharata: Where Krishna Is, There Is Victory* (Columbia: University of South Carolina Press, 1989), 3.

human behaviour. Like most pre-modern 'histories', therefore, part of its task is to legitimize the present (whenever that happens to be). However, in the case of the *Mahābhārata* the interpretation of that 'history' is vastly complicated, not only by the fact that it contains so much material, both narrative and didactic (some of which may date, even in its present form, to *c*.900 BCE or earlier), but also because that material has apparently been gathered together, edited, added to, and re-edited over a period of perhaps 900 years (*c*.500 BCE to 400 CE).[10] This chronology, and long process of composition, at least provides an explanation for the occurrence of the apparent contradictions and inconsistencies that arise at all levels of the text. It is precisely this encyclopaedic or cornucopian quality that has led one modern translator to characterize the *Mahābhārata* as a 'library' rather than a single literary work.[11]

If the clear implication of this is that the *Mahābhārata* as we now have it could not possibly be the work of an individual, the text itself (and thus Indian tradition), nevertheless, identifies the brahmin *ṛṣi* (sage or seer) Kṛṣṇa Dvaipāyana,[12] known as Vyāsa, as its composer. But since the compilation of other ancient texts, including the uncreated Vedas, is also attributed to him, and since he appears as an apparently immortal character in his own narrative (in Chapters 13 to 16 of the *Sauptikaparvan*, for instance), his authorship is probably intended to be symbolic.[13] The fact that the 'author' may not be the individual named in the text does not, however, necessarily mean that the text was never subject to an individual shaping intelligence. Indeed, many Indian scholars are unhappy with the near consensus view of recent western scholarship (following the pioneering work of E. W. Hopkins[14]) that the text has neither a single composer nor an individual editor, since they see this both as an inappropriate fracturing of the text's organic unity, and as a barrier in itself to discerning such unity. They find a partial ally in the great French scholar Madeleine Biardeau, who has argued for the single

[10] This, it should be noted, is the consensus view on the dating of the *Mahābhārata* as we have it now.

[11] J. A. B. van Buitenen, *The Mahābhārata* (Chicago: University of Chicago Press, 1973–8), i: *The Book of the Beginning*, p. xxv.

[12] Not to be confused with the god Kṛṣṇa, otherwise known as Kṛṣṇa Vāsudeva.

[13] See van Buitenen, *The Mahābhārata*, i, p. xxiii.

[14] E. W. Hopkins, *The Great Epic of India: Its Character and Origin*; (1901; Calcutta: Punthi Pustak, 1969); for a summary of his views, see ch. 6.

editorship of a 'brahmin of genius',[15] on the basis that the didactic and narrative portions of the epic are integrated and complementary, one consciously illustrating the other in order to produce a work of instruction for a king. Whatever the case (and Biardeau's claim here seems overstated), it is not essential to regard the text as a totally or consciously unified work in order to distinguish many of its major themes and preoccupations, or even to discern 'a central guiding force'.[16] Part of the *Mahābhārata*'s fascination lies in the way in which its juxtaposition of seemingly incompatible views and 'solutions', and its unexpected, although not necessarily illogical, interpolations, reveal a process of historical development and change. Indeed, it is often precisely the attempt to include or reconcile competing views in some all-encompassing, 'changeless' unity that reveals most vividly the process of change. If we ask, therefore, what the 'authorship' of Vyāsa is symbolic *of*, an answer which may achieve some measure of approval from both camps is that he is 'the symbolic representative of all the epic poets . . . who perceived correspondences between the epic they were composing and the myths and rituals of their heritage'.[17]

So far, I have considered the general nature of the text—its unity or otherwise—but not the related although separable question of the way in which it may have evolved. What follows is a short summary of the work of a number of scholars on this question; for a more detailed exegesis, I refer the reader to the works mentioned in the footnotes.[18]

This account assumes that the text of the *Mahābhārata* has evolved over a long period of time. As with all evolutionary patterns,

[15] In, for instance, her introduction to Jean-Michel Péterfalvi's translation: *Le Mahābhārata* (Paris: Flammarion, 1985–6), i. 27—'un seul brahmane de génie'.

[16] Katz, *Arjuna in the Mahabharata*, 10.

[17] Bruce M. Sullivan, *Kṛṣṇa Dvaipāyana Vyāsa and the Mahābhārata: A New Interpretation* (Leiden: Brill, 1990), 24, summarizing Alf Hiltebeitel, *The Ritual of Battle: Krishna in the Mahābhārata* (1976; Delhi: Sri Satguru Publications, 1991), 359.

[18] My principal sources have been: John D. Smith, 'Old Indian: The Two Sanskrit Epics', in A. T. Hatto (ed.), *Traditions of Heroic and Epic Poetry*, i: *The Traditions* (London: The Humanities Research Association, 1980); Mary Carroll Smith, *The Warrior Code of India's Sacred Song* (New York: Garland Publishing, 1992); the introduction to Katz, *Arjuna in the Mahabharata*; and the introduction to van Buitenen, *The Mahābhārata*, i. To avoid cluttering the text with even more notes, I have not given precise references to these works throughout. It is probably therefore necessary to record that, while my debt to them is very substantial, I alone am responsible for the the truncation, juxtaposition, and reformulation of their ideas here.

the basic driving force must have been adaptive; that is to say, the text in any particular shape and at any particular time was the product of the needs of certain groups and communities. With the advent of written texts (see below), it was at least possible for the history of those needs, even if they were no longer felt, to be recorded (i.e. become fossilized), although, as we have seen, the *Mahābhārata* has continued to evolve in various ways (and not necessarily in the form of written texts) up to the present. All adaptations, however, have unintended consequences, notably in the form of incompatibilities and contradictions; and from our point of view it is often impossible to say what is the result of adaptation, and what is an 'unintended' consequence. Nevertheless, the broad influence or concerns of certain dominant groups in Indian society, and their attempts to 'take over' the text, or parts of it, are not difficult to detect in much of the *Mahābhārata*.[19] It is for this reason that textual scholars have been able to offer reconstructions of the stages through which the text has evolved.

For some time it has been noted that there are close analogies between the basic narrative of the *Mahābhārata* and Persian, Scandinavian, and other Indo-European epic traditions. This has led to speculation that the Indo-Āryans, those early Sanskrit-speaking peoples, who are presumed, by most scholars, to have entered northern India sometime during the second millennium BCE, brought with them the core stories of some kind of Indo-European heroic epic. Given this possibility, Alf Hiltebeitel has written of the *Mahābhārata* that: 'Its story, at least in some of its basic contours and episodes, may thus be very old. Indeed, it may be our best preserved "record" of the Indo-Europeans' heroic age.'[20]

[19] To take the present instance (the *Sauptikaparvan*), Ruth Katz has suggested that, in the epic as we now have it, this episode 'is a tale moulded by the Pancharatrins to illustrate their own doctrine symbolically' (*Arjuna in the Mahabharata*, 253). (The Pancharatra [Pāñcarātra] is a Viṣṇu worshipping tradition, the earliest evidence for which is in the *Mahābhārata* itself.) For a further account of this, see Ruth Katz, 'The *Sauptika* Episode in the Structure of the *Mahābhārata*', *Journal of South Asian Literature*, 20 (1985), 109–24.

[20] Hiltebeitel, *The Ritual of Battle*, 59. It is this view concerning the *Mahābhārata*, and the related one of Georges Dumézil—that it is the Indian expression of a deep-seated Indo-European way of structuring the world—which leads to the conclusion that it is an entirely mythic composition. For an extended and highly influential analysis of the *Mahābhārata* from the 'mythic' perspective, see Georges Dumézil, *Mythe et épopée*, i: *L'Idéologie des trois fonctions dans les épopées des peuples indo-européens* (Paris: Gallimard, 1968), 33–257.

The Indo-Āryans brought with them, or developed, not just the Sanskrit language and its orally preserved religious texts, the Vedas (the earliest of which is the collection of hymns known as the *Ṛg Veda*), but also a social structure based on hierarchy and (in theory, at least) complementarity of function. At the top of this hierarchy were, on the one hand, the hereditary guardians of the Vedic and priestly tradition, the brahmins, and, on the other, the practitioners of the *kṣatriya* tradition, the warriors and princes. The interplay between these two classes, and subgroups within them, comes to dominate much of social and political life. Certainly, members of these sometimes antagonistic classes, brahmin and *kṣatriya*, play the key roles in the *Mahābhārata* as we have it.

If the Veda was the 'property' of the brahmins, then the earliest detectable version of the epic[21] was the 'property' of the warriors, or *kṣatriyas*. Like the Veda it was an oral composition, but purely heroic in character, dealing with legendary warrior heroes, and concerned with the warrior *dharma*, or code of conduct, and problems arising from its violation. Mary Carroll Smith has argued that a relatively small number of verses in a non-regular form of the Vedic *triṣṭubh* metre,[22] which she has excised from the current text of the *Mahābhārata*, constitute this 'warrior kernel'—a kernel that became, through many transformations and accretions, the text we have today. (Or, to put it the other way round, this distinctive narrative and linguistic core represents an 'archaic, Aryan, warrior song imbedded in the vast brahmanical or priestly redaction of the *Mahābhārata*'.[23] It would, of course, betray a basic misunderstanding of the nature of the text to equate such an excised core or kernel to some hypothetical 'real' or 'true' epic.)

Although this 'original' heroic epic was warrior 'property', it appears to have been composed and recited for the *kṣatriyas*, with musical accompaniment, by the *sūtas*—members of a class, or caste, of bards, who, according to the *Mahābhārata* itself, also acted as charioteers, and so were well placed, as technically inviolable observers, to 'report' battles.[24] These core verses, like the Veda, were

[21] i.e. a version deduced by scholars: no such text exists in its own right.

[22] See 'A Note on the Sanskrit Text, its Translation, and its Metre' (below), for a discussion of metre in the *Mahābhārata*.

[23] Smith, *The Warrior Code of India's Sacred Song*, p. xii.

[24] *Sūtas* are said to have been the issue of mixed brahmin and *kṣatriya* unions—for a discussion, see Biardeau in the introduction to Péterfalvi's translation: *Le Mahābhārata*,

memorized (i.e. 'fixed') at an early time; subsequently a more fluid, but likewise orally transmitted, body of additional material was accrued, in its most basic form acting as a commentary on, and expansion of, the fixed core. It is this additional material, recognizable from its use of different kinds of metre (predominantly *śloka*), and only perhaps 'fixed' when written down in the literary form that initiates the manuscript tradition, that makes up 95 per cent of the text as we now have it.

The sequence of events that, between its oral composition and literary redaction, caused the text of the *Mahābhārata* to undergo 'a massive expansion which not merely at least quadrupled its size, but also radically altered its character',[25] may be impossible to trace with any certainty. Some initial editing possibly took place in the environment of a royal court; at some stage the text was 'brahminized', and then, or at another time, filled (almost indiscriminately) with didactic and devotional material; and there was probably considerable interaction between written and oral versions before anything like a 'settled' text appeared.[26] What we do know, however, is that, 'By the end of the process, the text had, so to speak, changed hands: it was now the "property" of the Brāhmaṇs' (brahmins).[27]

At this point in its evolution, the Sanskrit *Mahābhārata*, in the form of numerous regional variations, had spread throughout India, initiating a process that, alongside the continuing oral traditions, crystallized into various related manuscript traditions, or recensions. The oldest versions of the epic to survive as physical objects (i.e. as manuscripts) all date from the medieval period, after the creation of the two major extant recensions: the northern and the southern, each of which is made up of versions written in a number of different scripts.[28]

i. 3 f. Saṃjaya, the blind king Dhṛtarāṣṭra's charioteer, who recites the first part of the events of the *Sauptikaparvan* to him, is a *sūta*.

[25] Smith, 'Old Indian: The Two Sanskrit Epics', 50.

[26] For a picture of the evolution of the *Mahābhārata* that attempts to reconcile traditional Indian views with those of western scholarship, see Katz, *Arjuna in the Mahabharata*, 11 ff.

[27] Smith, 'Old Indian: The Two Sanskrit Epics', 50.

[28] As mentioned earlier, the *Mahābhārata* also has a long history in various vernacular (non-Sanskritic) forms, which may be drawing on sources and material that are non-Āryan in origin (i.e. anything but Sanskritic or Brahminical). Such material may, of course, have found its way into the Sanskrit tradition as well. See, for instance, Alf Hiltebeitel on the influence of south Indian goddess myths and rituals, in *The Cult of Draupadī*, i.

The Poona Critical Edition, upon which the present translation is based, is the result of the collation of a large number of manuscripts from both recensions, which the editors concluded all originated from some single source text of about the sixth century CE. Their aim, therefore, was not to reconstruct some 'Ur-*Mahābhārata*', but to re-create what they considered to be the 'ancestor' of all the manuscripts they examined and collated.[29]

Narration and Narrators (the Text's Own Account)

Mahābhārata

The *Mahābhārata* is said to have been composed by Vyāsa (Kṛṣṇa Dvaipāyana), who is himself an essential character in the story. At his bidding, his pupil Vaiśaṃpāyana recites it for the first time to Janamejaya, a direct descendant of the Pāṇḍavas (and therefore of Vyāsa himself), at his snake sacrifice.[30] This is the core narrative dialogue of the text. Subsumed within it is Saṃjaya's report of the battle (Books 6–10) to the blind king Dhṛtarāṣṭra. At the snake sacrifice it is heard by the bard Ugraśravas, who repeats it to the Bhṛgu brahmin Śaunaka and his colleagues, who are engaged in a twelve-year sacrificial session in the Naimiṣa forest.

The Massacre at Night (*Sauptikaparvan*)

Chapter 1 opens with King Dhṛtarāṣṭra's mixed-caste (*sūta*) driver Saṃjaya continuing his description of the battle and its aftermath for the benefit of his blind master. Saṃjaya took over most of the immediate narration from Vaiśaṃpāyana in Book 6 (*Bhīṣmaparvan*),[31] when Vyāsa granted him the divine sight necessary to follow the events of the war (including the *Bhagavadgītā*). At the end of Chapter 9 of the *Sauptikaparvan* that gift is withdrawn and the narrative reverts to Vaiśaṃpāyana, who once again addresses Janamejaya.[32]

[29] See V. S. Sukthankar, 'Prolegomena', in *The Mahābhārata*, Critical Edition, ed. V. S. Sukthankar *et al.* (Poona: Bhandarkar Oriental Research Institute, 1933–72), i: *Ādi Parvan*, pp. cii–ciii.

[30] He is avenging the death of his father Parikṣit, who was killed by a snake.

[31] After a kind of 'trial-run', at Dhṛtarāṣṭra's request, at the end of Book 5: 'Preparations' (*Udyogaparvan*).

[32] There have, in fact, been occasional interventions from this layer of the narrative throughout Saṃjaya's story. For more on Saṃjaya, see the note on 9. 57–9.

The *Sauptikaparvan* in the *Mahābhārata*

Given the nature of the *Mahābhārata*, its lengthy evolution, and library-like construction, it would be a task beyond a short introduction to attempt a thematic summary of its contents (a condensed narrative summary is given in the Appendix). What follows is not, therefore, an attempt to say what the *Mahābhārata* in general 'is about'; rather it tries to provide pointers to some of the major epic themes and preoccupations where these are raised in the *Sauptikaparvan*. Nevertheless, because at some levels this short book marks the culmination of the epic narrative, the questions it raises, and sometimes answers, are to a significant extent those crucial to the epic as a whole. This may, therefore, serve as a selective introduction to some of the *Mahābhārata*'s major preoccupations, and some of the approaches taken to it in recent scholarship.

Fate

Aśvatthāman's despair in the face of ineluctable fate (which, through the Pāṇḍavas, has destroyed the Kaurava army and its leaders), indeed, his attack of explicit 'fatalism', and Kṛpa's reply,[33] are merely further additions to a debate about the relationship between fate and individual human action which continues throughout the entire epic. The Sanskrit term translated here as 'fate' is *daiva*—literally, 'what comes from the gods'. *Daiva* is derived from *deva*, the term used to refer to the Vedic gods. In the Vedic hymns these are both manifestations and counterparts of natural entities and cosmic powers—Agni, for instance is both fire and the god of fire—but they also exhibit human characteristics. In developed Brahminical religion, the *devas* are the recipients of sacrifices made by human beings, giving various things in return. This distinguishes them from the *asuras* or anti-gods, who do not accept offerings and do not give help. The *devas* are never absent from Indian myths and stories, but their cosmic roles are taken over and developed by the great gods ('God') of sectarian Hinduism, Viṣṇu (Kṛṣṇa) and Śiva. Crucially for the history of Indian religions, devotion to these gods, or God, becomes a major instrument of salvation or liberation.[34]

33 *Sauptikaparvan* 1. 56–65, and Ch. 2.

34 For more details see the general accounts of Hinduism listed in the Select Bibliography.

Viṣṇu and Śiva (or Rudra, to give him his Vedic name) appear as minor deities in the Vedic pantheon, but in the *Mahābhārata* as we have it Viṣṇu (Kṛṣṇa) in particular, and to a lesser extent Śiva, are the pre-eminent divine powers. The five Pāṇḍava brothers, and others, are partial incarnations, 'sons' of various Vedic deities, and share in or exhibit some of their 'divine' characteristics: Yudhiṣṭhira is, at some level, Dharma; Arjuna 'is' the warrior king Indra. However, in the *Mahābhārata, daiva* or fate—'what comes from the gods'—refers essentially to cosmic matters. That is to say, it refers to some overall cosmic plan, which is at best opaque to human beings, even those with divine parents. It is therefore not surprising to find that Kṛṣṇa's will (God's will) and fate become virtually indistinguishable as the narrative core of the *Mahābhārata* comes to its conclusion in the *Sauptikaparvan*. For Kṛṣṇa-Viṣṇu has not only taken over the collective cosmic powers of the Vedic gods, but he also intervenes in human affairs in a personal way to guarantee cosmic outcomes (see the section on '*Dharma*', below).

In the *Mahābhārata*, it is therefore not a dead metaphor to say that something was or is fated—that it comes from the gods—for it provides a different level of explanation from that given by the twentieth-century man or woman who shrugs their shoulders and says, 'It's in the lap of the gods.' While the latter is essentially a way of indicating that we cannot control or predict what might happen, the former is an avowal that there is a real and active cosmic power that shapes or blocks the results of human actions, even when the actors have willed or expected something else. In other words, the plans and actions of individuals, separately and collectively, are subordinate to an all-encompassing cosmic or universal plan. To a greater or lesser extent, and at some times and not others, human beings may recognize the existence of that plan, but they cannot alter it. As the blind king Dhṛtarāṣṭra says, realizing with hindsight the inevitability of his son Duryodhana's defeat: 'fate cannot be overruled by men.'[35]

This does not mean that humans are constrained in all their actions, simply that fate—'the will of the gods'—demands certain outcomes. Some actions accord with fate while others do not: Aśvatthāman realizes (again with hindsight) that the Pāṇḍava

[35] *Sauptikaparvan* I. 9.

victory was 'fated' and the entire Kaurava effort was therefore useless.[36] His uncle Kṛpa argues for the necessity of human effort on the grounds that you cannot know what is fated in advance, but you do know that inaction will get you nowhere at all. True, you may be completely blocked by fate in the end, but that would be exceptional; according to Kṛpa most actions fail, not through the intervention of fate, but through lack of effort.[37]

Sensible as it may seem in terms of general advice, this argument turns out to have something of a hollow ring to it in the context, which as we shall see is cosmic and eschatological.[38] Aśvatthāman, who has played a relatively minor role in the epic up to this point, is shortly to become a major instrument of fate himself. Both he and his companions think he is planning an act of inspired, but individually willed revenge for the deaths of his father and Duryodhana;[39] but like all other acts of revenge in the epic, this too turns out to be part of, indeed, in this case the culmination of, the cosmic plan. In short, it is fated. As John Smith has pointed out, the events of the *Mahābhārata* are doubly accountable: 'they must make sense as deeds performed by human beings, and they must make sense as components of the cosmic plan.'[40] So, in theory, any single epic event must have two motives: a human motive looking to the past (in this case, as in many, revenge—the payment of a 'debt' due to one's slaughtered kinsmen and allies), and a cosmic motive looking to the future (ultimately the restoration of universal order or *dharma*).[41]

So important is it for the universal plan that this particular action —the destruction of the Pāṇḍava armies—should succeed, that Aśvatthāman is possessed by God (Śiva as destroyer) to ensure that he will be able to complete it.[42] In this way, fate and the will of God are shown to be one. In a process that reflects a crucial development in

36 Ibid. 1. 65.

37 Ibid. 2. 33.

38 David Shulman suggests that this whole argument has a comic side to it: he describes it as 'a gloomy parody of a learned debate, replete with proof texts and logical claims and counterclaims', *The King and the Clown in South Indian Myth and Poetry* (Princeton: Princeton University Press, 1985), 132.

39 *Sauptikaparvan* Ch. 3.

40 Smith, 'Old Indian: The Two Sanskrit Epics', 70.

41 See ibid. for the application of this principle of 'double accountability' to the other great epic, the *Rāmāyaṇa*. On *dharma*, see below.

42 *Why* this act of total destruction is necessary at the cosmic level will be discussed below.

the history of Indian religions,[43] the powers of the Vedic gods are subsumed under the will of the one God of devotion (*bhakti*), who intervenes more or less directly in human affairs.[44] Aśvatthāman thereby becomes the complete, and yet barely self-conscious, instrument of fate, whose strength to achieve his purpose is in inverse proportion to his autonomy. As the *Sauptikaparvan* itself puts it:

And so they [the Pāṇḍava armies], who had already been condemned
To death by fate, were now assailed by Droṇa's son [Aśvatthāman].
(8. 68)

Aśvatthāman's 'human' or individual powerlessness when he attempts to act without the concordance of fate/God becomes clear when, later, he launches the catastrophic *brahmaśiras* weapon, but cannot recall it.[45] Not only that, but fate/God, in the shape of Kṛṣṇa, actively opposes Aśvatthāman in this case, intervening directly to ensure that his intention—the annihilation of the Pāṇḍavas and their line—is thwarted.

It is indicative that, in the *Sauptikaparvan*, the Sanskrit word for 'fate', *daiva*, only appears in the first part of the book, 'The Sleepers' (Chapters 1–9). The reason for this is clear: in the second part, 'The Arrow Made from Stalks', Kṛṣṇa and fate are indistinguishable and so not distinguished—'what comes from the gods' is the 'will of God'. In other words, in the second part of the *Sauptikaparvan*, Kṛṣṇa resumes the role he has played throughout most of the epic as (in John Smith's phrase) 'Fate's own representative in the action which Fate has instigated', fate's 'stage-manager'.[46] But as the great theophany of the *Bhagavadgītā* (*Mahābhārata* 6. 23–40) has already made clear, Kṛṣṇa is, to extend the metaphor, the director and the actors as well: he *is* fate, Viṣṇu incarnate, '*the* god of the *Mahābhārata*'.[47] Even his absence from the camp to make way for the destructive capabilities of the other great god of devotion, Śiva, is engineered

[43] This development is perhaps not just mirrored in the *Mahābhārata*, but may also be partly engendered there.

[44] Usually Kṛṣṇa-Viṣṇu in the epic, but, for reasons discussed below, in this instance Śiva. In any case, it is essentially Kṛṣṇa's removal of the Pāṇḍava brothers from the camp that allows the massacre to take place, as Saṃjaya informs Dhṛtarāṣṭra (*Sauptikaparvan* 8. 146–7).

[45] Ibid., Ch. 15.

[46] Smith, 'Old Indian: The Two Sanskrit Epics', 71.

[47] Ibid. 72.

by Kṛṣṇa himself as part of the wider pattern of fated events. For precisely by being absent himself, and ensuring the absence of the five Pāṇḍava heroes, he enables the massacre to take place.[48]

With the destruction of the Pāṇḍava camp, and the death of Duryodhana, fate in the epic has almost run its course: what needed (and had) to happen has. But Kṛṣṇa, who has shaped the course of events at every crucial point in the war and its antecedents, has one more essential intervention to make: he guarantees the future birth (the 'resurrection') of Parikṣit, and with him the survival of the Lunar Dynasty into a new age.[49] Although, in terms of the narrative, his promise is not fulfilled until the *Aśvamedhikaparvan* (Book 14: 'The Horse Sacrifice'), Kṛṣṇa's intervention in the *Sauptikaparvan* is the last necessary divine intervention in the *Mahābhārata* story, the rest merely follows from what has already happened. In this sense, at the very least, the events of the *Sauptikaparvan* mark the culmination of the epic, and perhaps the first in what might be considered a whole series of endings.

Dharma

Another way of describing the concluding events of the *Mahābhārata* would be to say that *dharma* has been restored. *Dharma* is often identified as a key concept of the epic: the battle is fought on 'the field of *dharma*'. (*Bhagavadgītā* 1. 1), and after it, King Dharma himself, Yudhiṣṭhira, rules a united realm. But what does the term signify, and how does it relate to what has already been said about fate and the will of God in the *Sauptikaparvan*?

At one level, *dharma* is a cosmogonic term associated with the maintenance of universal order. What are thought to constitute the foundations of such an order shift with the historical transition (which is also partly an incorporation) of Vedic and 'Brahminical' religion into what becomes known as 'Hinduism'. The *Mahābhārata* as we have it spans and represents much of this reformulated tradition; as Alf Hiltebeitel puts it:

> the epic narrative ... has been structured in part to bridge the gap between Vedic and Purāṇic mythologies,[50] conserving the former (and conserving

[48] As Saṃjaya tells Dhṛtarāṣṭra at *Sauptikaparvan* 8. 146–7.

[49] Ibid., Ch. 16.

[50] i.e. myths that come to be developed and reworked in a vast category of literature known as the *Purāṇas*, traditionally dealing with subjects such as the creation,

pre-Vedic themes as well) and embracing it within the new 'universe of *bhakti*'[51] of the great gods of epic and Purāṇic Hinduism.[52]

As we have seen, 'what comes from the gods' (fate) and 'God's will' exist side by side in the epic, with the historically earlier, polytheistic, but somewhat abstract concept being assimilated to, or merging with, the later, monotheistic one. In a similar fashion, and as a result of the same compositional process (which in itself reflects a wider synthesizing process), the concept of *dharma* and the apprehension of God's cosmically ordering action tend to run together, although each may originate from a historically separable source. Again the *Bhagavadgītā* provides the clearest example of this amalgamation. In the theophany of *Bhagavadgītā* 11, Kṛṣṇa is eulogized by Arjuna as 'the unchanging protector of the perpetual law [*dharma*]' (11. 18). Earlier, Kṛṣṇa himself has explained his protective function:

Whenever there is a falling away from the true law (*dharma*) and an upsurge of unlawfulness (*adharma*), then... I emit myself. I come into being age (*yuga*) after age (*yuga*), to protect the virtuous and to destroy evil-doers, to establish a firm basis for the true law (*dharma*). (*Bhagavadgītā* 4. 7–8)

In other words, what God wills ('fate') is willed precisely for the preservation of *dharma*, the perpetual law. This provides the key to all Kṛṣṇa's interventions: only he sees the full picture, only he sees in its entirety what is necessary for the working out and ultimate restoration of *dharma*.

The situation is, however, complicated by *dharma* operating at both a cosmic and a social (and thus also an individual) level. Again, what we are presented with in the *Mahābhārata* reflects various changes, reinterpretations, and tensions within the tradition. Attempting to define *dharma*, from within this kind of historical perspective, one scholar has written:

The term refers to the primeval cosmogonic 'upholding' and opening of the world and its fundamental divisions, and then to the repetition and human analogues of the cosmogonic acts in the ritual, as well as the extension of the ritual into the sphere of social and ethical norms. Subsequently, there is an

preservation, and destruction of the world, but effectively the encyclopaedias of sectarian and devotional Hinduism, the earliest of which were coming into existence in roughly the same period as the epic.

[51] Madeleine Biardeau's phrase.

[52] Hiltebeitel, *The Ritual of Battle*, 139.

increasing emphasis on the 'upholding' of the social and religious status quo, of the distinction between hereditary groups and levels of qualification... The rituals and social norms which were once associated with the upholding of the universe are now primarily a means of upholding the identity and continuity of the Aryan tradition.[53]

In the *Mahābhārata* the cosmogonic and social understandings of *dharma* are placed in apposition; this results in a fundamental tension between the two, which at every narrative crux is resolved in favour of the cosmogonic.[54] Using traditional Sanskrit terminology, the *dharma* that upholds the religious and social status quo is designated *sva-dharma*. The term signifies one's inherited identity and status in a society divided into a hierarchy of classes. One's *sva-dharma* is therefore one's class-specific *dharma* or inherent duty. Most significantly in terms of the *Mahābhārata*, it is the warrior's duty to fight: i.e. he must conform to the *sva-dharma* of the warrior or *kṣatriya* class. This generally prescribed role, or *sva-dharma*, is regulated in practice by various rules of conduct governing the manner and means of waging war etc. which are themselves considered part of the *kṣatriya dharma*, and so constitute, loosely speaking, a 'warrior code'. So although it is Aśvatthāman's general duty to fight, he should do so in accordance with the rules, and an attack on the sleeping warriors by night would, according to his uncle Kṛpa, constitute a violation of that *dharma* (5. 9). Aśvatthāman, however, has already seemingly convinced himself that it is his duty as a warrior to massacre the sleepers (1. 48), even producing some dubious proof-texts to support his case (1. 51–2). (Although later, when confronted by a spirit he cannot identify, he freely admits that killing the sleeping contravenes *dharma* (6. 19 f.).) More compellingly, perhaps, he cites a long list of the Pāṇḍavas' own violations of the warrior code (5. 16 f.). By implication his particular violation would, therefore, be only the most recent such infringement in a long line formed by both sides.[55]

[53] Wilhelm Halbfass, *India and Europe: An Essay in Understanding* (New York: State University of New York Press, 1988), 332.

[54] One of the differences between Vedic cosmogonic thought and that of the *Mahābhārata*, however, is that, for the latter, it is God who is the ultimate arbiter of *dharma*. Consequently, devotion to God, rather than ritual in the Vedic sense, is the appropriate human response.

[55] Later, Aśvatthāman uses a similar 'excuse' for his launching of the *brahmaśiras* weapon: it is a response to Bhīma's violation of *dharma* in the manner in which he killed Duryodhana (15. 14).

From this last example, two further considerations arise, which illustrate the relationship of 'cosmogonic' *dharma* to *sva-dharma* in the *Mahābhārata* very well. First, although Aśvatthāman follows the warrior's *dharma* he is, like his father Droṇa, actually a brahmin (i.e. his prescribed or inherited function is priestly and instructional).[56] The relation between brahmins and *kṣatriyas* is complex and has been much discussed.[57] Aśvatthāman's seemingly anomalous position may reflect, historically speaking, an earlier relationship between the classes, more fluid than that found in the later rigid divisions, based on birth. However, in terms of the epic drama, such mixing of *sva-dharmic* functions merely serves to mirror, and is indicative of, the general rupture in the cosmic order whose apotheosis is the *Mahābhārata* war. In other words, at this level Aśvatthāman represents *adharma*, that great and general upsurge of unlawfulness and chaos which is a cosmic event rather than an individual characteristic, although it may well manifest itself through individuals and their actions. In general, violations at the *sva-dharmic* level are thought to indicate, as well as contribute to, *dharmic* imbalance at the cosmic level (i.e. an upsurge of *adharma*).

This leads to the second point: the *Mahābhārata* crisis is a crisis for *dharma* at both the cosmic and the social levels, but its resolution can only take place at one of those levels, the cosmic. This means that actions and events that work for the restoration of *dharma* at the cosmic level can and do override any specific *sva-dharmic* action. It is no surprise, therefore, that *adharma*, and the agents of *adharma*, such as Aśvatthāman and Duryodhana, also turn out to be part of the cosmic plan. The essential difference between them and the agents of *dharma* (prototypically Yudhiṣṭhira, but also the other Pāṇḍavas) is not that they contravene their *sva-dharma* and the warrior code (even Yudhiṣṭhira is guilty at times of that), but simply, and tautologically, that their role in the cosmic play requires them to perform in that *adharmic* way. What makes epic heroes 'good' or 'bad', therefore, is not their subscription to or deviation from some

[56] See *Sauptikaparvan* 3. 21–5; cf. 16. 16–17.

[57] See for instance, J. C. Heesterman, *The Inner Conflict of Tradition: An Essay in Indian Ritual, Kingship and Society* (Chicago: University of Chicago Press, 1985); cf. Louis Dumont, 'World Renunciation in Indian Religions', printed as an appendix in *Homo Hierarchicus: The Caste System and its Implications* (Chicago: University of Chicago Press, 1980), 267–86.

universal moral code (in a formal sense there is no such code), but their acting in accordance with, or against, *dharma*. Yet such actions are ultimately prescribed, not chosen. Just as at the *sva-dharmic* level what counts as a good or bad action is relative to one's class, which is prescribed, so at the cosmic-*dharmic* level one's actions are ultimately *dharmic* or *adharmic* as a result of the part one has been allotted in the cosmic drama, and for no other reason.

In other words, at the narrative level certain things have to happen in order for the 'good', or lawfulness (*dharma*), to triumph. Kṛṣṇa ensures that such actions take place, even when they contravene specific *sva-dharmas*, notably the warrior code and Yudhiṣṭhira's own understanding of his inherent duty. Violations of *sva-dharma* must nevertheless be paid for at the individual, karmic level,[58] even if they have been 'forced', through the needs of *dharma*, at the cosmic level. So, although a *dharmic* end always justifies the means, those involved in acting in this way must still accept the personal consequences. It is significant that Aśvatthāman himself is quite aware of and prepared to accept the possible personal (i.e. karmic) repercussions of his proposed action (he envisages rebirth as a worm or a moth).[59] What he does not, and cannot, see is its cosmic significance. Still blind to this, he is later condemned by Kṛṣṇa to wander for 3,000 years for his (in cosmic terms) necessary destruction of the Pāṇḍava camp and Pāṇḍava children (16. 9–10).[60] Even Yudhiṣṭhira has to suffer karmically for his *sva-dharmic* infringements. Duryodhana, on the other hand, who is the chief instrument of *adharma* in the epic,[61] is discovered by Yudhiṣṭhira enjoying the delights of heaven,[62] since in general he has conformed to his *kṣatriya dharma*, and has died on the battlefield. Indeed, his ascent to heaven is recorded in the *Sauptikaparvan* (9. 55). Just as much as his *kṣatriya* adversaries, the Pāṇḍavas, Duryodhana's job was the battle, and that is now over.[63]

[58] The law of karma being the mechanism by which individuals experience the good and bad results of their good and bad actions.

[59] *Sauptikaparvan* 5. 25.

[60] Although in this particular instance Aśvatthāman is still following a pattern of Śiva-like behaviour—see below.

[61] Duryodhana is in fact said to be the partial incarnation of an *asura* or anti-god, stressing his necessarily *adharmic* role in the cosmic drama.

[62] See the summary of Book 18: 'The Ascent to Heaven' in the Appendix.

[63] See Smith, 'Old Indian: The Two Sanskrit Epics', 67.

At some level, therefore, *dharma*, like its instrument, fate, remains inscrutable even to partially divine characters. It might be argued that the Pāṇḍavas, unlike Aśvatthāman or Duryodhana, act with knowledge of the overall cosmic plot, since they have the guiding intelligence of Kṛṣṇa. But on those occasions when some of that 'plot' is apparently revealed to a Pāṇḍava, as in the theophany of the *Bhagavadgītā*, for instance, the experience proves to be more disabling than enlightening. (The practical religious message in that particular case is of course quite clear: devote yourself to God, who is the only *real* actor. But the answer to the metaphysical question of why things are as they are—why *dharma* is as it is—is again tautological.) Each actor in the drama knows his or her own part, but the rest of the script remains largely hidden from them. As Yudhiṣṭhira, the king of *dharma* himself, confounded by the sudden draining away of the Pāṇḍava victory in Aśvatthāman's massacre, laments:

> Even for those with divine sight, the course of
> Events is hard to discern ...[64]

It is the view of some scholars that it will never be possible to know with certainty the full meaning of the *Mahābhārata* at the cosmic level, for, as John Smith has remarked, the text is for the most part silent on its own *raison d'être*.[65] The most influential modern students of the *Mahābhārata*, have, however, been more sanguine (some would say more speculative) about the possibility; and because of its pivotal role in the epic, the *Sauptikaparvan* has often been at the centre of their exegesis, as we shall now see.

A cosmic crisis

Why do the battle books of the *Mahābhārata* conclude in the *Sauptikaparvan* with such a catastrophic massacre? At one level, this is clearly a crisis for the Lunar Dynasty, for the Kuru succession, but, as we have already seen, such a crisis at the narrative or

[64] *Sauptikaparvan* 10. 10. Madeleine Biardeau, however, argues that Arjuna is an exception in this respect: '[he] is the only actor in the drama to see beyond the cards and discern the divine game behind the human play. This is not by accident; in particular it shows this warrior's depth of detachment at the very heart of the action: he does not attribute the ability to perform his lofty deeds to himself, he knows that in reality he does nothing.' My translation of Biardeau, 'Études de mythologie hindoue (IV)', *Bulletin de l'École Française d'Extrême Orient*, 63 (Paris, 1976), 211 n. 3.

[65] Smith, 'Old Indian: The Two Sanskrit Epics', 71.

epic level seems to mirror a greater cosmic crisis. To understand this we have to consider in more detail the nature of the *dharmic*, i.e. cosmic, imbalance which the events of the epic may be an attempt to remedy.

At the beginning of the *Mahābhārata* Earth (personified as a goddess) finds herself overrun by *asuras* (anti-gods) and other demons.[66] Defeated by the devas in heaven, they have taken embodiment among men, especially among *kṣatriyas*, disrupting a golden age. They multiply to such an extent that the Earth can no longer support herself. (In more abstract terms, *adharma* is in the ascendant.) Tyrannized in this fashion, Earth appeals to the god Brahmā for help.[67] He instructs the gods to help relieve Earth's burden by being born with a part of themselves among men. Thus the cosmic battle against the *asuras* will be fought out on earth, *dharma* will be pitted against *adharma* in the world of men. Most significantly, this entails the 'descent' (*avatāra*) of the great god Viṣṇu, who is embodied with a portion of himself as Kṛṣṇa Vāsudeva.[68] Here and in the *Bhagavadgītā* passage (4. 7–8) quoted above, a pattern is established in which Viṣṇu makes regular 'descents' to relieve the earth of *adharma*.[69] As Biardeau points out, the *avatāra* often takes the form of a prince—or a brahmin 'with warlike qualities—who provokes the destruction of humanity through war, so as to enable the world to start anew'.[70] The other partial incarnations are listed in *Mahābhārata* 1. 61; notable among them are Yudhiṣṭhira as Dharma, Arjuna as Indra, Duryodhana as the *asura* Kali (with his brothers as creatures of the demonic *rākṣasas*), and Aśvatthāman as portions of Mahādeva (Śiva), Death, Desire, and Rage.

As a result of these incarnations (or at least, as a result of them in the *Mahābhārata* as now constituted) the cosmic battle between *asuras* and *devas*, between *dharma* and *adharma*, is fought out at

[66] *Mahābhārata* 1. 58–9.

[67] Brahmā is the 'Grandfather' and 'creator' or demiurge. Sheerly as a rule of thumb, we may follow Biardeau and say that he is superior to the Vedic devas, the gods of heaven, but inferior to Viṣṇu and Śiva, the gods ('God') of devotion (*bhakti*) (Péterfalvi and Biardeau, *Le Mahābhārata*, i. 54).

[68] *Mahābhārata* 1. 61. 90.

[69] In the *Purāṇas* and some forms of classical Vaiṣṇavism (the form of sectarian Hinduism which regards Viṣṇu as supreme 'God'), this idea is developed into lists of *avatāras* and a full-blown doctrine of 'descents'.

[70] Madeleine Biardeau, *Hinduism: The Anthropology of a Civilization*, trans. Richard Nice (Delhi: Oxford University Press, 1989), 102–3.

the epic or heroic level in the form of a struggle for control of the Lunar Dynasty, the war between the Pāṇḍavas and Kauravas. According to Georges Dumézil there is, however, a further causal layer in this chain of events, in that the epic crisis is essentially the transposition of an Indo-European eschatological myth to do with the events that accompany a threatened end of the world, or at least the end of a world age, followed by a rebirth, or the beginning of the next age.[71] The form in which this ancient myth appears in the text, however, has an Indian and classically 'Hindu' framework. To understand this, it is necessary to know something about Indian cosmology.[72]

An idea which is well known to the *Mahābhārata* (in, for instance, Book 12) is that time is divided into cycles, each consisting of four world ages, or *yuga*, named after pieces used in games of dice or the throws of the die themselves (4—*kṛta*, 3—*tretā*, 2—*dvāpara*, 1—*kali*). As the values descend, the ages become shorter, and, in *dharmic* terms, worse. The first age in each cycle, the *kṛta yuga*, is thus a golden age in which *dharma* 'stands on all four feet'; the last, the *kali yuga*, is a morally atrophied, dharmically 'one-footed' age. This *adharmic kali* age—the one we are living through at present—is traditionally thought to have started with the conclusion of the *Mahābhārata* war. Time, as already noted, is thought to be cyclical, so with the end of the *kali yuga* a new golden age will be initiated, and so on. In developed Purāṇic cosmology, a cycle of four *yuga* taken together is known as a 'great *yuga*' (*mahāyuga*), and a thousand *mahāyuga* constitute one day of Brahmā. This day begins with the creation of the world, and ends with its destruction by fire and/or flood, issuing in an equally long night of Brahmā—a period of quiescence before the next cycle of cycles begins (and so on *ad*

[71] See Dumézil, *Mythe et épopée*, i, esp. chs. 8 and 9.

[72] In the *Purāṇas* especially, there are numerous variations on the basic cosmological plan or, as A. L. Basham puts it, 'an imperfect synthesis of more than one independent doctrine'—*The Wonder That Was India* (New York: Grove Press, 1959), 321. What follows is a simplification, and merely one version intended to give some idea of the prevalent pattern. I have not listed the thought-stopping numbers of years involved, but thousands, hundreds of thousands, and millions are the common currency. For an overview of Indian cosmologies, see R. F. Gombrich, 'Ancient Indian Cosmology', in C. Blacker and M. Loewe (eds.), *Ancient Cosmologies* (London: George Allen & Unwin, 1975), 100–42. See also Madeleine Biardeau, 'Cyclic Time', in *Hinduism*, 100–4; and *Études de mythologie hindoue*, i: *Cosmogonies purāṇiques* (Paris: Publications de l'École Française d'Extrême Orient, 128, 1981), ch.1.

infinitum). A day and night of Brahmā together are known as a *kalpa* or 'world period' (although, taken strictly, *kalpa* refers only to the 'day'). The destruction of the whole world at the end of a *kalpa* is called the *pralaya* or 'dissolution'.

Reading the *Mahābhārata* in these terms, the crisis for the Lunar Dynasty conforms to a crisis in the history of the universe, namely the destruction that comes with the end of a *kalpa* or world period (or according to some accounts, simply with the end of a *mahāyuga*),[73] followed by a rebirth, i.e. the beginning of a new age. Thus, according to Dumézil, the whole Kurukṣetra war, including the massacre at night, is an Indo-European eschatological conflict between good and evil, transposed to the battle between the Pāṇḍavas and the Kauravas. The massacre and its aftermath provide the key moments: the holocaust, followed by Kṛṣṇa's 'resurrection' of the line through the unborn Parikṣit.

This can be unpacked further. Dumézil argues that the main gods have not been related in a secondary way to the main heroes, rather the former are the models for the latter, and their conceptual connections are expressed through parentage, partial incarnations, alliances, etc.[74] As events come to a crux in the *Sauptikaparvan*, the two major actors are Kṛṣṇa Vāsudeva and Aśvatthāman. Kṛṣṇa is explicitly an incarnation of the great god Viṣṇu, and Aśvatthāman is closely connected to the other great Hindu god Śiva or Rudra (he is possessed by him, as well as being his partial incarnation). Although Dumézil is concerned to stress their Vedic antecedents, he points up the roles that, according to Hindu mythology, each of these great gods plays in cosmic and eschatological events. When a cycle of cosmic time comes to an end, it is Śiva's role to bring about the destruction of the universe. (This is precisely what he is doing in the famous south Indian sculpture of Śiva as *naṭarāja*, 'lord of the dance'—dancing the universe to destruction in a cosmic fire-storm.)

[73] Dumézil actually refers to this as the end of a *yuga*, ignoring the developed 'long' Purāṇic cosmology in favour of an earlier version; but whatever the terms used, he is referring to the *destruction* of the universe at the end of an age—*Mythe et épopée*, i. 218 ff.

[74] Ibid. 238. In this he follows the pioneering work of Stig Wikander (see Select Bibliography), who demonstrated that the Pāṇḍava heroes were essentially transpositions of Vedic gods. Further, Dumézil connects the five Pāṇḍava brothers, and their divine prototypes, with each of the three functions he posits as underlying Indo-European social and ideological structures. Thus Yudhiṣṭhira (Dharma) mirrors religious sovereignty and law, Bhīma (Vāyu) and Arjuna (Indra) warfare, Nakula and Sahadeva (the Aśvins) economic welfare and service. See ibid., chs. 1 and 2.

And here, in the *Sauptikaparvan*, it is really Śiva who destroys the Pāṇḍava camp, as Kṛṣṇa reveals to Yudhiṣṭhira (Chapters 17 and 18). It is also Śiva-Aśvatthāman who threatens to make the destruction complete by releasing the catastrophic *brahmaśiras* weapon. Viṣṇu, on the other hand, has the mythological role of preserver and regenerator of the universe, who at the end of each world period (or *mahāyuga*, depending upon one's reading) reabsorbs the universe and then causes it to be reborn (traditionally through the offices of Brahmā as demiurge or 'creator'). Kṛṣṇa, as we have already seen, also intervenes ('descends') to restore *dharma* from *yuga* to *yuga*;[75] in other words, he is specifically linked to the cosmic process at two closely related levels: as the restorer of balance, of *dharma*, when it has declined within a cycle, and also as the restorer of the universe to its 'golden' *dharmic* state at the beginning of a new cycle. If we accept the suggestion that, at some level, either a world cycle or a *yuga* is coming to an end with the night massacre and the deaths of the unborn Pāṇḍava children, then Kṛṣṇa's 'resurrection' of Parikṣit marks either the rebirth of the universe or the beginning of a new *yuga*. As Dumézil remarks, Aśvatthāman-Śiva and Kṛṣṇa-Viṣṇu each does his office (i.e. they complement each other in the cosmic scheme of things), but it is the saviour god who has the last word at both the epic and cosmological levels.[76]

For Dumézil none of these events would have developed in this way and this order if they had not been transposed from an 'end of an age' myth.[77] Madeleine Biardeau agrees that the epic has an underlying mythic structure, and that it is eschatological. However, she differs from Dumézil in stressing the Purāṇic and therefore Hindu nature of the structuring myth, as opposed to Dumézil's Vedic cum pre-Vedic and Indo-European model. At the centre of her analysis is the Purāṇic myth of cosmic dissolution (*pralaya*), already noted by Dumézil, but seen by him as secondary.

In general, Biardeau reads the epic as a *bhakti* (devotional) text, or more precisely as a text in which Vedic mythology and Brahminic

[75] See *Bhagavadgītā* 4. 7–8, quoted above.

[76] *Mythe et épopée*, i. 219. Madeleine Biardeau takes this dominance of Kṛṣṇa-Viṣṇu a step further, arguing that Śiva is always ultimately subservient to, i.e. simply the instrument of, Viṣṇu in the epic. See, for instance, 'Études de mythologie hindoue (IV)', 211–12. Others, including Hiltebeitel, stress their complementary roles and functions.

[77] *Mythe et épopée*, i. 219.

sacrifice are re-routed or re-assembled from a *bhakti* perspective, the focus of devotion being Kṛṣṇa, the *avatāra* ('descent' or incarnation) of Viṣṇu. From this perspective, the two great gods of *bhakti*, Śiva and Viṣṇu (Aśvatthāman and Kṛṣṇa in their epic guises), are not simply complementary—at a cosmic level they are collaborative and not competitive—but they are virtually one and the same God: Viṣṇu (in the shape of his *avatāra* Kṛṣṇa). This explains Kṛṣṇa's 'absence' from the night camp, which allows Aśvatthāman-Śiva to carry out the massacre. As Śiva himself tells Aśvatthāman, '[the Pāñcālas] have fallen under the power of Time'.[78] Time (*kāla*) is an epithet of Śiva, but it is also, as Biardeau points out (and as we know from the *Bhagavadgītā*), Kṛṣṇa-Viṣṇu himself.[79] Thus although Śiva apparently dominates the entire battle—killing for Arjuna as well as for Aśvatthāman—he does so with the 'permission' of Kṛṣṇa,[80] i.e. he acts for the ultimate restoration of that cosmic *dharma* which is identical with Viṣṇu's will. Nevertheless, in the *pralayic* scheme of things, the hour of total or universal destruction has arrived,[81] and that is Śiva's job, just as it is Kṛṣṇa-Viṣṇu's job to usher in the new age with the promised revival of the dead Parikṣit, and the re-establishment of the reign of *dharma* in the person of Yudhiṣṭhira.

One consequence of viewing the shaping myth as *pralayic*, rather than simply *yugic*, is that the traditional reading of the end of the *Mahābhārata* war as marking the transition to the *kali yuga* becomes problematical. According to the *pralayic* scheme, the new age with which the world begins again should be a *kṛta yuga*, a 'golden age'; that is to say, the war and its aftermath are at the juncture between two world periods (and therefore also between the *kali* and the *kṛta* ages), not—as would be the case if it were simply a *yuga* rather than a *mahāyuga* or *kalpa* that was ending—the juncture between two *yugas*, traditionally the *dvāpara* and *kali yugas*. Because of Biardeau's stress on the idea of Kṛṣṇa as *avatāra*, she regards the tradition that the *Mahābhārata* marks the transition from the *dvāpara* to the *kali*

78 *Sauptikaparvan* 7. 63.

79 Biardeau, 'Études de mythologie hindoue (IV)', 211. See *Bhagavadgītā* 11. 32: 'I am time run on, destroyer of the universe, risen here to annihilate worlds', from a passage that in itself is an image of *pralaya*. Taken from W. J. Johnson (trans.), *The Bhagavad Gita* (Oxford: Oxford University Press, 1994).

80 Biardeau, 'Études de mythologie hindoue (IV)', 211.

81 See Biardeau in Péterfalvi and Biardeau, *Le Mahābhārata*, ii. 272–3.

yuga as both later and incoherent. It is incoherent because it would destroy the very idea of an *avatāra* (i.e. that God descends to restore *dharma*), since the preceding age (the *dvāpara yuga*) would have to have been better than the present one, and Kṛṣṇa would have come to earth effectively to engender an upsurge in *adharma*. On the contrary, according to Biardeau, the Kṛṣṇa-inspired victory of Yudhiṣṭhira as *dharmarāja*, his celebration of the horse sacrifice, and Parikṣit's eventual birth are all indicative of the restoration of *dharma*, and so point to a *kṛta yuga* or golden age,[82] which follows on the *kali-yuga*-like catastrophic war, and the 'cosmic night' of Aśvatthāman's nocturnal raid. Others, however, while agreeing that *dharma* is restored, conform to the traditional Hindu view that the accession of Parikṣit marks the beginning of the *kali yuga*. So although Parikṣit is, indeed, an ideal king, the age he rules over is an attenuated one.[83]

It may be possible to accept that the epic as a whole, and the *Sauptikaparvan* in particular, has at one level a *pralayic* structure or counterform, without necessarily attempting to find exact parallels in every detail. Indeed, some of the logical conundrums melt away if one accepts, with Biardeau's follower Jacques Scheuer, that in the epic the *imagery* of universal dissolution or *pralaya* is also applied to the end of a *yuga* (i.e. the end of every *yuga* becomes a small *pralaya*), although Scheuer too thinks the passage in the *Sauptikaparvan* is from the *kali* to the *kṛta yuga*.[84] At the very least, the fact that epic action is commonly expressed in terms of *pralaya* imagery demands attention.[85]

In summary, therefore, Biardeau (like Dumézil) regards the *Sauptikaparvan* episode as a symbolic reprise and clarification of the meaning and structure of the entire conflict, as well as its completion. And that meaning resides in the idea that the total destruction

[82] Biardeau in Péterfalvi and Biardeau, *Le Mahābhārata*, i. 42. See also Jacques Scheuer, *Śiva dans le Mahābhārata* (Paris: Presses Universitaires de France, 1982), 332 f.

[83] Hiltebeitel, *The Ritual of Battle*, 308.

[84] Scheuer, *Śiva dans le Mahābhārata*, 328–9. Biardeau herself, in fact, describes the *Mahābhārata* war as presenting itself as 'a *pale image* of the reabsorption of the world at the end of a kalpa'—*Hinduism*, 102–3 (my italics). See also 'Études de mythologie hindoue (IV)', 121 ff. ('*Yuga* épique et *kalpa* purāṇique'), esp. 133; and Hiltebeitel, *The Ritual of Battle*, 310, commenting on Biardeau's perception that the epic is 'concerned more with the cycle of yugas and the appearance of *avatāras* and less with the *kalpa* cycle, which it leaves in the background'.

[85] See, for instance, Hiltebeitel, *The Ritual of Battle*, 311.

of the war is a kind of end of the world, albeit one that prefigures a new beginning in the promised resurrection of Parikṣit.[86]

A universal sacrifice

There is, however, another way of looking at both the epic war and the *Sauptikaparvan* episode, one that may be compatible with the eschatological model outlined above, but that operates in a different metaphoric and symbolic field. According to this reading, sacrifice provides the basic paradigm for understanding the apparent catastrophe. The events of the *Sauptikaparvan* have been interpreted, as we have seen, as a *pralaya*, a destruction of the world at the end of time; but that destruction in itself (like the war as a whole) can, at another level, be interpreted as a sacrificial activity. Madeleine Biardeau is again responsible for using sacrificial symbolism as a key to interpreting the epic, an approach which has been developed in their differing ways by Scheuer and Hiltebeitel, especially in connection with the *Sauptikaparvan*.

According to this mode of analysis, much of the epic can be understood as a symbolic reworking (in a *bhakti* context) of the ideology of Vedic and Brahminical sacrifice. In general terms, how does this work? First it is necessary to realize the centrality of sacrifice and its 'theology' to Vedic and Brahminical religion and society.[87] At the individual, social, and cosmic levels sacrifice was perceived to be the mechanism that regulated and guaranteed the desired outcome of all significant actions (*karman*). Indeed, *dharma* in general—as cosmic order, the *most* desired outcome—was itself thought to be maintained through correct sacrifice. So pervasive was this view of the world that, in post-Vedic times, any significant or simply elaborate activity was (re)interpreted as 'sacrificial', including the renouncer's (*saṃnyāsin*'s) 'renunciation' of external ritual itself.

[86] Biardeau, 'Études de mythologie hindoue (IV)', 209. The destruction is total in so far as Aśvatthāman destroys the unborn Pāṇḍava children with the *brahmaśiras* weapon, and, but for Kṛṣṇa's intervention to revive Parikṣit, would thereby ensure the lingering extinction of the Lunar Dynasty. In *yuga* terms, one age ends with the destruction, another begins with the rebirth.

[87] 'Vedic and Brahminical' indicate that society whose social and religious practices were authorized and exemplified in the category of texts known as 'the Veda'—a society dominated ideologically by the hereditary class of ritual specialists, the brahmins. 'Hinduism' is a label used here to designate the expansion and alteration of this world-view from the epic and Purāṇic period onwards, especially in the form of devotion (*bhakti*) to a supreme God.

According to the orthodox Brahminical interpretation, it was necessary to be qualified by birth (one had to be a member of one of the three higher classes) and training (one had to have access to the Veda) to be a sacrificer,[88] and the extent and nature of such a man's sacrifices were likewise quite specific, depending upon his depth of initiation and (practically speaking) his wealth. However, according to the more generalized or universal view of sacrifice (that all actions, external and internal, have a sacrificial quality), just as each class has its *sva-dharma* or inherent duty, which is congruent with *dharma* at the cosmic level, so each also has its own 'particular sacrifice', which is congruent with the sacrificial nature of existence in general. (Sacrifice and *dharma*, as we have seen, are part of the same ideological complex.) A potential problem arises, however, in that, with the universalization of sacrifice, every specific action is believed, like every specific sacrifice, to have a specific result. This happens through the law of karma (which, indeed, probably developed out of sacrificial thought): good actions have good results, bad actions have bad results.

Partly due to the influence of the renouncer movements of Buddhism and Jainism (sacrifice and sacrificial theology are two of the things they are renouncing), violence in particular was thought to bring bad results (although at some level it seems always to have presented problems for sacrificial theology). While Brahminical orthodoxy regarded the violence inherent in sacrifice (in the specifically ritual sense) as justified, or technically not even 'violence' at all, it is less easy to justify the violence of war or battle, of which the *Mahābhārata* war is the archetype. How will such a conflict not bring bad results for the warriors involved in it? In a general sense, this is the disabling question that overcomes Arjuna in the *Bhagavadgītā*. The resolution Kṛṣṇa proposes there is, in fact, consonant with the view of the epic in general, namely that the warriors' particular or ascribed 'sacrifice' is the 'sacrifice of battle'.[89] War—the violence of battle—is therefore justified because it is sacrificial; that is to say, it accords with *dharma*, and works ultimately to

[88] This is a simplification; for a more detailed discussion see the general works cited in the Select Bibliography, especially P. V. Kane's *History of Dharmaśāstra* (Poona: Bhandarkar Oriental Research Institute, 2nd edn. 1968–75).

[89] See, for instance, the introduction to my translation of *The Bhagavad Gita*, pp. xv–xvi.

preserve cosmic order. At the individual level, the fruit (the result) of the sacrifice is either the enjoyment of the earth (for the victors) or the attainment of heaven (for the vanquished), as Kṛṣṇa points out in the *Bhagavadgītā* (2. 37).

The king (the *kṣatriya*) is the sacrificer *par excellence*, and the *Mahābhārata* war is framed by two great royal sacrifices (the royal consecration or *rājasūya*, and the horse sacrifice or *aśvamedha*) performed by the king of *dharma* himself, Yudhiṣṭhira.[90] It is the king's function to protect the Earth, to relieve her of her burden, and this is how he does it, through sacrifices, the most comprehensive of which is the 'sacrifice of battle'. As Biardeau has pointed out, the horse sacrifice in particular is a ritual reprise of the war, a 'total sacrifice', performed by Yudhiṣṭhira, not for himself, but for the good of the universe, and to assure the succession of Parikṣit. These two goals amount to the same thing, for his purpose is to ensure the continuity of royal *dharmic* power precisely because it is only that power which can guarantee cosmic order. This is why Kṛṣṇa, as *avatāra*, protects and guides the Pāṇḍavas in general, delegating his powers on earth to Arjuna, the archetypal *kṣatriya* prince and devotee (*bhakta*), in particular: *dharma* is at stake, and it is the duty of the king—of the Pāṇḍavas—to restore it through the sacrifice of war.[91] Again we can see how *all* the participants—Pāṇḍavas and Kauravas, good and bad alike—ultimately work for the restoration of *dharma*, for a proper and successful completion of the sacrifice.

But as Biardeau shows, the presence of the *avatāra*, of Kṛṣṇa, throughout the story is not just a sign that *dharma* is at stake, but also that men are not the masters of their fate.[92] The king's duty, the power of the Pāṇḍavas, and God's will coincide only *because* it is God who wills it. In other words, the participants' roles—they are at the same time instigators (patrons), celebrants, and victims of the 'sacrifice of battle'—are ascribed to them by God.[93] God (as the

[90] See summaries of Bks. 2 and 14 in the Appendix.

[91] See Biardeau, 'Études de mythologie hindoue (IV)', 214 ff.

[92] Ibid. 217.

[93] In accordance with Brahminical practice, all larger-scale sacrifices require the sacrificer (the patron or instigator of the sacrifice) to pay brahmin priests (the celebrants) to perform the sacrifice on his behalf. Theoretically, at least, the victim (typically an animal) is offered into the fire as a substitute for the sacrificer himself. With the sacrificer's death, this process of substitution comes to an end and he is finally offered

Bhagavadgītā makes clear) is the only real agent, the only real sacrificer, and therefore the fruits too are his. In the light of this, the appropriate human response is to act in accordance with one's inherent duty, perform one's 'inherent sacrifice', and hand over the apparent fruits of one's sacrificial action to their real agent (God) in a spirit of devotion (*bhakti*). Such a response guarantees personal salvation (*Bhagavadgītā* 18.65–6). The warrior's duty, the violence of his inherent sacrifice, is thereby made yogic, a matter of renunciation (a giving up to God), and so a way to salvation, not, as Arjuna fears, a path to hell (*Bhagavadgītā* 1. 44). In short, as the pivot of *dharmic* society, sacrifice serves as a key to justify the violence of the war.[94]

Turning to the *Sauptikaparvan*, we find that, in addition to its depiction of the culmination and conclusion of the (sacrifice of) battle, it is shot through with a thread of more specific sacrificial imagery. Indeed, Madeleine Biardeau sees the *Sauptika* episode as not really part of the war at all (although Aśvatthāman has been consecrated as general of the Kaurava army), but as a sacrificial session of the kind associated with Śiva Paśupati—Śiva as 'lord of animals'.[95] This is borne out by the way the principal victims are put to death: far from following the usual pattern of warrior conflict, Aśvatthāman, in word and deed, slaughters Dhṛṣṭadyumna, and others in the camp, like sacrificial animals (*paśu*) (5. 34, 8. 18, 8. 35–6, 9. 51). Indeed, he specifically refuses Dhṛṣṭadyumna's request to be killed like a warrior (8. 19–20). The three Kaurava warriors are likened to three enkindled sacrificial fires (5. 37, cf. 9. 7), and, later, Kṛpa and Kṛtavarman have, in Biardeau's words, 'done their work as acolytes of the sacrifice so well' that they set fire to the camp in three places (8. 103), ensuring that no one escapes.[96] These three fires are thus the triple fires of the solemn sacrifice,[97] as well as the fire of the cosmic holocaust.

in the 'sacrifice' of the funeral pyre. In the sacrifice of battle, victorious warriors have therefore offered their defeated foes as substitutes for themselves; whereas the defeated have 'offered' themselves directly. See ibid. 255.

94 Scheuer, *Śiva dans le Mahābhārata*, 349.

95 See Biardeau in Péterfalvi and Biardeau, *Le Mahābhārata*, ii. 283–4; and *Sauptikaparvan* 8. 122.

96 Biardeau in Péterfalvi and Biardeau, *Le Mahābhārata*, ii. 284, my translation.

97 According to Brahminical orthopraxy, all solemn or *śrauta* sacrifices require at least three properly installed fires. This distinguishes them from the domestic (*gṛhya*) rites which require only a single fire.

Significantly, Aśvatthāman is described in the midst of the slaughter as being 'drunk' or 'maddened' with sacrifice (8. 81), for this is a sacrifice that has run out of control. At the level of myth, it is Śiva's destruction of the sacrifice of the gods (Dakṣa's sacrifice—retold in Chapter 18) which provides the prototype of just such an out of control sacrifice. In David Shulman's words, 'the excluded Śiva of the myth proceeds from an emotional stance similar to Aśvatthāman's to destroy—and thereby complete—his opponents' sacrifice'.[98] Indeed, it is Śiva *through* Aśvatthāman who is responsible for the near total slaughter of this near total 'sacrifice'. For after Aśvatthāman offers himself to the god, a golden sacrificial altar with a blazing fire springs up before him, and, entering it as an oblation, he is immediately possessed by Śiva (Chapter 7). Thus it is Śiva himself who becomes both instigator and celebrant of this abnormal 'sacrifice', in which the sacrificial fire overruns the entire sacrificial sphere (i.e. the entire universe). As Jacques Scheuer remarks, it is no longer a question of the violence necessary to the life of society (normal sacrifice), but of the destruction of that society (an excessive and 'savage' sacrifice, which destroys the normal sacrificial world). This is sacrifice transposed from a Vedic and Brahminical framework to a Purāṇic one: the destruction of the world at the end of an age is presented as a sacrifice which has gone out of control, and the 're-creation' at the beginning of a new age as a return to sacrificial order.[99]

As a number of commentators have pointed out,[100] until the *Sauptika* episode, the battle has been presided over by Kṛṣṇa, but now, in his absence, Śiva (in the form of Aśvatthāman) claims his 'share' of the 'sacrifice of battle'. The 'shares' in this case are the human victims of the battle: just as Droṇa was Dhṛṣṭadyumna's share, so Dhṛṣṭadyumna in his turn is Aśvatthāman's, and 'the sacrifice of battle will not be complete until Aśvatthāman has claimed [his share]'.[101] As already noted, the connection at this level between the Kaurava warrior and the god is made explicit at the

[98] Shulman, *The King and the Clown*, 138. Wendy Doniger O'Flaherty points out the ambivalence of Śiva's action in this myth from the standpoint of orthodoxy: he simultaneously *destroys* the sacrifice 'as demons were said to try to do... and actually *completes* it as the sacrificial butcher would do; thus he restores it at the end' (*Hindu Myths* (Harmondsworth: Penguin Books, 1975; repr. 1980), 118).

[99] See Scheuer, *Śiva dans le Mahābhārata*, 351–2.

[100] See, for instance, Hiltebeitel, *The Ritual of Battle*, 311.

[101] Ibid. 319.

conclusion of the *Sauptikaparvan* itself (Chapter 18), when Kṛṣṇa retells the myth of Śiva's destruction of the sacrifice of the gods (Śiva's way of claiming his share) in order to demonstrate to Yudhiṣṭhira how Aśvatthāman on his own could have managed such slaughter.[102]

If the events of the *Mahābhārata* war in general represent a sacrifice, then those of the *Sauptikaparvan* represent that sacrifice finally threatening to run out of control and consume the entire world, i.e. that social and cosmic order (*dharma*) which has been at risk throughout the entire narrative. The destruction of the Pāṇḍava camp and its aftermath is therefore, at one level, perceived as corresponding to Śiva's destruction of the world at end of a *kalpa*, and, at another, to Śiva's takeover and threatened destruction of the sacrifice of the gods when he is deprived of his share. But either way, order is finally restored: Earth is relieved of her burden and renewed, the sacrifice—paradoxically but properly completed by Śiva-Aśvatthāman's violent intervention—has, in the shape of Parikṣit, a remnant or survivor. Thanks to Kṛṣṇa, there is a king to come, and the maintenance of *dharma* is thereby guaranteed.

Whether this is simply a matter of eschatological and sacrificial imagery complementing the epic story as cosmological and sacrificial metaphors, or whether one or both of these 'lends form to the story as a background myth',[103] is the subject of continuing scholarly debate.[104] Whatever the case, it would be a mistake to underestimate the sophistication of those who helped to shape this multi-layered and multivalent text. If as Alf Hiltebeitel suggests, the epic poets were 'seers', with the faculty to see and draw all kinds of correspondences, equivalences, and connections,[105] then, as modern scholars

[102] This is usually known as the myth of the destruction of Dakṣa's sacrifice, although Dakṣa himself does not appear in the *Sauptikaparvan* version. Alf Hiltebeitel has argued that this myth, rather than simply complementing, echoing, or evoking the *Sauptikaparvan* as we now have it, has actually had a shaping influence on it, although the extent of this has been disputed by others, notably Scheuer. Hiltebeitel's argument is too detailed to present here; interested readers are referred to *The Ritual of Battle*, 312–45, and Scheuer's discussion of this approach in *Śiva dans le Mahābhārata*, 333–9. For further references, see the relevant Explanatory Notes.

[103] Hitlebeitel, *The Ritual of Battle*, 312.

[104] See for instance, Scheuer: It is 'not so much a question of the destruction of the sacrifice as of a sacrifice of destruction, not so much the end of the sacrifice as a sacrifice of the end' (*Śiva dans le Mahābhārata*, 339, my translation).

[105] Hiltebeitel, *The Ritual of Battle*, 359.

and readers, we have good reason to continue exploring the possible range of such correspondences. That their full significance continues to escape definitive analysis is neither a defeat, nor a conundrum, but simply a testament to the extraordinary shifts in perspective to be found in this epic mirror to the human condition, held up for so many centuries and through so many retellings.

SELECT BIBLIOGRAPHY

This is not intended to be an exhaustive or authoritative bibliography for *Mahābhārata* studies. The works listed here are those I have consulted and found useful for my translation, introduction, and notes. Many have extensive bibliographies in their own right, and the reader wishing to venture further into this field will need to consult them. As will be evident from their titles, a number of general and introductory works on Indian culture and Hinduism have also been included.

Texts (*Mahābhāraṭa*, including *Sauptikaparvan*)

Sukthankar, Vishnu S., Belvalkar, S. K., Vaidya, P. L., *et al.* (eds.), *Mahābhārata.* (Critical Edition), 19 vols. plus 6 vols. of indexes (Poona: Bhandarkar Oriental Research Institute, 1933–72).

Velankar, Hari Damodar (ed.), *The Sauptikaparvan*, Critical Edition, vol. xii, pt. 1 (Poona: Bhandarkar Oriental Research Institute, 1948).

Translations

Ganguli, Kisari Mohan (trans.) [early edns. ascribed to the publisher, P. C. Roy], *The Mahabharata of Krishna-Dwaipayana Vyasa*, 12 vols. (1884–99; 2nd edn. Calcutta, 1970; repr. New Delhi: Munshiram Manoharlal, 1970 (5th edn. 1990)). Vol. vii: *Sauptika Parva*. This is a complete translation of the vulgate text, not that of the Critical Edition, which, of course, it pre-dates.

Johnson, W. J. (trans.), *The Bhagavad Gita* (Oxford: Oxford University Press, Oxford World's Classics, 1994).

Péterfalvi, Jean-Michel (trans.), and Biardeau, Madeleine (introd. and commentary), *Le Mahābhārata*, 2 vols. (Paris: Flammarion, 1985–6). This is a translation of extracts from Ramachandrashastri Kinjawadekar's edition: *The Mahābhāratam with the Bharata Bhawadeepa Commentary of Nīlakaṇṭha* (Poona: Chitrashala Press, 1929–36; repr. New Delhi: Oriental Book Reprint Corporation, 1978). Readings have been corrected by reference to the Critical Edition, although there is no indication (deliberately) where this occurs. Biardeau provides a linking commentary and an interesting introduction. Effectively, the translation ends with Book 11 (Books 12–18 are given in *résumé* form).

van Buitenen, J. A. B. (trans. and ed.), *The Bhagavadgītā in the Mahābhārata: Text and Translation* (Chicago: University of Chicago Press, 1981).

——*The Mahābhārata*, Books 1–5, 3 vols. (Chicago: University of Chicago Press, 1973–8). This is a translation of Books 1–5 of the Critical Edition, with introductory material and notes.

Other Works

Basham, A. L., *The Wonder That Was India* (New York: Grove Press, 1959).

Benjamin, Walter *Illuminations*, ed. Hannah Arendt, trans. Harry Zohn (London: Fontana/Collins, 1973).

Biardeau, Madeleine, *Études de mythologie hindoue*, i: *Cosmogonies purāṇiques* (Paris: Publications de l' École Française d' Extrême Orient, 128, 1981).

——'Études de mythologie hindoue (IV)', *Bulletin de l'École Française d'Extrême Orient*, 63 (Paris, 1976), 111–263.

——*Hinduism: The Anthropology of a Civilization*, trans. Richard Nice (Delhi: Oxford University Press, 1989).

Blurton, T. Richard, *Hindu Art* (London: British Museum Press, 1992).

Brook, Peter, *The Mahabharata* (Connoisseur Video, 1989).

Carrière, Jean-Claude, *The Mahabharata: A Play Based upon the Indian Classical Epic*, trans. Peter Brook (London: Methuen, 1987).

Coulson, Michael, *Sanskrit: An Introduction to the Classical Language* (New York: Teach Yourself Books, Hodder & Stoughton, 1st pub. 1976; numerous reprints).

Doniger, Wendy, with Smith, Brian K. (trans.), *The Laws of Manu* (Harmondsworth: Penguin Books, 1991).

Dumézil, Georges, *Mythe et épopée*, i: *L'Idéologie des trois fonctions dans les épopées des peuples indo-européens* (Paris: Gallimard, 1968).

Dumont, Louis, 'World Renunciation in Indian Religions', printed as an appendix in *Homo Hierarchicus: The Caste System and its Implications* (Chicago: University of Chicago Press, 1980), 267–86.

Flood, Gavin, *An Introduction to Hinduism* (Cambridge: Cambridge University Press, 1996).

Gombrich, R. F., 'Ancient Indian Cosmology', in C. Blacker and M. Loewe (eds)., *Ancient Cosmologies* (London: George Allen & Unwin, 1975), 100–42.

Halbfass, Wilhelm, *India and Europe: An Essay in Understanding* (New York: State University of New York Press, 1988).

Hardy, F., *The Religious Culture of India: Power, Love and Wisdom* (Cambridge: Cambridge University Press, 1994).

Heesterman, J. C., *The Inner Conflict of Tradition: An Essay in Indian Ritual, Kingship and Society* (Chicago: University of Chicago Press, 1985).

Hiltebeitel, Alf, *The Cult of Draupadī. Mythologies: From Gingee to Kurukṣetra*, i (Chicago: University of Chicago Press, 1988).

——'Mahābhārata', in M. Eliade (ed. in chief), *The Encyclopedia of Religions* (New York: Macmillan, 1987).

——*The Ritual of Battle: Krishna in the Mahābhārata* (1st pub. Ithaca, NY: Cornell University Press, 1976; repr. Delhi: Sri Satguru Publications, 1991).

Hopkins, E. W., *The Great Epic of India: Its Character and Origin* (1st pub. 1901; repr. Calcutta: Punthi Pustak, 1969).

Kane, P. V., *History of Dharmaśāstra*, 5 vols. (Poona: Bhandarkar Oriental Research Institute, 2nd edn. 1968–75).

Katz, Ruth C., *Arjuna in the Mahabharata: Where Krishna Is, There Is Victory* (Columbia: University of South Carolina Press, 1989).

——'The *Sauptika* Episode in the Structure of the *Mahābhārata*', *Journal of South Asian Literature*, 20 (1985), 109–24.

Klostermaier, Klaus K., *A Survey of Hinduism* (Albany: State University of New York Press, 2nd edn. 1994).

Kramrisch, Stella, *The Presence of Śiva* (Princeton: Princeton University Press, 1981).

Laine, James W., *Visions of God: Narratives of Theophany in the Mahābhārata* (Vienna: Publications of the De Nobili Research Library, XVI, 1989).

Malamoud, Charles, *Cooking the World: Ritual and Thought in Ancient India*, trans. David White (Delhi: Oxford University Press, 1996).

Monier-Williams, M., *A Sanskrit–English Dictionary* (Oxford: Oxford University Press, 1st pub. in this edn. 1899; numerous reprints).

O'Flaherty, Wendy Doniger, *Hindu Myths: A Sourcebook Translated from the Sanskrit* (Harmondsworth: Penguin Books, 1st pub. 1975; repr. 1980).

Olivelle, Patrick (trans.), *The Pañcatantra* (Oxford: Oxford University Press, Oxford World's Classics, 1997).

Scheuer, Jacques, *Śiva dans le Mahābhārata*, Bibliothèque de l'École des Hautes Études, Section des Sciences Religieuses, LXXXIV (Paris: Presses Universitaires de France, 1982).

Shastri, J. L. (ed.), *Manusmṛti, with the Sanskrit Commentary of Kullūka Bhaṭṭa* (Delhi: Motilal Banarsidass, 1983).

Shulman, David, *The King and the Clown in South Indian Myth and Poetry* (Princeton: Princeton University Press, 1985).

Smith, Brian K., *Classifying the Universe: The Ancient Indian Varṇa System and the Origins of Caste* (New York: Oxford University Press, 1994).

——*Reflections on Resemblance, Ritual, and Religion* (New York: Oxford University Press, 1989).

Smith, John D., 'Old Indian: The Two Sanskrit Epics', in A. T. Hatto (ed.), *Traditions of Heroic and Epic Poetry*, i: *The Traditions* (London: The Humanities Research Association, 1980).

—— 'Scapegoats of the Gods: The Ideology of the Indian Epics', in S. H. Blackburn, *et al.* (eds), *Oral Epics in India* (Berkeley and Los Angeles: University of California Press, 1989).

Smith, Mary Carroll, *The Warrior Code of India's Sacred Song* (New York: Garland Publishing, 1992).

Sørensen, S., *An Index to the Names in the Mahābhārata, with Short Explanations and a Concordance to the Bombay and Calcutta Editions and P. C. Roy's Translation* (1st pub. 1904; repr. Delhi: Motilal Banarsidass, 1963).

Stutley, Margaret, and Stutley, James, *A Dictionary of Hinduism* (London: Routledge & Kegan Paul, 1977).

Sullivan, Bruce M., *Kṛṣṇa Dvaipāyana Vyāsa and the Mahābhārata: A New Interpretation* (Leiden: Brill, 1990).

Wikander, Stig, 'Pāṇḍava-sagan och Mahābhāratas mystika förutsättningar', in *Religion och Bibel*, 6 (1947), 27–39 (translated into French by Georges Dumézil in *Jupiter Mars Quirinus*, iv (Paris: Presses Universitaires de France, 1948), 37–53).

NOTE ON THE SANSKRIT TEXT, ITS TRANSLATION, AND ITS METRE

Most scholars have recognized that the Poona Critical Edition represents a valuable tool, as long as its preferred text is not mistaken for some definitive version or the 'real' *Mahābhārata*. I have, accordingly, used it as the basis for my own translation. In the Explanatory Notes I have indicated where I have deviated from or added to the editors' preferred version. When I have used variant readings or additional material, I have done so not because I believe they represent the 'true' or 'original' text, but simply because sometimes they seemed to make better sense, or added, in my opinion, something of narrative or poetic interest. The Sanskrit text of my translated version may, therefore, never have existed up till now in *precisely* that form or combination of lines (although all those lines exist individually in the manuscript traditions). The same may perhaps apply to the Critical Edition's preferred text, but that reflects the nature of the epic and the way in which, historically, it has been transmitted, not (in either case, I trust) some defect in scholarship.

In its Sanskrit form the *Sauptikaparvan* (*The Massacre at Night*), like nearly all of the rest of the epic, is in unrhymed verse. Most individual verses have thirty-two syllables, a metre known as *śloka* or *anuṣṭubh*; this divides into printed lines of sixteen syllables each, subdivided for further analysis into 'quarters' (*pāda*) of eight syllables each. Rhythm is provided by the variation of light and heavy syllables, although their pattern is not fixed throughout the whole line. This makes it a particularly flexible metre for both epic and didactic purposes. Chapter 10, verses 17–30 (a 'purple' passage evoking Yudhiṣṭhira's grief) is, however, in another metre, known as *triṣṭubh*. This has forty-four syllables to the verse, eleven syllables to the line, and is here based on a fixed rhythmical pattern known as *upajāti*.[1]

[1] For a more detailed discussion of epic verse forms, see Smith, *The Warrior Code of India's Sacred Song*; for a general introduction to Sanskrit metre, see ch. 15 of Michael Coulson's *Sanskrit: An Introduction to the Classical Language* (New York: Hodder & Stoughton, 1976).

My version does not attempt to reproduce these metres, either in the number of syllables per line, or in particular patterns of light and heavy syllables; it is, nevertheless, based on a syllable count, worked out in the process of translation. This results in a mixture of irregularly accented ten-, eleven-, and twelve-syllable lines, plus the occasional half-line. The exception is the passage at the end of Chapter 10, in the longer *triṣṭubh* metre in the original, which I have echoed with proportionately more English syllables to the line.

This compromise in terms of prosody has enabled me to stay close to the literal meaning of the Sanskrit original, while permitting an overall pattern to emerge that, from time to time, develops a strong enough regular accent to differentiate it from 'ordinary' cadenced prose. By this means I have tried to modify that prosaic 'translator's tone' which, in the process of advertising its fidelity, risks the most elementary betrayal: persuading the reader that monotony is a quality of the original, not a defect of the translation.[2]

For similar reasons I have supplied line breaks, indentations, and other typographical conventions where there are none in the original. Apart from the indication of the ending of a line or a verse, there is no punctuation in the Sanskrit text. Since the translator is therefore obliged to provide his or her own punctuation, it seems quite consistent to make use of other non-Sanskritic typographical conventions as well, providing these help to clarify the narrative, or contribute to its rhythm in another language. In other words, typography has to suggest what, in the oral tradition, would have been supplied by the reciter-performer. (The text has always seemed to me much more like a prompt-book than, for instance, a novel.)

Ultimately, of course, a translation neither stands nor falls by such devices. Walter Benjamin wrote that 'all great texts contain their translation between the lines'.[3] The *Mahābhārata* is, by any standards, a great text (according to some, the greatest), and I can only hope that a small part of its interlinear potential has been realized in what follows.

[2] To be accurate, variety of tone in the original is obtained by varying the pattern of short and light syllables within the basic constraints of the metre. In English prose, this variety is almost inevitably ironed out, leading, as van Buitenen admits, to a certain predictability and syntactic monotony (*Mahābhārata*, i, p. xxxviii).

[3] Walter Benjamin, *Illuminations*, trans. Harry Zohn (London: Fontana/Collins, 1973), 82.

I am grateful to Kate Crosby for reading through the complete manuscript with such care, and for making a number of acute suggestions.

NOTE ON THE PRONUNCIATION OF SANSKRIT WORDS

The following may act as an approximate guide, but for detailed information on the pronunciation of Sanskrit the reader should consult chapter 1 of Michael Coulson's *Sanskrit: An Introduction to the Classical Language*. In the Introduction and Explanatory Notes some terms have been Anglicized: 'brahmin' for *brāhman* (a priest), and so 'Brahminical' instead of 'Brahmanical', etc.

Pronounce Sanskrit	as in English
a	c*u*t
ā	f*a*r
i	s*i*t
ī	m*e*
u	p*u*t
ū	t*oo*
ṛ	*ri*sk
e	pr*ay*
ai	s*i*gh
o	h*o*pe
au	s*ou*nd
c	*ch*urch
v	close to the English *w*
ś	*sh*ame
ṣ	di*sh*
ḥ	as in English but with a faint echo of the preceding vowel
ṭ etc.	as in English, but with the tongue further back in the mouth
ṅ, ṇ	have a nasal quality
ñ	ca*ny*on
kh, gh, ch, jh, ṭh, ḍh, th, dh, ph, bh	aspirated—as in 'ho*th*ouse', (*not* 'wi*th*'), 'she*ph*erd', 'clu*bh*ouse', etc.
ṃ	nasalizes the preceding vowel sound, as in French *bon*

THE *SAUPTIKAPARVAN* OF THE *MAHĀBHĀRATA*

The Massacre at Night

PART I

The Sleepers

CHAPTER 1

Saṃjaya said:

1 Those heroes* then struck out towards the south,
And at the sunset hour came near the warriors' camp,*
2 Where filled with dread, in haste they let their horses roam,
And crawled into a thicket, unobserved.
3 Close by the camp they crouched, not far at all,
Bruised and tenderized by blades, all seeping wounds.
4 And panting, long and hot, they thought on Pāṇḍu's sons
Whose shouts of dreadful triumph filled the air.
5 Then overcome by fear, to check pursuit
They harnessed up and rode towards the east.

After an hour their horses tired, in need of drink.
6 Sullen with rage, unable to bear their fate,
Still burning with the murder of their king,*
Those great bowmen now paused
To catch their breath.

Then Dhṛtarāṣṭra said:

7 This thing that Bhīma's done defrauds belief—
My son,* ten thousand elephants in strength, cut down!
8 His body was adamantine, he was young—
He, whom not a creature in this world could harm,
Has been destroyed by Pāṇḍu's sons in war
— My son, Saṃjaya!

9 But fate cannot be overruled by men—
Once joined in fight with Pṛthā's kin my son was dead.
10 My heart must be a granite stone indeed,
For even the news of one hundred slaughtered sons
Does not break it to a thousand separate shards.

11 Yet what is left for parents of a murdered child?
I cannot bear to live in Pāṇḍu's son's domain.

12 How should I, the father to a king—a king myself—
Exist a slave at Pāṇḍu's son's diktat?
13 Shall I, who ruled the whole world, standing at its head,
Join at the last with slaves and make an obscure end?
14 How shall I stomach Bhīma's taunts—Bhīma,
Who alone has killed all my hundred sons?
15 The words of great-souled Vidura* are now made truth—
The words my son ignored . . .

16 But go on, old friend, tell me what Kṛtavarman,
Kṛpa, and Droṇa's son did next, after my son,
Duryodhana, was felled, in contravention
Of everything that's natural, right, and good.

Saṃjaya continued:

17 Before they had gone too far, your men pulled up.
Stretched out before them was a forest's dreadful tract,
Knotted with many kinds of creepers, roots, and trees.
18 Resting a while, letting their thoroughbreds drink,
They reached that forest as the sun began to set.

19 Crowded with roosting birds, swept by herds of wild deer,
Choked with trees and creepers, prowled by beasts of prey,
20 Shimmering with tracts of water, chained with lakes,
A flood of ponds quilted with blue lotus beds,
21 —That was the forest they entered and gazed on.

And there they saw a fig tree with a thousand limbs . . .
22 Great warriors that they were, and peerless among men,
They recognized that fig tree as their forest peer.
23 Descending from their chariots there, they freed
Their horses, bathed themselves and then performed
Their evening ritual,* in the proper way.

24 Then, when the sun had set behind the western hills,
Night, mother of the universe, came down.
25 The sky's dark resplendent hem, stitched with stars,
With meteors and planets, stretched out above.

26 Below, creatures that walk the night roamed at will,
While those that walk the day were caged in sleep.
27 The cries of the prowlers rose to a ghastly pitch,
Flesh-eaters were gladdened, and the night turned to dread.

28–9 Faced with that dreadful darkness, choked with grief,
Kṛtavarman, Kṛpa, and Droṇa's son
Huddled deep in their gloom beneath the tree,
Lamenting that disaster which had overrun
The Kurus and the Pāṇḍavas alike.
30 Then limbs dragged down by sleep, they lay on the bare earth,
Overcome by fatigue, wounded by many shafts.
31 And in this fashion, king, the two great warriors,
Kṛpa and Kṛtavarman, gave in to sleep—
Fit for happiness, unworthy of suffering,
Yet stretched on the bare earth, crammed with fatigue and grief.

32 But Droṇa's son, O Bhārata, overpowered
By shame and wrath, could not sleep, and lay there
Hissing like a snake.
33 Burnt up by rage, sleep lay beyond his grasp—
Instead, great-armed Aśvatthāman surveyed
The terrible forest and its lurid sights.
34–5 Peering at one particular, teeming spot,
The warrior saw a fig tree covered in crows—
Crows in their thousands, perched on that banyan* abreast,
Crows innocently sunk that night in happy sleep.
36 But as those oblivious, trusting crows slept on,
Aśvatthāman beheld a terrible owl.*
Sight-rending and sudden in its fell approach,
37 Plummet-bodied, green-eyed, and tawny-plumed,
It stooped as swift as Garuḍa, screeching loud,
Unnaturally taloned, freakishly beaked.
38 Then uttering soft, deceitful cries, like any bird
Come down to roost, it fell upon the tree—
39 Stooped on a branch, and slaughtered countless sleeping crows—
That sky-goer, that crow-destroying owl—

40 Slicing the wings off some, beheading the rest,
And shattering the talons of others
With his own lethal claws.
41 Such was his power, O king, that those who fell
Into his field of sight perished in an instant,
Their limbs and bodies drifting in an ever-
Widening pool around the banyan's trunk.
42 And now the crows were dead, the owl was full of joy—
A foe-destroyer, his foe-destroying slaked.

43 Then, Droṇa's son, a witness to that guileful deed
Accomplished by the owl at night, resolved
To do a similar thing himself, reflecting:

44 'This owl has tutored me in war. My thoughts
Are locked onto my enemies' death, and
Now the time has come.
45 The Pāṇḍavas seem like winners, and as things stand
Cannot be killed by me. They have perseverance
And strength; their marksmen are proven, their warriors skilled;
Yet in the presence of Duryodhana, the king,
I promised to destroy them* all, to the last breath.
46 It is a moth-like course, a suicidal dive
Into the flame to fight them fairly—certain death.
But through deceit success may come, and with it
The obliteration of all my foes.
47 In this, those who know the treatises on statecraft*
Prize certain means above those subject to doubt.
48 It matters not at all what worldly blame
And censure such an action draws: for a warrior
Following the warrior's code*, it is a duty
And it must be done.
49 At every turn the Pāṇḍavas, those spiritual dwarfs,
Have perpetrated guileful, reprehensible,
Utterly foul, and contemptible deeds.
50 Those familiar with the universal law,*
Who see into the heart of things, and know
What acts are proper in the light of truth,
Refer to two time-honoured stanzas—thus:

51 *'The enemy's army, even when exhausted
And wounded by its foes, even when eating
And drinking, even when marching away
Or resting in the camp, should be attacked.*

52 *'The same applies to forces when they sleep at night,
Those leaderless or broken,- and those divided
By an error when they should be joined as one.'**

53 And by this line of reasoning, Droṇa's powerful son
Resolved himself to massacre at night*
The Pāṇḍavas and Pāñcālas as they slept.
54 Binding himself, vow upon vow, to this cruel deed,
He woke his sleeping uncle and the Bhoja king.*
55 But when their reaction was not as he had hoped,
He bristled with shame, and after a moment's pause,
Addressed them once more, his eyes filled with tears:

56 'That singular hero, the mighty king—
Duryodhana, for whose sake we have fought
The Pāṇḍavas without respite, has been destroyed.
57 Lord of eleven armies, pure strength, cut off
In battle, he was felled by Bhīmasena
And a rabble host.
58 Then—such vile cruelty—the low Vṛkodara*
Crushed with his foot the head of that anointed king.
59 The Pāñcālas are buzzing, they bellow and laugh—
Jubilant, they blow their conches by the hundred,
And batter their drums,
60 As though the wind had fused the regions of the air
To one great cacophony of conch and drum.
61 A gale of lion-voiced warriors, of elephant roars,
Of horses whinnying, deafens our ears.
62 The shuddering of wheels, the violent cry
Of the exultant charioteers breaks from the west.
63 And we three alone have survived that slaughter—
The massacre of Dhṛtarāṣṭra's men
By the Pāṇḍava hordes.

64 Some had the strength of a hundred elephants,
Others had mastery of lethal weapons—
All have been destroyed by the Pāṇḍavas' minions.

'And now I feel the whirligig of Time:
65 For in reality this has fallen out
Just as it had to; whatever the effort—
However exceptional—the result would have
Been precisely the same.
66 But if distraction has not withered up your minds,
Tell us how we may best proceed in this great—
Yet so greatly corrupted—enterprise!'

CHAPTER 2

Kṛpa said:

1 'Mighty Aśvatthāman, you have argued well,
And with good reason—but now consider this:
2 There are two forces: fate and human effort*—
All men depend on and are bound by these,
There is nothing else.
3 *Two*, since actions succeed neither by fate,
Nor sheer exertion alone, but through their bond.
4 All purposes, from low to high, depend upon
These two together. In every case, men
Are engaged or disengaged in action
By virtue of this pair.

5 'What happens when it rains on a mountain?
What happens when it rains on a ploughed field?
6 It is clear in every case: exertion
When something is not fated is as useless
As restraint when it is.
7 But just as rain, falling by fate on a field
Properly prepared, gives rise to more abundant seed
And higher yield—so it is with human success.
8 Of the two, fate once determined proceeds alone;
But the wise, with skill, employ themselves in effort.
9 For through these two, all ends of human action
Are attained. And in respect of these, men are thought
Active or restrained.
10 Activated, human effort succeeds through fate,
And then that action's fruit falls to the actor.
11 But even the effort of industrious men,
Working together, is fruitless in the
World devoid of fate.
12 Because of this, idle and unperceptive men
Despise exertion—the wise know better.

13 For generally action bears some productive fruit,
While to abstain altogether produces
Nothing but the heavy fruit of suffering.

14 'Two kinds of men are seldom found*—those who achieve
Their ends fortuitously, without exertion,
And those who, having acted, still do not succeed.
15 The industrious man, rejecting idleness,
Is fit to live; it is he, and not the idler,
Who increases happiness—it is he
Who desires the welfare of his fellow beings.
16 If the industrious man, through taking action,
Does not succeed, he should not be blamed for that—
He still perceives the truth.

17 'The man who succeeds in the world without acting
Is the exception; as a rule, the inactive
Lay themselves open to blame and revulsion.
18 So the man who flouts this rule garners to himself
Misfortune—and there is nothing wise about that.
19 Exertion can be fruitless in two ways:
When it is devoid of human effort
Or when it's not fated. But as this world goes,
Action cannot succeed without human effort.
20 And in fact, the industrious, skilful man,
Who, having made due obeisance to the gods,
Strives to obtain his ends the proper way, never
Exerts himself in vain.
21 Likewise the person who attends on the elders,
Questions them on what is conducive to welfare,
And uses their advice to advantage,
Has done the right thing.
22 For every time you plan to exert yourself,
Those acknowledged elders should be consulted—
They are the ultimate source of practice:
Success is defined as what is rooted in that,
23 Since the man who practises exertion,
Following the advice of the elders,
Quickly attains the full fruit of his action.

24 Whereas the man who tries to attain his ends
Through passion, greed, fear, and anger—the man
Who is supercilious and not to be advised—
Is soon deprived of wealth.

25 'And it was just such an ill-thought out enterprise
Which was undertaken by the avaricious
Duryodhana, without corroboration,
Without foresight, and out of sheer folly.
26 Ignoring the well-disposed, and consulting
With the dishonest, being frustrated,
He began a feud with the Pāṇḍavas,
Who in their qualities outranked him by far.
27 From the first he was exceptionally volatile—
Unable to humble himself, he failed to act
On the advice of his friends, and now he burns
In the ruins of his ambitious folly.
28 And because we have followed that wicked man,
We too have suffered this most harsh misfortune.

29 'This disaster has scorched our minds: thinking for
Ourselves no longer shows us the best way to go.
30 The perplexed should consult knowledgeable friends,
Question them, and then act on their advice.
31 So let's approach Dhṛtarāṣṭra and Gāndhārī,
And clever Vidura—let's consult with them.
32 Questioned, they may say what is best for us,
And we can act on it at once—I'm certain this
Is what we must now do.

33 'The purpose fails because the proper step
Is never taken—only those whose actions stall
After all human effort has been made
Can claim that their affliction stems from fate.'

CHAPTER 3

Saṃjaya said:

1 Once he had heard Kṛpa's speech, so beneficial,
So full of gain and good, Aśvatthāman,
Great king,* was overcome with discontent and grief.
2 Consumed with anguish as if set alight,
He scorched all pity from his mind, and said:

3 'Intelligence differs from one man to the next,
And yet each is happy with his own insight—
4 Each thinks himself much brighter than the rest,
Each values and praises himself to the height.
5 All think their own understanding the best—
Forever lauding their superior intellect,
Forever denigrating all the rest.

6 'Men who make common cause share common thoughts—thinking
Much of and ever praising one another.
7 But when reverses mount, those selfsame men
Find intellectual differences intervene.
8 Thanks to the unfathomable nature of their thoughts,
There is a difference between man and man—
Each is bewildered in a different way.
9 For just as a skilled doctor, having diagnosed
A disease according to the book, in practice
Prescribes a medicine to effect a cure
Specific to each case,
10 So men use their intellect, harnessed to insight,
To put their intended actions into practice—
And other men revile them because of that.

11 'One kind of consciousness misleads a man
In youth—some other sort in middle age—
And in his dotage another kind of thought
Is his obsession.

12 In the same way, a man who suffers some
Terrible distress or equally intense
Success, has his intelligence transformed.
13 So in one and the same person, intelligence
Differs at different times, and because his
Insight fluctuates, nothing is clear for him.

14 'Yet having determined some new idea
According to insight, one considers that thought
To be correct, and out of it a way of acting
Is produced;
So it is thought that leads to action,
15 For every person undertakes an action
With optimism, convinced of its rightness,
Even when such an action may prove fatal.
16 All men in the light of their own practice
And insight, exert themselves in various ways,
Which they believe to be advantageous.

17 'Today, in our hour of defeat, a thought
Came to me to banish grief. Listen to this:
18 Creator Prajāpati* emitted
Creatures and gave them work. Then he assigned
To each estate* its own best qualities:
19 To the brahmin* he gave cool self-control,
To warriors and rulers* energy supreme,
To merchants and farmers* industrious skill,
And to the labourer and serf* good will
To serve the rest.
20 An unrestrained brahmin is a foul disgrace,
A warrior without energy is most vile,
An unindustrious merchant is reviled—so too
The refractory serf.

21 'I was born into a brahmin family—
The best, the most highly honoured family—
But ill fortune has allotted me this
Kṣatriya duty.*

22 If, having followed the duty of a warrior,
I now reverted to the brahmin way, I might
Shake the world, but such an action would be worth
23 Nothing—for how could I, who have drawn the magic
Bow* and carried marvellous weapons into war,
Recite the mantra at the sacrifice?*
—I who have seen my father so vilely slain?

24 'And since I have honoured my warrior duty,
Which accorded precisely with my desires,
Tonight I shall tread the path that the king
And my glorious father trod before me*—
25 Tonight, like conquerors, the unsuspecting
Pāñcālas will unbuckle their armour
Unyoke their chariots, and sleep, crammed with joy,
Thinking us beaten and extinguished by the fight.
26 Then, as they are lying prone within their camp,
Among their own people, in the dead of night
I shall make an irresistible assault.
27 As they lie dead to the world, and senseless
In their tents, I shall attack and slaughter them,
Fell as Maghavat against the Dānavas.*

28 'Imagine a fire blowing through dry grass—
Attacking them tonight all in the one place,
I shall, like that fire, consume all those whose lord
Is Dhṛṣṭadyumna.* And then I shall be at peace,
For the Pāñcālas will have been destroyed.
29 As wrathful Rudra, bow Pināka* in hand,
Roams among his victims,* so shall I roam tonight
Among the Pāñcālas, slaughtering them in war.
30 And once I have cut through and killed all Pāñcālas,
Still wrathful, I shall then torment in combat
Pāṇḍu's sons—tonight.
31 When the earth is buried in Pāñcāla bodies,
When I have battered them down, one by one,
I shall be freed then from that debt I owe
My father*—tonight.

32 Tonight, I shall make the Pāñcālas tread
That self-same stony path already trodden
By Duryodhana, Karṇa, Bhīṣma, and
The great king of Sindh.*
33 Tonight, in the darkness before the dawn,
I shall, through sheer force, tear from the shoulders
Of Dhṛṣṭadyumna, the Pāñcāla king,
His head, as though he were a tethered goat.*
34 Tonight, in the dark, with my whetted sword,
I shall strike in battle the sleeping sons
Of the Pāñcālas and Pāṇḍavas alike.
35 Tonight, having destroyed in darkness, in their sleep,
The Pāñcāla army, I shall have then discharged
My duty to the full—
And I shall rest.'

CHAPTER 4

Kṛpa said to The Unfallen (Aśvatthāman):

1 'Thank heaven you've been inspired to take revenge—
Indra himself could not restrain you now.
2 At daybreak we shall follow you, but for tonight
Lay down your standard, unstrap your mail, and rest.
3–4 Tomorrow, armed and standing in our chariots,
Kṛtavarman of the Sātvatas and I
Shall follow you towards the foe, where, with our aid,
In the press of battle, you shall, great warrior,
Showing your valour, cut down the Pāñcāla foe,
With all their retinue.
5 Rest tonight, sleep tonight, dear lord—you have the strength
To rise to this, but you have been awake too long.
6 Rested, alert, and joined in battle with a clear mind,
You shall, beyond all doubt, destroy the foe.
7 For no one, not even the god of war* himself,
Has power to overcome you—best of warriors,
Wielder of the greatest weapons of war.
8 For who would fight Droṇa's son in battle,
With Kṛpa and Kṛtavarman at his side?
—Not even the king of heaven* himself.

9 'So we three, having rested up at night, shall
Assail the enemy with the rising sun,
Our spirits lifted, and our minds alert.
10 For you clearly have magical weapons—
And so do I. And this great Sātvata archer,
Kṛtavarman, has always been skilled in battle.
11 Then, once the three of us have violently dispatched
The entire congregation of our foes in war,
Our joy shall be complete.
So rest tonight
In safety, lord, and happy be your sleep!

12 'Best of men, once you've set out in your chariot
In haste, Kṛtavarman and I, archers
And foe-torchers both, shall follow you in our
Chariots, fully armed.
13 And once you've gained their camp, and given your name
In challenge, then you should fight—for then you'll make
A shambles of the foe.
14 And when you've killed them in the bright dawn air,
You shall divert yourself in pleasure, like Śakra
When he had dispatched the great *asuras*.*
15 For you, it will be as nothing to conquer
The Pāñcāla troop in battle—no more
Than for the fierce killer of the Dānavas*
To destroy the entire Daitya army.*
16 Going into battle side by side with me,
And guarded by Kṛtavarman, even mighty
Indra* himself could not prevail against you.

17 'My dear lord, never shall Kṛtavarman or I
Withdraw from combat until the Pāṇḍavas
Are dead.
18 So killing them in battle, killing
The vile Pāñcālas too, we shall live again—
Or being killed by them, all go to heaven.
19 For, by every means within our power,
We shall be your helpers in the morning light.
Strong-armed, sinless man, I tell you this in truth.'

20 Responding to his uncle's beneficial speech,
Eyes bulging with rage, Droṇa's son said this:

21 'Where is sleep for the man who is suffering?
For the angry? For those anxious about wealth?
Or for the man who has gone the way of desire?
22 Can't you grasp that *all* these are now at work in me,
When one alone would be enough to cancel sleep?
23 How in this world can a man express the grief
Remembrance of his father's murder brings?
My heart burns night and day, but never burns it out.

24 'That special way in which my sire was slain*
By evil men—you saw it all. And it is that
Rips my vitals now.
25 How can a man like me, even for a moment,
Stomach a world where one may hear that Pāñcāla
Refrain: "Droṇa is dead"?

26 'Life is unbearable until I've killed
Dhṛṣṭadyumna in battle. He murdered
My father, and so he must be killed by me,
Along with all his Pāñcāla allies.
27 And again, whose heart is so pitiless
It would not burn to have heard, as I have,
The wailing of the king whose thigh's been shattered?*
28 Indeed, where is that man without compassion
Whose eyes would not fill with tears having heard
Such a sound from the king with shattered thighs?
29 That he, who took sides with me and mine, lives vanquished
Swells my grief, as a tidal wave the sea.
My mind is weathered to a single point of grief—
Whence shall sleep come tonight? And whence content?

30 'Uncle, I believe even great Indra himself
Cannot subdue them while Vāsudeva
And Arjuna are there for their protection.*
31 So the question of my holding back now doesn't
Arise. No man in this world can deflect me
From this, my duty. My mind is made up,
My thought is unerring.
32 The defeat of my friends
And the Pāṇḍavas' triumph is the messengers'
Report, and my heart burns.
33 But I shall sleep
And my grief shall be dispelled, when in their sleep,
This very night, I have slaughtered all my foes.'

CHAPTER 5

Kṛpa responded (to Aśvatthāman):

1 'It's my belief that an ignorant man,
Even though he attends upon his superiors,
Cannot, if his senses are uncontrolled,
Discover everything there is to know
About the pursuit of worldly ends and *dharma*.*
2 It's the same for even a man of learning
Who doesn't practise discipline: he ascertains
Nothing certain at all about *dharma*
And the pursuit of wealth.
Even though he waits on
His teacher forever, a strong but stupid man
Never understands his duties; he is like the
Ladle in the soup—oblivious to its flavours.
But a man with insight, waiting on that teacher
For just an instant, understands his duties
Directly, like the tongue the soup's flavours.*

3 'That's to say, a man of learning, who attends
On his superiors—a person whose senses
Are controlled—may come to understand all
Established teachings, and does not oppose
What should be accepted.
4 But he who is cynical and ungovernable,
That perverse and wicked man who has abandoned
Prescribed virtue, perpetrates a great evil.
5 Friends restrain a friend from sin; the fortunate man
Turns back, the unfortunate carries on.
6 For just as the man whose mind is distracted
Is restrained by soothing words, so it is
With the man subdued by a friend—but the
Unsubdued sinks down.
7 So when an intelligent friend is preparing
An evil action, those with insight restrain him—
For as long and in so far as they can.

8 'Concentrate on the acquisition of virtue,
Restrain your self with the self. Do as I say,
My boy, and you'll not regret it later.
9 In this world, the slaughter of the sleeping
Is not respected as conforming to *dharma*.
The same applies to those whose arms have been laid down,
To those whose fighting chariots have been unyoked,
10 To those who have declared their allegiance,
To refugees, and those with dishevelled hair,*
To those, as well, whose chariots have been destroyed.

11 'Tonight, my lord, the Pāñcālas will sleep,
Their armour unbuckled, unconscious as the dead,
All unsuspecting through the dark till dawn.
12 The wicked man who seeks to harm them in that state,
Without a doubt, would dive into a raftless,
Fathomless, shoreless hell.
13 You are celebrated throughout the world
As peerless in your skill with weapons, and yet
In this world you have never done the slightest wrong.
14 So when the sun has risen on the morrow
On all beings alike, you, like another sun,
Shall beat your foes in war, in broad daylight.

15 'For in you an unworthy action would inspire
Revulsion—like blood splattered on a white tunic,
So it seems to me.'

Aśvatthāman replied:

16 'It's as you've said, uncle, and I would restrain
Myself, if long before this the limits had not
Been pulled apart in a hundred ways by the
Pāṇḍavas themselves.
17 In the presence of kings, and of yourself, my lord,
My father, who had laid aside his sword, was felled
By Dhṛṣṭadyumna.
18 And that great warrior Karṇa, when his chariot's wheel
Was stuck, and he was motionless in supreme
Distress, was killed by the Gāṇḍīva bow.

19 In the same way, Bhīṣma, Śāṃtanu's son, unarmed,
His sword laid down on Śikhaṇḍin's account,
Was killed by Arjuna.
20 So too the great archer Bhūriśravas,
While fasting to death on the field of battle,
Was felled by Yuyudhāna though kings cried out.
21 And Duryodhana, confronted in battle
By Bhīma with a mace, was unlawfully felled
In clear sight of all the lords of the earth.*
22 Surrounded by the great warriors, there alone,
That tiger of a man was stricken down
By lawless Bhīma.
23 Even in the messengers' reports, the cries of
The king, his thigh-bones shattered, cut me to the quick.

24 'Thus it is with the unrighteous and evil
Pāñcālas, who have broken all the limits—
So why doesn't your honour censure them,
Who have so shattered the bonds of morality?

25 'Truly, if killing my father's murderers,
The Pāñcālas, as they sleep in the night, means
Rebirth for me as a worm or a moth, I shall
Suffer it gladly.
26 Tonight my purpose drives me on, and driven so,
What place is there for sleep, what time for happiness?
Never in the world has that man been born—
Nor will he be—who may rescind my will
To their destruction.'

Saṃjaya continued:

28 With these words, great king, Droṇa's son, filled with power,
Yoked his horses in a place apart, then,
Ready to advance, turned towards the foe.
29 At which those great-souled men, the Bhoja and the son
Of Śaradvat, asked:
'Why is your chariot yoked,
And what do you intend?

30 Our aim is just the same as yours, bullish man—
Truly, we are one in suffering and joy.
So don't distrust us.'

31 But remembering the death of his father,
Incensed Aśvatthāman told them his true intent.

32 'With his sharp arrows my father killed warriors
In their hundreds and thousands. But when his weapons
Were laid aside, Dhṛṣṭadyumna felled him.
33 And so indeed, tonight, when he has laid aside
All protective armour, I shall kill him—
Dhṛṣṭadyumna, the Pāñcāla king's evil son—
In just such a way, with just such a wicked act.
34 And then how, I wonder, shall that evil
Pāñcāla attain the worlds reserved for those
Conquered in war by arms,* when he has been destroyed
By me, like an animal at the sacrifice?

35 'Now best of warriors, incinerators
Of the foe, take up your bows and swords, buckle
Your armour without delay, and wait on me.'

36 Mounting his chariot with these words, he then set out
Towards the foe. And Kṛpa and the Sātvata,
Kṛtavarman, my king,* both followed him.
37 Shining like three enkindled sacrificial fires*
Fed with ghee,* those three advanced towards the foe,
38 And came, my lord, close to the sleeping camp,
Before whose gates Aśvatthāman arose
In his great chariot.

CHAPTER 6

Dhṛtarāṣṭra asked Saṃjaya:

1 'When the Bhoja and Kṛpa saw Droṇa's son
Stationary before the gates, what did they do?'

But Saṃjaya went on:

2 Once he had taken leave of Kṛtavarman
And the great warrior Kṛpa, Droṇa's son,
Brimming with wrath, went to the threshold of the camp.
3 There, his hair rose on his scalp, for he saw
Guarding the gate, a great-bodied spirit, bright as
The sun and moon combined.
4 It was draped in a tiger's skin soaked in blood,
Its upper garment, black antelope skin,
Its sacred thread, a snake.
5 Its arms were exceptionally long and muscular,
Each with its own particular arsenal,
And another great snake encircled its bicep.
Its mouth was a cave, wreathed in garlands of flames,
6 Its gaping jaws and their jutting tusks spoke terror—
Brilliant eyes in their thousands stared from its face.
7 Its body and dress were indescribable—
The mountains themselves would sunder, and shatter
When they beheld it.
8 From every orifice—from its mouth, its nostrils,
Its ears, from those thousands of eyes—there licked high
flames.*
9 Then, from those particles of fiery energy
There rose Hṛṣīkeśas* in their hundreds and
Thousands, each bearing a conch, a disc, and a mace.*

10 Seeing that prodigious spirit, the world's terror,
Droṇa's son was quite unshaken, drenching it
Beneath a cloudburst of magic arrows.

11 But that great being swallowed up the shafts discharged
By Droṇa's son, as the mare's-mouth fire* swallows streams
Of water from the sea.
12 Then seeing those floods of arrows disappear,
Aśvatthāman hurled a war javelin, tipped
With a blazing fire.
13 Like a great meteor that strikes the sun as an age
Of the world comes to an end,* and falls from heaven—
So his flame-tipped javelin struck that spirit and broke.
14 Instantly, Aśvatthāman pulled from its sheath,
Like a blazing snake from its pit, a heavenly,
Golden-hilted sword, lustrous as the sky.
15 Cannily the warrior cast that radiant sword
At the spirit—and, like a mongoose into
A hole,* the weapon vanished without trace.
16 Incensed, Droṇa's son cast next a blazing club,
Resembling Indra's flagpole—and that too
The spirit devoured.
17 Then, when all his weapons had been repulsed,
Looking around, he saw the entire sky
Had darkened with teeming Janārdanas.*
18 Beholding that extraordinary wonder,
Disarmed and in torment, Droṇa's son recalled
How Kṛpa had counselled him, and cried aloud:

19 'A man like me, who ignores the unwelcome
But salutary advice of friends, laments,
As I do now, when disaster befalls.
20 Bypassing the precepts of *śāstra** completely,
He desires to kill those who should not be killed,
And, falling from the ordained path, sets foot
Upon an evil road.
21–2 For a man should not bear weapons against cattle,
Against brahmins or kings, against a woman,
A friend, his mother, his teacher, the old,
Against children, the moronic, the blind,
Against the sleeping, and those rising from sleep,
The terrified, drunk, insane, and distracted—
Such was the constant teaching of the past masters.

23 But by neglecting the path laid down in *śāstra*,
I have come by a bad route to great distress.

24 'Yet those who know say the worst distress is felt
By the man who undertakes a great deed,
And then turns back from it, in fear of danger.
25 But here below, who can do the impossible
Through sheer force? What they say is true—human
Action is not more powerful than fate.
26 If a man's action does not succeed through
The workings of fate, he falls from the ordained path,
And encounters ruin.
27 Those who know say it is the opposition
Of the unknown which turns a man back in fear
Once he has begun an action in this case.
28 But this danger has befallen me through my own
Misconduct, otherwise Droṇa's son would never
Turn back in battle.
29 Like fate's instrument,
This towering spirit prepares to strike—and yet
I cannot recognize it, however
Deep I rake my mind.
30 Surely this terrible being that comes
To obstruct me is the fruit of my impure
Intention,* produced with no regard for *dharma*.
31 So my turning back from battle has been
Determined by fate: fate alone can check me here.
32 Tonight I put myself under the protection
Of mighty Mahādeva; he will destroy
For me this terrible instrument of fate.
33 I resort to Umā's lord,* the god of gods,
Kapardin—he of the braided and knotted hair,
Skull-garlanded Rudra*—Hara—destroyer
Of Lord Bhaga's sight.*
34 For in his asceticism and strength, this god
Far surpasses all the rest. And so it is
To the trident-bearing mountain god* I go
For protection now.'

CHAPTER 7

Saṃjaya said to Dhṛtarāṣṭra:

1 With this avowal Droṇa's son, my lord,
Stepped down from his chariot's driving box, and stood,
Head bowed, before that supreme god of gods.

Droṇa's son said:

2–5 'By an act beyond the unintelligent—
By an act which, even for those with a mind,
Is barely imaginable—I shall offer
Myself in sacrifice to the destroyer
Of the triple citadel*—fierce, immovable,
Auspicious* Rudra, Śarva, Īśāna,
Īśvara, Giriśa, the boon-giving god,
Creator of life, imperishable,
Blue-throated,* unborn, Śakra, the destroyer
Of Dakṣa's sacrifice*—three-eyed Hara,*
Whose body is the universe, multiform
Husband of Umā, wild inhabitant
Of the cremation grounds, the mighty
Lord of myriad troops of spirits, brandishing
The skull-topped pole,* the celibate with matted locks—
Rudra.
6 Celebrated in the past, the present,
And the future, unerring, skin-robed, red-haired,
Blue-throated, singular, irrepressible,
7 All-making Śakra, Brahman,* celibate—
The avowed vower, incessant devotee
Of austerities, the infinite goal
Of all ascetics,
8 Multiform director of troops of spirits,
Three-eyed focus of your retinue's love,
Yours is the face seen by Gaṇeśa, which is
Dear above all to the heart of Gaurī;

9 Kumāra's tawny father, whose wonder-
Vehicle is the bull,* whose scent is most delicate,
So very fierce, and yet so eagerly engaged
In adorning Umā,
10 Higher than the high—so highest—for nothing
Higher is known, master of the most lethal
Bolts and arrows—Death,
11 A god in golden armour, crested by the moon—
This is the god I go to for refuge, with
Supreme concentration.

12 'Tonight I shall traverse this great obstruction,
This terrible calamity: with a pure
Oblation of all five of my elements,*
I shall offer myself to the god who is pure.'

13 And because his will to offer up himself
Was clear, a golden sacrificial altar
Sprang up before great-souled Aśvatthāman—
14 An altar upon which a blazing fire was lit
That spread across the sky and every point in space.*
15 And in the same place there appeared troops of creatures,*
With blazing jaws and eyes, and multiple heads
And feet and arms, like elephants or mountains.
16 They had the cast of dogs, wild boars, and camels,
The heads of horses, jackals, cattle, tigers, and
Panthers, the faces of wild cats and bears; there were
17 Duck-heads, monkey-heads, parrot-heads, white goose-faces,
And those with the mouths of great constricting snakes;
18 There were woodpecker heads and blue-jay faces,
Tortoise-, crocodile-, and porpoise-headed beasts.
19 They had the faces of whales, and great sea monsters;
They were lion-faced, curlew-beaked, and pigeon-headed.
20 They had the tongues of turtle doves, they had the beaks
Of cormorants; some had ears in their hands,
Some a thousand eyes, some a hundred bellies;
21 Others were fleshless, wolf-headed, or hawk-visaged;
Some were without heads at all, my king,* and some
Had the terrible heads of human bears.

22 Some had licking flames for eyes, some fire-mouths;
Others had the faces of rams or goats.
23 Some were conch-faced, conch-complexioned, and conch-eared;
Their retinues were garlanded with conches, and
They roared like conches too.
24 Some wore matted locks, others five tufts of hair;
Some were bald and hollow-bellied, others
Four-fanged, four-tongued, diademed, and ass-eared.
25 Some had top-knots, some were curly-haired, some crowned;
Some had beautiful faces, finely adorned;
26 Full of majesty, in their hundreds and thousands,
They were wearing blue lotus blossomss, they were decked
In white water-lilies.
27 Some brandished clubs, some the spiked *śataghnī* disc,*
Some maces, others nooses, and some, Bhārata,*
The *bhuśuṇḍī* weapon.*
28 Some had quivers slung on their shoulders, bulging
With different kinds of arrows, some had banners,
Some flags, some bells, some axes—all maddened with war.
29 Some spun great nooses, some brandished clubs, or swords,
Or stakes; some were diademed with striking snakes.
Some wore bright jewels, and others serpents, coiled
About their upper arms.
30 Some were wreathed in white garments, smeared with mud,
And shrouded in dust; some had fresh faces,
And rosy limbs, and some again were blue.

31 Rejoicing, bright as gold, that great god's retinue,
Their bodies* kettledrums, conches, and tabors,
Played upon horns, and drums, and double-drums.
32 Full of a boundless vigour, some sang while others danced,
Some leapt about, some skipped, some capered round.
33 Hair flowing in the wind, fierce and swift, they trampled
Like mighty elephants in rut, thundering
And bellowing, bellowing and thundering.
34 Very terrible, most dreadful to see, armed
With whetted spears and pikes, they were variously dressed
In motley, brightly garlanded and unguent smeared,

35 Their bejewelled and braceleted arms were raised
Ready to strike—those great foe-destroyers,
Irresistibly strong.
36 Drinkers of blood, marrow, and other remains,
Diners on entrails and flesh, some wore earrings,
Some a lock of hair on the crown of the head,
Some were pot-bellied, others seemed starved.
37 Some were dwarfs and some were giants, some were
Very powerful and fierce; some had monstrous
Blackened under-lips, some huge penises, erect.
38 Some had many precious crowns, some shaven heads,
Some matted hair. They could bring the sun, the
moon,
The planets, stars, the very sky itself to earth;
39 They had the power to kill the fourfold host*
Of living things. Forever free from fear,
Those slaves to Hara's frowns,
40 Behaving as they pleased, attainers of their ends,
The lords of the lord of the triple world* are
Perpetually immersed in sensual pleasures,
Yet untouched by passion. Masters of speech,
41 Eight kinds of superhuman power* are theirs—
Thus they are bewilderment free. Lord Hara
Is forever made proud by their actions.
42 The Lord is devoted to them in thought, word,
And deed, for they are as children produced
By himself; and they forever worship him
In thought, word, and deed, with loving devotion.
43 Some are fierce, perpetual drinkers of the
Bone-marrow and blood of the impious;
And there are those ever-drinking *soma*,*
To the ritual chant in twenty-four parts.*
44 They have propitiated the trident-bearing
Śiva with Vedic recitation,* and
Celibacy, and asceticism, and
Self-restraint—and now they are absorbed in Bhava.

45 So together with Pārvatī, the lord
Maheśvara, master of past, present,

And future, enjoys, through the beings that are
Himself, the multitude of living creatures.

46 Filling the universe with resonant cries,
Bellowing aloud with peculiar, distinctive
Laughter, roaring, they approached Aśvatthāman.
47 Praising Mahādeva, radiating light,
Wanting to increase the glory of the
Great-souled son of Droṇa,
48 Wanting to assess his lustre and energy,
Wanting to witness the sleeping warriors
Massacred at night, that ghastly crowd of spirits
Approached from all sides, their terrible and fierce clubs,
Their firebrands, spears, and lances at the ready.

49 It was a sight to terrify the triple world,*
But for mighty Aśvatthāman it held no fear.
50 Bow in hand, his arm and fingers bound with
Iguana skin,* Droṇa's son of his own accord
Offered himself as an oblation to Śiva.

51 In that sacrifice bows were the fuel, whetted
Arrows the filters,* and the self of that
Completely self-possessed man the burnt offering.
52 Then the inflamed son of Droṇa, with a mantra
To *soma*,* offered himself as oblation.
53 Having worshipped that high-souled Rudra, whose deeds are
Ferocious, with imperishable rites no less
Terrible themselves, he joined his hands and said:

54 'I, born of the Āṅgirasa clan,* offer
Tonight this very self into the fire.
O Lord, accept me as a sacrifice!
55 Great god, universal self, with devotion
To you, with extreme concentration in
This my distress, I consecrate in your
Presence, a sacrifice!
56 All creatures are in you, and you are in them—
For all essential qualities are one in you.

57 Refuge of all beings, I come before you, lord,
As an oblation—accept me, O god,
Since I cannot overcome my enemies.'

58 With these words, Droṇa's son, giving himself up
Entirely, mounted that sacrificial altar
Where the fire was blazing, and entered the flames.

59 Seeing him as an oblation, arms uplifted,
Unmoving before him, Lord Mahādeva
In person* addressed him, with the hint of a smile:

60 'With truth, purity, and sincerity,
With renunciation, austerity, and vows,
With patience, devotion, and resolution,
With both thought and word,
61 I have been duly worshipped by Kṛṣṇa,* whose deeds
Are pure; and therefore there is no one dearer
To me than Kṛṣṇa.
62 And so to honour him, and put you to the test,
I have forcibly protected the Pāñcālas,
Often employing my magical powers.

63 But the honour I did him in protecting
The Pāñcālas is now complete, and so
They have fallen under the power of Time,* and
Tonight their lives are done.'

64 With these words Lord Śiva gave the warrior
A spotless sword, and entered his body.*
65 Then, being possessed by God, Aśvatthāman
Blazed with divine energy, and with that fiery,
God-engendered power, he was transformed
Into the embodiment of battle.

66 So like Śiva in person, he bore down on
The enemy camp, invisible spirits
And *rākṣasas** streaming before and behind him.

CHAPTER 8

Dhṛtarāṣṭra said:

1 'While Droṇa's son approached the camp, I trust
Those great warriors, Kṛpa and the Bhoja,
Did not hold back through fear.
2 I hope the two of them were not observed
Vilely warded off by guards, or that such great
Men did not turn back, thinking the task beyond them.
3 I would rather that, in destroying the camp,
And slaying Somakas and Pāṇḍavas alike,
They followed the true example Duryodhana
Set, and died in battle.

4 'But I trust the Pāñcālas have not slain them,
Or that they lie exhausted in sleep. Did they
Achieve anything? Tell me that, Saṃjaya.'

Saṃjaya said:

5 As the great-souled son of Droṇa advanced
Towards the camp, Kṛpa and Kṛtavarman
Waited by the gate.
6 Then seeing those two great warriors ready
For action, Aśvatthāman thrilled with delight,
And whispered to them:

7 'You two alone could destroy the whole warrior class—
Never mind this remnant of a sleeping army!
8 I shall penetrate the camp and career about
Like Time the Destroyer. The two of you
Must ensure that not a man escapes alive—
I have decided that it must be so.'*

9 With these words, Droṇa's son, shedding all fear,
Ignored the gate, and leapt into the vastness
Of the Pārthas' camp.

10 Having penetrated the camp like this,
The great warrior then discerned, and stealthily
Approached, Dhṛṣṭadyumna's own resting place.
11 Meanwhile the Pāñcālas, exhausted by great deeds
Done in the intensity of battle,
Slept unconcerned, surrounded by their fellows.
12 So entering Dhṛṣṭadyumna's tent, Aśvatthāman
Saw the prince of the Pāñcālas sleeping
On a bed close by—
13 On a great bed covered with a priceless quilt
Of spotless linen, fragrant with powder
And incense, and hung with beautiful garlands.
14 Then with a kick Aśvatthāman awoke
High-souled Dhṛṣṭadyumna, sleeping in his bed,
Secure and trusting.
15 Roused by the impact of that blow, Dhṛṣṭadyumna—
A soul beyond measure, so arrogant in war—
Rose up and recognized that great warrior,
Droṇa's son.
16 But as he rose from bed, mighty
Aśvatthāman seized his hair in both his hands and
Ground him into the earth.
17 Crushed by that force and his own fear, the Pāñcāla
Prince was trapped half out of sleep, quite paralysed.
18 So one foot on his chest,* the other on his throat,
Aśvatthāman prepared to kill him, groaning
And quivering like a sacrificial beast.*
19 Then Dhṛṣṭadyumna, tearing with his nails
At Droṇa's son, cried in a muffled way:

'Son of the teacher, best of men, kill me
With a weapon. Quickly! Strike! So by your hand
I may reach the worlds of those whose deeds were good.'*

20 Hearing those garbled words, Droṇa's son spat back:

'There are no worlds for those who kill their teachers,
Defiler of your race. And that is why,
Bad-minded man, you do not merit death by arms.'

21 So speaking, enraged Aśvatthāman drummed
Violently on that hero's vitals with his heels,
Like a lion mauling an elephant in rut.
22 Then at that hero's dying cries,* his guards
And wives, who also lay within the tent, awoke
23 To see a being with superhuman power
Pummelling the body of their lord, and yet from fear
They uttered not a single cry for help.
24 In this way Aśvatthāman dispatched him
To the house of Death; and full of power
And spirit-force, then issued out to mount
His shining vehicle.
25 How the directions resounded, mighty king,
As Aśvatthāman issued from that tent,
Bent upon the destruction of his foes, to scour
The camp by chariot.

26 Then, after that great warrior, Droṇa's son, had gone,
The women and the guards began to cry out loud.
27 For realizing that their king had been
So violently dispatched, the *kṣatriya* wives*
Of Dhṛṣṭadyumna keened, scarfed up in grief.
28 And at that sound, the mighty warriors, near at hand,
Cried

'What's afoot?'

And armed themselves at speed.

29 Terrified at the sight of Aśvatthāman,
Of Bharadvāja's heir, the women implored them
In a piteous tone:

'Follow him quickly—
30 Whether *rākṣasa** or man we cannot say, but
Having killed the Pāñcāla king he has mounted
A chariot, and is waiting out there still.'

31 Then the leading warriors precipitately
Surrounded him—
And instantly with the Rudra
Weapon* he crushed them all.

32 So now, having slain both Dhṛṣṭadyumna
And his attendants, he turned his attention
To Uttamaujas,* asleep on a bed nearby.
33 Bestriding him vigorously, one foot pinning
His throat, the other his chest, he put to death
That roaring conqueror of his enemies.
34 Then Yudhāmanyu arrived, and believing
His brother killed by a *rākṣasa*, raised his mace
And struck Droṇa's son violently in the chest.
35 Counterattacking, Aśvatthāman seized him
And threw him to the ground, where he slew him,
Writhing like a victim at the sacrifice.
36 And when he had killed him, that hero attacked
The other great warriors sleeping nearby,
And slaughtered them as a butcher slaughters
The struggling, quivering beasts at a sacrifice.

37 Then with his sword like a sacrificial knife,*
This expert swordsman slew the others, man by man,
Careering through the camp, path after path.
38 Thus seeing two divisions of exhausted men
Slumbering on the bed of their cast-aside
Weapons, he in an instant crushed them all.
39 Like Death himself let loose by Time, his limbs
Painted with their blood, he cut down with his
Mighty sword, warriors, elephants, and steeds.
40 So as they struggled, and as he plunged and raised
And stabbed convulsively, Aśvatthāman
Was triple-dyed in blood,
41 And shone most horribly, as though inhuman,
Wielding his brilliant, blood-wet sacrificial sword.

42 And those he woke, stupefied by the din,
Stared at one another and trembled at
This sight of Droṇa's son.

43 Seeing that foe-tormentor's* form, and thinking him
A *rākṣasa*, those warriors shut their eyes,
44 While in this terrible shape he careered
Like Time about the camp, until he saw
Draupadī's sons* and the Somaka remnant.*

45 Frightened by that noise, and told of Dhṛṣṭadyumna's
Death, Draupadī's great warrior sons, armed with bows,
Fearlessly deluged Aśvatthāman in shafts.
46 Then Śikhaṇḍin and the Prabhadrakas,*
Awakened by that noise, distressed with *their* arrows
Droṇa's mighty son.
47 But seeing those arrows raining down, he roared
A terrible roar, lusting to destroy
Those intransigent men.

48 Horribly enraged at the remembrance
Of his father's death, he stepped down from his
Chariot and ran at speed towards his foes—
49 Ran towards the sons of Draupadī and attacked
Them with his long celestial sword, embossed with gold,
Holding aloft his shield, wide as a thousand moons—
Mighty Aśvatthāman.
50 Then that tigerish man crushed in combat
Prativindhya's abdomen, my king, and
He fell to earth, dead.
51 Next, the glorious Sutasoma wounded
Aśvatthāman with a javelin, and, raising
His sword, rushed Droṇa's son.
52 But that bullish man lopped Sutasoma's sword-arm
To the ground; then he stuck him in the ribs,
And so he too fell to earth, with a skewered heart.
53 Then Śatānīka, the son of Nakula,
Bursting with strength, seized the wheel of a chariot
In both his hands and hurled it at Aśvatthāman,
Striking him on the chest.
54 But in his turn, twice-born* Aśvatthāman
Struck Śatānīka, the hurler of the wheel,
So that, reeling, he fell to the ground, where
He cut off his head.

55 Next Śrutakarman took up an iron bludgeon,
And running at Droṇa's son, struck him violently
On the left shoulder-blade.
56 But with his great sword he struck at Śrutakarman's
Jaw: disfigured and senseless, he fell dead on the earth.
57 Alerted by this noise, the heroic archer
Śrutakīrti, approaching Aśvatthāman,
Rained arrows on his head.
58 But warding off that hail of arrows with his shield,
Aśvatthāman severed from its body
Śrutakīrti's glittering, earringed head.
59 Then mighty Śikhandin, Bhīṣma's bane, with all
The Prabhadrakas, assailed that hero
On every side with arsenals of weapons,
Hitting him between the eyebrows with an arrow.
60 But, filled with rage, Droṇa's mighty son closed
With Śikhandin, and with his sword split him in two.*
61 And when he had killed Śikhandin, that torcher
Of the foe, possessed by rage, violently
Overran the entire host of Prabhadrakas,
And attacked the remnant of Virāṭa's force.
62 Crammed with strength, no sooner did he see the sons,
Grandsons, and friends of Drupada, than he loosed
A terrible carnage.
63 And as new waves of men advanced to meet him,
Skilled as he was in the way of the sword,
Droṇa's son butchered them all with his blade.

64–5 Then, chanting,* there appeared before them a black-skinned
Woman, the Night of all-destroying Time,*
Whose mouth and eyes were the colour of blood,
Whose garlands and unguents were just as crimson,
Who wore a single blood-dyed garment, and
Held in her hand a noose.
They saw horses,
Elephants, and men, bound by terrible cords,
Driven by her as she carried away
All kinds of hairless spirits, roped together
With the great warriors, divested of their arms.*

66 On other nights, the greatest of those warriors
Had seen her in their dreams, leading the sleepers
Away—and Droṇa's son forever killing them.
67 Ever since the war between the Kuru
And Pāṇḍava hosts began, they had dreamt
Of that baleful goddess,* and of Droṇa's son.

68 And so they, who had already been condemned
To death by fate, were now assailed by Droṇa's son,
Terrifying every being, roaring
Bhairava*-like roars.
69 And those fate-afflicted heroes, remembering
Such former sights, understood that what they had dreamt
Then was now being realized in fact.

70 Then the archers in the Pāṇḍava camp
Awoke at that noise in their hundreds and thousands.
71 And Aśvatthāman split the feet of some,
The hips of others; some he pierced between the ribs,
Like the End-Maker, Death, let loose by Time.
72 O Lord, the earth was covered by men roaring
In great affliction, flattened by overwhelming
Savagery, crushed by elephants and horses,
Crying out:

73 'What?—What's happened? What's that noise? What's this?
Who's this?'

And so for those men too, Droṇa's son
Proved the god of Death.
74 Yes—Droṇa's son, best of dispatchers, dispatched
The confused Pāṇḍu and Sṛñjaya hordes,*
Weaponless and armourless, to the realm of Death.
75 Terrified by his sword, jumping up sick with fear,
Blinded by sleep and befuddled, some hid
Wherever they could,
76 Legs paralysed, and drained of strength by despair,
Crying out harshly in fear, they crushed each other.

77 Then once again Droṇa's son mounted his chariot,
Whose churning wheels appalled the world, and, bow in hand,
Shot others with his arrows into Death's own realm.
78 And excellent, valiant men, who had risen
From their beds and rushed to meet him, he killed
From afar, and offered them to the Night of Time.*
79 So he ran through his enemies, dragging them
Under his careering chariot, burying them
Beneath a hail of assorted arrows.
80 And still he drove on, his shield brilliant with
A hundred moons, his scimitar the colour
Of the noonday sky.

81 O mighty king, drunk with sacrifice, Droṇa's son
Stirred up their camp, like an elephant clouding
A great tank of water.
82 Aroused by that noise, the senseless warriors,
Oppressed by sleep and fear alike, scattered
Hither and thither.
83 Many others cried out
Discordantly, jabbering incoherently;
84–5 Some, their hair dishevelled, did not know each other;
Others, having risen, wandered, quite terrified.
Urinating and defecating, horses
And elephants broke their tethers; and some men
Threw themselves into a terrible crush.
86 Among those, some clung with terror to the ground—
And elephants and horses crushed them where they lay.

87 While this was happening satiated *rākṣasas*
Bellowed cries of intensive joy, O bullish man,
O best of Bharatas*—
88 A sound projected by hordes of spirits possessed
By joy, so great it filled all the directions
And rolled through the sky.
89 Terrorized by the cries of those in pain,
Escaped elephants and horses careered about,
Crushing those encamped,

90 Stirring up dust with their hooves as they ran around,
Doubling the darkness of the night for those in camp.
91 As that darkness thickened, the whole world was lost:
Fathers failed to recognize their sons, and
Brothers their own brothers.
92 Elephants, riderless, trampled on elephants,
Horses on horses—so they wounded, shattered, crushed...
93 And killing each other, broken and toppling,
They brought others down, and crushed them as well.
94 Shrouded in gloom, barely conscious, filled with torpor,
Men killed their own comrades there, impelled to it
By Time the Destroyer.*
95 The gatekeepers abandoned their gates, the soldiers
Their platoons, and so they fled senseless, at random,
Lost, and crying out:

96 'My father! My son!'

No longer recognizing each other,
Their spirits crushed by fate.

97 Fleeing in all directions, abandoning even
Their own kinsmen, they cried out to one another
With their own names and those of their families.
98 Others lay on the earth wailing in grief;
Enraged in battle, Droṇa's son found them out
And stopped their tongues for good.
99 During the massacre, other warriors
Went completely astray—insensible,
Eclipsed by fear, they flew from their bases.
100 But those who fled the camp in terror, striving
To save their lives, were cut down by Kṛpa
And Kṛtavarman waiting at the gate.
101 Without weapons, instruments, or armour,
Hair dishevelled, as suppliants they joined their hands,
Harrowed, and grovelling on the earth; but not
A man of them was spared—
102 No, great king, not a single man who fled the camp
Was spared by Kṛpa or bad-minded Hārdikya.

103 Then desiring to do what was most dear
To Droṇa's son, in three places they fired the camp.*
104 Upon which, dexterous Aśvatthāman,
The delight of his fathers, careered, sword in hand,
Through the blazing tents.
105 Some brave opponents rushed him, others ran:
That best of brahmins, with his sword, parted them
From their vital breath.
106 Enraged, heroic Droṇa's son struck other
Warriors with his blade, slicing them in two
Like sesame stalks.
107 The earth was covered with the fallen—the
Foremost men, the greatest elephants, and horses—
Thrashing about violently and crying out.

108 And when thousands of men had fallen dead, many
Headless trunks stood up,* only to fall again.
109 Droṇa's son lopped off heads, and hands and feet,
And braceleted forearms still brandishing weapons,
And thighs with the muscle of elephants' trunks.
110 Assailing some, he broke their backs, smashed their heads, and
Shattered their ribs; and others he made flee the fight.
111 Some he pierced through the midriff, others through the ears;
Some he struck between the shoulder-blades; the heads
Of others he forced deep into their trunks.

112 While he careered so, killing men in their hundreds,
The awful night became thick with ghastly shadows.
113 The earth was smothered with dead and dying
In their thousands—men, elephants, and horses—
Terrible to see.
114 Cut off by the enraged son of Droṇa,
They fell on the dreadful earth, strewn with chariots, with
Horses and elephants, *yakṣas** and *rākṣasas.*
115–16 Men called upon their mothers, their fathers,
Their brothers; others cried out:

'The furious sons of
Dhṛtarāṣṭra could not do in open battle
What these cruel *rākṣasas* have done to us in sleep.
We die because the sons of Pṛthā* are away.
117 There's not a god, anti-god, *gandharva,* yakṣa*,
Or *rākṣasa* who could overpower Kuntī's
Son—for he is protected by Janārdana.
118 Pārtha Dhanaṃjaya is a devotee
Of sacred knowledge, he speaks the truth, is
Self-restrained, and shows compassion to every
Creature—he would never kill the sleeping,*
The distracted, those who have laid down their arms,
Supplicants, those in flight, or those with trailing hair.
119 This atrocity is done to us by cruel
And bloody *rākṣasas*.'

Many men, lying down
To die, lamented thus.

120 Then, in a little while, the great tumultuous
Din—the roaring of men, and other, lower moans—
Faded and died away.
121 And that terrible swirling dust, my king,
Was in a moment absorbed by the blood-drenched earth.

122 Cruel Aśvatthāman had killed men in their thousands—
Huddled together, shuddering, and powerless—
Like Paśupati* destroying his victims.
123 Droṇa's son had killed them all, whether they were
Embracing each other, sleeping, or in flight,
The cowering and the fighting alike.
124 Thus, consumed by the flames and killed by him,
The warriors led each other into Yama's realm.*
125 So, by the middle of the night, he had dispatched
The great Pāṇḍava host to the house of Death.

126 That night, so terrible and destructive for men,
For elephants, and horses, only increased
The joy of those beings that love the dark:

127 A multitude of *rākṣasas* and *piśācas**
Were seen, devouring human flesh, and drinking blood.
128–9 Gaping-mouthed, tawny, fierce, with teeth of stone,
Full of passion, matted-locked, long-thighed, five-footed,
Swollen-bellied, fingers reversed, deformed,
Emaciated, terrible-voiced, knees
Swollen like jars, dwarfish, blue-throated, horrible,
130 Very cruel, and fierce, impossible to gaze on
For long, these many kinds of *rākṣasas*,
Together with their sons and wives, appeared.
131 And rapturous from drinking blood, some danced in troops,
Crying:

'How good this is, how pure, how sweet!'

132 Replete with flesh, fat, marrow, bones, and blood,
These corpse-consuming scavengers who live
On flesh devoured the body in all its parts.
133 And other vicious scavengers, flesh-eating
Demons with many kinds of faces, having gorged
On flesh-marrow, ran around with bloated guts.
134 Unbounded millions and tens of millions
Of terrible, bloody-deeded, gigantic
Rākṣasas were there,
135 Satiated and delighting in such great
Slaughter, and a congregation of many ghosts.

136 At dawn, Droṇa's son, bedewed with human blood,
The hilt of his sword plastered to his hand
As though they were one, desired to quit the camp.
137 With everything consumed, he reigned over
The massacre of those men, like the fire
At the end of a world age, when it has reduced
All beings to ash.*
138 And now he had done that deed as he had vowed
He would, Droṇa's son, via that evil path,
Broke the fever caused by his father's death.

139 And just as at night he had entered a silent
And sleeping camp, so now at dawn he left
A silent camp again, with all its sleepers dead—
That bull among men.

140 Outside, the other two rejoined that hero;
In raptures he told them everything he'd done,
Thrilling them through and through.
141 And those two, so dear to him, pleasured him in turn
With tales of their shredding of thousands of
Pāñcālas and Sṛñjayas. Then, with high-pitched cries
Of joy, they exulted and clapped their hands.

142 Such was that overwhelmingly dreadful night
In which the Somakas, who had been asleep
And heedless, were massacred to a man.
143 For without a doubt, Time's revolution
May not be stopped—they massacred us,* and now
They too have been destroyed.

Dhṛtarāṣṭra interrupted here:

144 'Why was it that this mighty warrior, Droṇa's son,
Could not achieve so great a feat before,
Although he had resolved on victory
For Duryodhana, my son?
145 And why, only
When the warrior Duryodhana was dead,
Was the great archer, Droṇa's son, committed to
This action?—Tell me that!'

Saṃjaya said:

146–7 It was because he feared the Pārthas, O son
Of Kuru's race, that he was not committed;
And it was because they, with wise Keśava
And Sātyaki, were absent that this feat
Was done by Droṇa's son. For in the presence
Of those heroes, no one could have killed them,
Not even the lord of the Maruts himself.

148 Besides, this was only achieved because the men
Were sleeping.

Then having engineered this
Great massacre of the Pāṇḍavas, the mighty
Warriors greeted one another, exclaiming:

'Well done! Well done, indeed!'

149 Saluted by the others, Droṇa's great son
Embraced them, and, with joy, uttered this high speech:

150 'To the last man the Pāñcālas and the sons
Of Draupadī have been dispatched, and all
The Somakas and the Matsya remnant
Have been killed by me.
151 Now right has been done, let us go to our king*
Without delay, and, if he still lives, tell him
This great and precious news.'

CHAPTER 9

Saṃjaya said:

1 So having slain the Pāñcālas and the sons
Of Draupadī to the last man, they went
There, where Duryodhana had fallen.
2 Approaching, they saw that life still flickered
In the king, and, leaping from their chariots, gathered
Round your son, my lord.*
3 He lay there on the bare earth, his thighs broken,
Gasping painfully, barely conscious, blood
Vomiting from his mouth.
4 Appalling beasts of prey and packs of jackals
Circled him, anxious to devour his body.
5 But, rigid in agony, with great pain, he
Rotated his body in the dust, frustrating
Their carrion eagerness to eat his flesh.
6 And as that great man lay on the earth, soaking
In his own blood, the three heroes, remnants
Of the slaughter—Aśvatthāman, Kṛpa,
And the Sātvata, Kṛtavarman—embraced him,
Loaded down with grief.
7 And so, like a sacrificial altar
Enclosed by three fires,* the king was surrounded
By these three panting, blood-anointed men,
8 Who, beholding their king, so undeserving
Of such a fate, lying prone upon the earth,
Were filled with unbearable grief, and wept.
9 Then, wiping the blood from his face with their hands,
They keened piteously for their lord, stretched out
Upon the field of war.

Kṛpa said:

10 'If Duryodhana, the lord of eleven
Armies, lies stricken in a pool of blood,
There is nothing fate cannot accomplish.

11 See! Next to the man who loved to wield it—
Who was as gold himself—his golden mace
Now lies on the earth;
12 That mace which, in battle upon battle,
Never failed its champion, and which, even now,
On the threshold of heaven, does not desert
So great a warrior.
13 See! That mace, adorned with pure gold from the river
Jambū,* lies down dutifully with the hero,
Like a loving wife beside her lord in sleep.
14 See the whirligig of Time! The scorcher
Of the enemy, who rode before a troop
Of consecrated kings, is stricken down,
And chews the sand and dust!
15 This king of all the Kurus now lies broken
By his foes upon the ground, when, formerly,
It was their part to fall to earth, cut down
By him in war.
16 The king to whom kings in their
Hundreds bowed down in fear, now lies on the couch
Of battle, encircled by beasts of prey.
17 Brahmins* used to wait upon this lord for wealth;
Now it is carnivores who wait for meat.'*

Saṃjaya said:

18 Then, O best of the Bharatas, Aśvatthāman,
Beholding that king of kings prone on the earth,
Lamented pitifully:

19 'Tigerish king, men invoked you as the greatest
Of bowmen, the pupil of Saṃkarṣana,*
In battle like Kubera, treasure-lord himself—
20 How then, sinless king, did Bhīma detect your flaws,
When you are ever-skilful, ever-powerful,
And he has a bad soul?
21 Without a doubt, great king, Time rules the world,
When we see that even you are felled by
Bhīmasena in war.

22 How was it that the low, wicked, and sluggish
Wolf-belly Bhīma struck you down through fraud*—
You who knew everything there was to know
About what's right? Truly, Time's irresistible.
23 Challenging you to a fair fight, that vigorous
Cheat Bhīma broke your thighs in battle with a mace.
24 Alas, that the wretch who connived at the trampling
Of the head of one stricken so unlawfully
In battle should be great Yudhiṣṭhira.
25 Truly, warriors in their battles will revile
Vṛkodara till the end of the world.
For fraud has brought you down.
26–7 Indeed, powerful Rāma of Yadu's race
Always said of you, my king: "No one matches
Duryodhana with the mace." And Vārṣṇeya
Eulogized you in assemblies, saying:
"The Kuru mace-warrior is my worthy pupil."

28 'You have attained that end which the great sages say
Is most auspicious for a warrior—you
Have died facing the enemy in battle.
29 Duryodhana, I do not grieve for you,
But for Gāndhārī and for your father—parents
Of a slain son, who shall wander this earth
As beggars in grief.
30 Shame upon Kṛṣṇa of the Vṛṣṇi race,
And shame upon the bad-minded Arjuna,
Who think themselves conversant with *dharma*,*
And yet looked on while you were being slain.
31 And what shall all those shameless Pāṇḍavas reply
To the kings of the earth, when asked about the way
King Duryodhana was killed by them?

32 'Son of Gāndhārī, you are fortunate, for you
Have been slain on the field of battle, advancing
Towards the foe, in accordance with *dharma*.
33 But what path will Gāndhārī take now, whose sons
Have been slain, whose kinsmen and relatives
Have been destroyed? What path will the blind king,
Unconquerable Dhṛtarāṣṭra, follow?

34 Shame upon me, upon the great warrior Kṛpa,
And upon Kṛtavarman—we who have stayed
This side of heaven, when you, a lord of the earth,
Have gone before us.
35 Shame on us wretches, who do not follow you—
The granter of all our wishes, the friendly
Shield of all his kinsmen.
36 It is through your power that our houses—mine,
My father's, our dependants', and Kṛpa's too—
Are stacked with jewels, O tiger of a man;
37 Through your grace, the abundant fees from many
Essential sacrifices* have been obtained
By us, our kin, and friends.
38 And where, and with whom, shall such a company
As ours obtain such things, when you have gone
Before us to join all the great kings of earth—
Gone to the highest goal?
39 And it is just
Because we three don't follow you, my king, that we
Suffer as we do.
40 Short of your heaven, destitute of wealth,
Remembering your bounty, what can we do
To follow in your steps?
41 Surely we shall wander this earth in grief—
For where is peace, where happiness for us without
You, great Kuru king?

42 'Mighty king, when you have gone from this world
To meet those great warriors, salute them in
My name, according to their rank and years.
43 And having honoured our teacher,* that greatest
Of all bowmen, tell him that Dhṛṣṭadyumna has
Been slain by me today.
44–5 Embrace King Bāhlika, that supreme warrior,
Embrace Saindhava and Somadatta,
Bhūriśravas,* and all the other great princes
Who have preceded you to heaven. And then,
Having embraced them in my name, ask how they
fare.'

46 Having said this to the barely conscious king,
Whose thighs were shattered, Aśvatthāman gazed
On him and spoke again:

47–8 'Duryodhana, if you are still alive
Listen to these words, balm to your ears: but
Seven Pāṇḍavas remain—the five brothers,
Vāsudeva, and Sātyaki—and we three
Followers of Dhṛtarāṣṭra—Kṛpa
Śāradvat, Kṛtavarman, and myself.
49 All the sons of Draupadī are dead, so too
The sons of Dhṛṣṭadyumna. Slain are all
The Pāñcālas, and the Matsya remnant!
50 See how their actions have been requited—
The Pāṇḍavas are childless now. Their camp has been
Destroyed, and with it all their sleeping men and beasts.
51 On the point of his evil deeds, Dhṛṣṭadyumna
Was skewered by me, great king,—entering the camp
At night, I killed him like a sacrificial beast.'

52 Then hearing these words, so dear to his heart,
Duryodhana, seeming to revive, replied:

53 'What neither Gaṅgā's son, nor Karṇa, nor your
Father could achieve for me, you have done
This night, with Kṛpa and the Bhoja at your side.
54 The chief commander of their army, the wretched
Dhṛṣṭadyumna has been slain, together with
Śikhaṇḍin, and because of this I now believe
Myself the equal of Maghavat himself.

55 'Goodbye my friends—and fare you well. We separate
To meet again in heaven.'*

With these words
The high-souled king of all the Kurus fell quiet;
So abandoning his grief for his kinsmen,
And then his vital breath, that hero died.

His soul flew up to sacred heaven, his body
Stayed below. So died Duryodhana, your son,
My king—the first to fight, and at the last
A warrior slain by his foes.*

56 Then the three heroes
Again and again embraced that king, until,
Gazing on him still, they each mounted their
Separate chariots.*

57 So I, having heard your son's dying words, came
Away towards the city in the hour before
The dawn, bowed down with grief.
In this way the Kuru and Pāṇḍava armies
Were destroyed.
Dreadful and fierce has been that slaughter,
Caused by your misguided policy, my king!*

58 And then, when your son had gone to heaven,
Blameless one, and while I was still grieving,
That divine sight, which the sage had given me,
Was withdrawn.

Vaiśaṃpāyana said:

59 At the news of his son's death, and the
Deaths of his kinsmen, the king sighed long and hot,
And then was lost in thought.*

PART II

The Arrow Made from Stalks

CHAPTER 10

Vaiśaṃpāyana continued:

1 When night had passed, Dhṛṣṭadyumna's charioteer
Relayed to Dharma's king, Yudhiṣṭhira,
The slaughter done on the warriors as they slept:

2–3 'The sons of Draupadī, great king, the children
Of Drupada himself, heedless* at night,
Unsuspecting, sleeping in their own quarters,
Have perished in your encampment at the hands
Of the evil Aśvatthāman, along with
Gautama's son Kṛpa,* and base Kṛtavarman.
4 With missile, lance, and axe they have massacred
Thousands—men, elephants, and horses: your force
Was utterly destroyed.
5 O Bhārata, such great tumult filled the air
When your army was felled like a great forest.
6 From that vast force I alone remain, escaped
Somehow from Kṛtavarman when he glanced away,
O king of the earth, O just and virtuous king!'

7 At this inauspicious news, Kuntī's son,
Inviolable Yudhiṣṭhira, fell on the earth,
Stunned with grief for his sons.
8 Then Sātyaki, Bhīmasena, and Arjuna,
And the two sons of Mādrī, the Pāṇḍava twins,
Approached the king and held him in their arms.
9 Recovering his senses, his voice trembling
With grief, he cried out in his suffering:

'We who were their conquerors have at the last
Been conquered by the foe.
10 Even for those with divine sight, the course of
Events is hard to discern: conquered, the foe
Conquers—and we are conquered, although conquering.

11–12 We have killed our brothers, our friends, our fathers,
Our sons, our kinsmen, and our followers,
Our relatives, grandsons, and ministers—
Defeated them all, and so now it is we
Who are the defeated.
Ruin wears the face
Of wealth, wealth seems like ruin; this victory
Has the figure of defeat—victory,
Therefore, *is* defeat.
13 Like some feeble-minded wretch, winning such
A victory, we are afterwards in pain.
How can we call it victory when we are the
Vanquished—more than our foe?

14 'Alas, we have sinfully slain our kinsmen*
For the sake of these seeming conquerors,
Who have now been vanquished by heedful foes.
15–16 They who escaped even angry Karṇa—
That lionish man, who never retreated
In battle, whose teeth were spears and arrows,
Whose tongue was a sword in combat, whose gaping mouth
Was a bow, whose fierce roaring was the slap
Of his palm on the bowstring—have through sheer
Negligence been slain.

17–18 'Those princes who crossed over the ocean that was Droṇa
On the ships of their manifold weapons—that ocean whose deep pools
Were chariots, whose waves were showers of arrows set with jewels,
Whose striped snakes were chariot horses, whose fish were spears and lances,
Whose alligators and serpent demons were banners, whose moon-rise
Was the meeting of armies, whose tide was the charge, whose roar
Was the slap of palms on the bowstring—have been slain through their own
Negligence.

19 In this world of the living, there is no greater
Killer of men than negligence. Riches utterly abandon
The negligent man, and ruin takes possession of him.
20–1 Even those princes who withstood that wild fire in a burning
Forest that was Bhīṣma, whose terrible quickness was the
Uncontrolled weaponry in his hands, which overpowered
As better than the best dry wood the great army, whose *homa**
Oblations were the various kinds of weapons and armour,
Whose roar was the slap of his palms and the bowstrings on his great bow,
Whose fanning wind was wrath, whose flames were arrows, whose wreath of smoke
Was the highest banner raised above his chariot—even they have
Been slain through their own negligence.

22 'For knowledge, asceticism, glory, and great fame are
Unobtainable by the negligent man. But see how
Great Indra prospered once he had, with care, killed all his foes.
23 And see how, through their negligence, the sons and grandsons of great kings,
Great Indras all, have been slaughtered by the remnant of our foe—
Like prosperous merchants crossing the ocean only to sink
Through negligence in a shallow stream. Yet though their bodies
Lie slain by those angry men, they have without a doubt ascended
To the third and highest heaven.

24 'No—it is for the virtuous princess Kṛṣṇā* that I grieve—
For how shall she not be drowned in a flood of grief today,
Learning that her brothers and her sons—her venerable father,
The king of the Pāñcālas—are all slaughtered? Surely, she
Shall fall to the earth and lie there inert, a slender stem
Emaciated by grief.

25 Unable to overcome the suffering to which such grief gives birth,
What shall then become of her—she who is used to happy things?
Shaking at the slaughter of her brothers, the loss of her sons,
She will be like a woman consumed by a raging fire.'

26 Thus afflicted and lamenting, that Kuru king turned to Nakula and said:

'Go now and bring here the ill-fated
Princess, together with her aunts!'

27 At that command, issued by the king—who through his *dharma*
Was like Dharma himself—Mādrī's son sped by chariot to that place
Where the queen and the wives of the Pāñcāla king were quartered.
28 Once Mādrī's son had gone, Ajamīḍha's scion, shaking
With grief and crying aloud, went with his kinsmen to the field
On which his sons had fought, now overrun with troops of ghosts.
29 Entering that cursed and terrible place, he saw his sons, his kinsmen,
And his friends, lying on the earth, their remains moist with blood,
Their beautiful limbs being dragged away, cleft and broken.
30 Beholding them, Yudhiṣṭhira, best of the bearers of *dharma*,
Was violently afflicted. Noble Kuru that he was,
He gave a high-pitched cry and, with his followers, fell to the earth,
Barely conscious.

CHAPTER 11

*Vaiśaṃpāyana said to Janamejaya:**

1–2 Janamejaya! When he had seen that his sons,
His brothers, and his friends had been slain in battle,
A great grief seized that king's great soul—a grief
That welled up with the memory of his sons,
His grandsons, his brothers, and his allies.
3 So his kinsmen, themselves distraught, comforted him,
His eyes brimming with tears, delirious and trembling.

4 Then, at daybreak, his chariot shining like the
Sun, Nakula arrived, with Princess Kṛṣṇā—
Greatly afflicted, for
5 At Upaplavya* she had heard that all her sons
Were dead, and still she reeled at that horrific news.
6 Shaking like the frail stem of the plantain
Buffeted by a gale, Kṛṣṇā approached
The king, then fell to the earth, crushed by grief.
7 And there her face, and her full dilated
Lotus-flower eyes, were precipitately
Overcome by sorrow, like the sun eclipsed.

8 Seeing her fall, irascible Vṛkodara—
Truly valorous Bhīma—rushed to her aid
And clasped her in his arms.
9 Thus comforted by Bhīma, passionately
Angry and weeping, Kṛṣṇā addressed the
Pāṇḍava,* surrounded by his brothers:

10 'How fortunate, my king, that you shall now enjoy
The whole wide world, obtained through offering your sons*
To Death, in accordance with the *kṣatriya* rule.*
11 How fortunate, that you, Pārtha, are prosperous,
That you have acquired the whole earth, and can forget
Subhadrā's* son Abhimanyu, who moved like
An elephant in rut.

12 How fortunate that you do not recall,
As I do, what I was told at Upaplavya—
That our heroic sons have been slain following
This *kṣatriya dharma*.

13 'O Pārtha, ever since I heard that they were
Slaughtered in their sleep by Droṇa's wicked son,
Grief burns me up, like fire running through a house.
14–15 If the life of this evil's author, Droṇa's son,
And the lives of his followers are not rubbed out
By you today in combat, on this very spot
I shall fast to death.
Don't doubt it, Pāṇḍavas—if Droṇa's son does not
Reap the fruit of his evil deed, I *shall* do this.'*

16 And with these words addressed to Yudhiṣṭhira,
The Pāṇḍava, to King Dharma himself,
Yājñasena's beautiful daughter Kṛṣṇā
Sat down to her fast.
17 When he saw his dear queen, seated in this way,
The Pāṇḍava—this royal sage, this pillar
Of *dharma*—said to the beautiful Draupadī:

18 'Fair lady, your sons and brothers have met their deaths
Virtuously, in pursuit of *dharma*.
You, who understand *dharma*, should not grieve for them.
19 What's more, my beautiful, noble queen, Droṇa's son
Has fled from here to a distant forest—so
How will you know if he has fallen in combat?'

Draupadī answered him:

20 'I have heard that Droṇa's son was born with a jewel*
On his head. When you have killed that evil man
In combat, bring the jewel to me, and when I
Have placed it on your head, my king, then may I live
Again, but not before.'

Vaiśaṃpāyana said:

21 Breaking off her address to the Pāṇḍava king,
The beautiful Kṛṣṇā, in agitation,
Approached Bhīmasena, and urged him thus:

22 'Bhīma, you must save me. Remember the
Kṣatriya dharma, and kill that evildoer,
As Maghavat killed the *asura* Śambara.*
For here no man can equal you in strength.
23 Throughout the worlds it has been told how you
Were the saviour of the sons of Pṛthā*
In their terrible plight in Vāraṇāvata
Town. And again you were the means of escape
When they encountered the *rākṣasa* Hiḍimba.*
24 Likewise, when I was gravely molested
By Kīcaka in Virāṭa's city,*
You rescued me from danger like Maghavat
His wife Paulomī.*
25 And just as you accomplished those great feats
Before, O Pārtha—slaughterer of foes—
So now kill Droṇa's son, and then rejoice!'

26 Supremely powerful Bhīmasena, Kuntī's son,
Hearing these many woes uttered in sorrow,
Could not endure it—
27 He mounted his great, golden-bodied chariot,
He took up his beautiful, shining bow,
He equipped himself with bowstring and arrows,
28 Then making Nakula his charioteer,
With an arrow ready drawn in his bow,
Pent up with the killing of Droṇa's son,
He immediately urged his horses on.

29 Thus impelled, tigerish man,* those thoroughbreds
Blew like a gale across the skin of the earth.
30 For as he left the camp, Bhīma had seen
The ruts made by Aśvatthāman's chariot,
And never leaving them, he tracked him at speed.

CHAPTER 12

Vaiśaṃpāyana said:

1 After the unassailable Bhīmasena
Had left, lotus-eyed Kṛṣṇa, the Yadu bull,
Spoke to Kuntī's son Yudhiṣṭhira, the king:

2 'O Bhārata, this Pāṇḍava brother of yours,
Unable to control his grief for his sons,
Goes in sorrow, hoping to kill Droṇa's son.
3 Bull of the Bhāratas, Bhīma, the dearest
Of all your brothers is now in danger, so why
Don't you fly after him?
4 The so-called *brahmaśiras* weapon,* which Droṇa,
That destroyer of hostile citadels, made known
To his son, can incinerate the entire world.
5 First the great-souled, most illustrious teacher,
The leader, the greatest of all bowmen, was pleased
With Dhanaṃjaya* and taught him that weapon.
6 Unable to stand that, Droṇa's son summarily
Begged to learn the secret too; unwillingly,
His father complied.
7 Great-souled Droṇa had never wished to take
His own son as a pupil, knowing very well
His volatility. So the teacher,
Who knew all about *dharma*, gave him this warning:

8 ' "My son, you must never launch this weapon,
Even when in battle mortal danger threatens,
And above all never against human beings."

9 'In this way *guru* Droṇa addressed his son,
And then, a little later, spoke again:

' "Bull of a man, it seems you cannot stay
In the way of truth . . ."

10 'Understanding too well his father's bitter words,
Malevolent Aśvatthāman, with no good
Prospects at all, wandered the earth, in misery.

11 'And then, Bhārata, best of the Kurus,
While you were in exile in the forest,
He came to Dvāraka and settled there,
Where he was greatly honoured by the Vṛṣṇis.
12 And one day, when he was living in Dvāraka,
He came to me alone as I walked by myself
At the margins of the sea. And with a smile
Playing on his lips, he addressed me thus:

13–14 ' "Kṛṣṇa, the weapon known as *brahmaśiras*,
Worshipped by gods and *gandharvas*,* which my father,
The teacher of the Bhāratas, whose strength was truth,
Obtained from the sage Agastya* through observing
Fierce ascetic penance, is now in me,*
Just as much, Kṛṣṇa, as it was in my father.
15 Foremost of the Yadus, if I give you
This divine weapon, will you, in return, give me
Your discus* which destroys all foes in battle?"

16 'While he, Bull of the Bhāratas, with joined hands,
Made a great effort to beg the weapon
From me, I, to gratify him, told him this:

17 ' "If you heaped gods, *dānavas,** *gandharvas*, men,
Birds, and snakes together, they would not equal
Even a hundredth part of my energy.
18 Here is my bow, my spear, my discus, and my mace*—
Whichever weapon you want, I give it you.
19 Forget that weapon you wanted to give to me—
Take whatever you can throw or wield in battle."

20 'Then, vying with me, he begged that thousand-spoked
Iron discus with the beautiful hub
And a diamond navel.

21 'So I said:
"Take the discus!"*
And he at once
Approached, and forcibly seized it with his left hand,
But he could not move it from where it was fixed.
22–3 Then he tried with his right hand—but even with
Total concentration, and grasping it
With all his strength, he could not move it in the least,
Let alone raise it up.
Exhausted by that
Supreme effort, and quite downcast, he pulled away.

24 'And when, perplexed, he had given up on
The attempt altogether, I addressed
The now deflated Aśvatthāman and said:

25 ' "He who is thought of as setting the highest
Standards among gods and men, whose bow is
Gāṇḍīva, whose horses are the purest white,
Whose banner is the most excellent of apes,*
26 Who, succumbing in single combat, appeased
Śaṃkara,* the blue-throated lord of Umā,*
The lord god of gods in bodily form himself,
27 That prince who is dearer to me than any
Other man alive, to whom I would refuse
Nothing—not even my wives and children—
28 Even he, my dear friend Pārtha, whose actions
Are untainted, would never have made the
Request that you, brahmin, have made of me.*
29–30 My lustrous son Sanatkumāra, called
Pradyumna, whom I gained through asceticism,
Practising strict celibacy for twelve years
On the side of Himavat—a son for
Rukmiṇī,* who had practised vows as hard as mine—
31 Even he has never solicited
This incomparable, super-divine discus
Of mine—this discus which you—you fool!—have asked for.

32 Rāma, for all his great strength, never mentioned
Such a thing. Neither Gada nor Sāmba
Asked what you have asked.
33 None of the great Vṛṣṇi and Andhaka warriors,
Or any others living in Dvāraka,
Have ever asked what you have asked of me.
34 Best of warriors, you are the son of the
Bhāratas' teacher, you are respected
By all the Yādavas—so whom, my child,
Do you wish to fight with this, my discus?"

35 'Questioned in this way, Droṇa's son replied:

' "After honouring you, Kṛṣṇa, it was in truth
You I would have fought with—
36–7 For that reason I wanted your discus,
Worshipped by gods and *dānavas** alike.
Thus, all-pervading one, I could have been
Invincible. That is the truth, Keśava,
But since you have thwarted me in my desire
To attain what was barely attainable
Anyway, I shall leave you now, my lord—
So bless me, Govinda.
38 This discus with its beautiful hub is borne
By you alone, its irresistible master,
Bull of the Vṛṣṇis: on earth there is no one else
Who can master it."

39 'Having said this much to me, Droṇa's son
Left Dvāraka, taking with him horses
And chariots, wealth, and many kinds of jewels—the fool!

40 'He's wrathful, wicked at heart, unpredictable,
And cruel—and he knows the *brahmaśiras* weapon.*
Vṛkodara must be protected from him.'

CHAPTER 13

Vaiśaṃpāyana said:

1–2 When he had finished speaking, Kṛṣṇa, greatest
Of warriors, the joy of all the Yādavas,
Mounted his great chariot, bristling with all
The most powerful weapons. To the pole of that
Perfect chariot, the hue of the rising sun,
Were harnessed the best, gold-garlanded Kāmboja
Horses: Sainya on the inner right, Sugrīva
On the inner left, and drawing the fore-
Axle, Meghapuṣpa and Balāhaka.
3 A magical construction—a celestial
Flagstaff, decorated with various gems, and forged
By Viśvakarman himself—was visible,
Erect on the chariot.
4 At its top, radiant in a circle of light,
Was Vainateya, for the enemy of snakes*
Was the flag of that embodiment of truth.

5 Then Hṛṣīkeśa, greatest of all archers,
Mounted that chariot, followed by true-actioned
Arjuna, and Yudhiṣṭhira, the Kuru king.
6 Seated on the chariot, either side of Kṛṣṇa,
Wielder of the bow Śārṅga, those two great men
Shone with the brilliance of the Aśvin twins
Next to Vāsava.
7 And as soon as the two of them had mounted
That chariot the whole world adored, Dāśārha
Whipped up his thoroughbreds, effortlessly swift,
8 And immediately they flew forward, dragging
The wondrous vehicle behind them, ridden
By the Yadu bull and the two Pāṇḍavas,
9 So that while the fleet horses bore away
The wielder of the Śārṅga bow, there arose
A great noise, like the beating wings of birds in flight.

10 Very quickly, those human tigers drew level
With the great archer Bhīmasena, whom they had
Pursued with such speed, Bull of the Bhāratas.
11 But even though they had caught him up, the great
Warriors could not check that son of Kuntī,
Who, fired with rage, was ready to attack his foe.
12 In sight of those glorious, unyielding bowmen,
Bhīma's swift horses bore him to the bank
Of the Bhāgirathī river, where, it was said,
The killer of these great men's sons, the son
Of their teacher Droṇa, could now be found.

13 There, sitting at the water's edge, surrounded
By seers,* he saw the celebrated,
And great, Kṛṣṇa Dvaipāyana Vyāsa.*
14 And near at hand, he saw, as well, Droṇa's
Cruel son, in a garment of *kuśa* grass,
Anointed with ghee,* hair covered in dust.
15 Then Kuntī's son, mighty-armed Bhīmasena,
An arrow ready-notched to his bow, rushed him,
Crying out:

'Stand! Stand!'

16 Seeing that frightful archer, bow at the ready,
And the two brothers behind him, standing
In Janārdana's chariot, Droṇa's son,
With his heart reeling, thought: 'This is the end.'
17 But not quailing at it, he called to mind
That celestial, ultimate weapon, all the while
Pulling up, with his left hand, stalks* to make
An arrow.
Thus threatened by calamity
He manifested the ultimate weapon.

18 Unable to bear the presence of those heroes
With their divine armaments, he spat out in rage
These dreadful words:
'For the annihilation
Of the Pāṇḍavas!'*

19 Having spoken thus, the fiery son of Droṇa
Loosed that weapon, to stupefy the universe,
My tigerish king,*
20 For in that arrow made of stalks, a fire
Was kindled that seemed ready to consume
All three worlds—
Like Yama as all-destroying Time.*

CHAPTER 14

Vaiśaṃpāyana continued:

1 By his gestures, mighty-armed Dāśārha
Immediately divined what Droṇa's son
Intended, and turning to Arjuna, said:

2 'Arjuna, Arjuna, Pāṇḍava—now
Is the time for that celestial weapon
Droṇa taught you,* which exists in your heart.
3 For the protection of your brothers and yourself,
Bhārata, discharge that weapon in battle,
For it can neutralize all other arms.'

4 So addressed by Keśava, the Pāṇḍava,
The slayer of enemy heroes, quickly
Stepped from the chariot* with his arrows and bow.
5 Then that incinerator of the foe blessed first
The teacher's son,* and afterwards, at once, himself
And all his brothers.
6 And having bowed to the gods and to all
His superiors, he launched the weapon, deeply
Intent on the auspicious, saying:

'May this
Weapon extinguish his!'

7 Then that missile, so violently discharged
By the wielder of the Gāṇḍīva bow, blazed great
Flames, like the fire at the end of a world age.*
8 In the same way, the weapon belonging
To Droṇa's intensely charged son ignited in
A halo of energy, enveloping
Its own towering flames.

9 There was thunder on thunder, and thousands
Of meteors fell; a great dread overwhelmed
All living creatures.
10 The air was pure noise and violent wreaths of flame;
In its mountains, forests, and trees, the whole earth shook.

11 Then, because they had seen that those weapons
Between them were incinerating all the worlds,
Two great seers showed themselves* there at once—
12 Nārada, the soul of *dharma*, and Vyāsa,*
Father of the Bharatas. Both sought to calm
Those heroes, Bhāradvāja and Dhanaṃjaya.
13 Desiring every creatures' welfare, those two
Sages, who knew all *dharma*, whose energy
Was supreme, stood between the blazing weapons—
14 Two illustrious, unassailable, and
Extraordinary seers, resembling two
Blazing fires themselves.
15 Celebrated by gods and *dānavas** alike,
Invulnerable to any living creature,
For the sake of the triple world,* they tried
To neutralize the power* of those missiles.

The seers spoke:

16 'Even when down, the great warriors, who know
All there is to know about weapons, have never,
Until now, used this weapon on human beings.
Then why, heroes, are you recklessly unleashing
Such a great evil?'*

CHAPTER 15

Vaiśaṃpāyana continued:

1 Seeing those two, whose energy was like fire,
That tiger of a man, Dhanaṃjaya,
Hastened to retract his divine missile.
2 Then, hands joined in reverence, great Arjuna
Addressed the two seers thus:

'I launched this weapon
With the wish—"May that missile be disarmed by this"—
3 When this ultimate weapon is withdrawn, it is
Inevitable that Droṇa's wicked son will,
Through the energy of his weapon, burn us up
To the last man, leaving not a trace behind.
4 Your honours are like gods—then you must be able
To lay hold of some means here for our protection
And that of the three worlds.'

5 In battle, even the gods find the recall
Of such a weapon nearly impossible, but
With these words, Dhanaṃjaya fetched back the weapon.
6 None other than the Pāṇḍava, not even
Śatakratu himself, is able to fetch back
That ultimate weapon once launched in battle,
7 For it was produced from *brahmic*-energy*—
Launched by the man whose spirit is unprepared,
It cannot be recalled. Only the man
Who has taken the vow of celibate
Asceticism* is capable of that.
8 For if a man who has not observed this vow
Tries to recall the weapon after its launch,
It cuts off his head and destroys his belongings.

9 Arjuna was a celibate ascetic
And an observer of vows, but having obtained
That weapon in spite of the difficulty,
He never launched it, even when afflicted
By extreme distress.

10 Yes—heroic Arjuna, the Pāṇḍava,
Was a celibate ascetic who kept the vow
Of truth*—he obeyed his superiors, and thanks
To that, was able to fetch the weapon back.
11 But Droṇa's son, beholding those seers in front
Of him, was unable likewise to recall
His terrible missile, launched in combat.
12 Powerless to make the ultimate weapon
Return in battle, Droṇa's son, dejected,
Addressed Dvaipāyana:

13 'Threatened by a supreme calamity,
And desiring to save my life, great sage, I launched
This weapon out of fear of Bhīmasena.
14 Holy one, *dharma* was violated* by this
Bhīmasena in the false way he killed
The son of Dhṛtarāṣṭra in battle.
15 Because of that I have launched the weapon,
brahmin,
Even though I was unprepared in spirit;
And for the same reason I do not, here
And now, have the power to recall it.
16 For this invincible, celestial weapon,
Which has the energy of fire itself,
Was sent on its way by me with a mantra
For the destruction of the Pāṇḍavas.
17 Thus charged with the obliteration of
The Pāṇḍava line, that weapon must now
Deprive all the sons of Pāṇḍu of their lives.
18 This sinful deed—the launching of this weapon
In combat for the slaughter of Pṛthā's sons—
Was done by me, O brahmin, when my mind
Was overwhelmed by wrath.'

Vyāsa said:

19 'My child—Pārtha Dhanaṃjaya, knowing
The *brahmaśiras* weapon,* launched it in battle
Neither in wrath nor with the desire to kill you—
20 Rather, he launched his weapon in this combat
Only for the purpose of neutralizing yours.
But now Arjuna has called his weapon back.

21 'The great-armed Dhanaṃjaya obtained that
Brahmic-weapon* through the teaching of your father;
Since then he has never wavered from his
Duties as a warrior.*
22 He is resolute and virtuous—a true
Connoisseur of weapons, so why do you want
To destroy him, along with his brothers?
23 Where the *brahmaśiras* is hit by another
Ultimate weapon, there is no rain in that
Kingdom for twelve years.
24 For this reason the mighty-armed Pāṇḍava
Did not ward off that weapon of yours, although
He had the power to do so—out of
Concern for the good of living creatures.
25 You,* the Pāṇḍavas, and the kingdom should always
Be protected, therefore, great-armed warrior,
You must call that celestial weapon back.
26 May your wrath subside and Pṛthā's sons be saved,
For Yudhiṣṭhira, the royal Pāṇḍava seer,
Has no wish to win through a sinful act.*

27 'Give the Pāṇḍavas that jewel* which stands on
Your head, and in return—
They will let you live.'

Droṇa's son replied:

28 'This jewel of mine is more valuable by far
Than any of those jewels and other wealth
Acquired in this world by Pāṇḍavas and
Kauravas alike.

29 He who bears it has nothing at all to fear
From arms, disease, hunger, gods, demons, or *nāgas**—
30 Troops of *rākṣasas** and robbers will hold no fears
For him—such is the power of this my jewel.
And nothing would have made me give it up—
31 Yet a holy man's commands should be carried out
At once.
Here is the jewel, and here am I!*

'But the arrow made of stalks will fall into
The wombs of the Pāṇḍava women,* for this
Weapon cannot be set off in vain, and I am
Unable, holy one, to call back what has once
Been launched. Therefore I'll discharge it in their wombs.

'But for the rest, I'll do as you command, great sage.'*

Vyāsa replied:

32 'Then do what you have promised—and nothing else:
Discharge this weapon into the Pāṇḍava
Wombs, and then leave off.'

Vaiśaṃpayana said:

33 So with Dvaipāyana's words ringing in his ears,
Aśvatthāman, convulsed with suffering, released
That ultimate weapon into their wombs.

CHAPTER 16

Vaiśaṃpāyana continued:

1 Then, realizing the evildoer had launched
That weapon, Hṛṣīkeśa turned to Droṇa's son
With triumph in his voice:

2 'Once a brahmin, faithful to his vows, seeing
Arjuna's daughter-in-law,* Virāṭa's daughter,
At Upaplavya, addressed her with these words:

3 ' "When the Kurus have been destroyed, you shall conceive
A son. This child you carry in your womb
Shall be called Parikṣit."*

4 'What that wise man said shall indeed come true—
The Pāṇḍavas, propagating their race
Anew, shall have a son called Parikṣit.'

5 Greatly enraged at Govinda's words, Droṇa's son,
Responded to that best of the Sātvatas thus:

6 'It will not be as you, lotus-eyed Keśava,
Have said, just because you are partial to the
Pāṇḍavas. No! It shall be as I have said—it
Cannot be otherwise!
7 For this weapon, activated by me,
Shall fall on the womb of Virāṭa's daughter,
Whom, Kṛṣṇa, you are so eager to protect!'

Vāsudeva replied:

8 'Indeed, this ultimate weapon will not fall
Without effect, yet that dead foetus will live,
And have a long life.

9 But as for you, the wise shall know you as a
Murderer of children and a coward,
Whose evil deeds are beyond all tally.
10 And so you must harvest those evil deeds:
For three thousand years you shall wander this earth,
Alone, and totally incommunicado.
11 You shall stray companionless in desert wastes,
For, villain, you have no place among men.
12 Stinking of blood and pus, driven to the
Inaccessible wilderness, you shall wander,
Subject to every plague that blows, you black-souled wretch!

13 'But heroic Parikṣit, his Vedic study*
Completed, shall, from Kṛpa,* son of Śaradvat,
Receive, in the prime of life, all his weapons.
14 And once he knows how to use these great weapons,
Vowing himself to the *kṣatriya dharma*,* that
Virtuous man shall rule the earth for sixty years.

15 'And so in the future, in spite of you,
Miserable man, the mighty-armed prince
Parikṣit will be king of the Kurus. Although
Consumed by the fiery brilliance of your weapon,
I shall make him live again.*
So behold, lowest
Of men, the strength of my austerities and truth.'

Vyāsa said:

16–17 'Since this dreadful deed has been done by you
Without regard for us, and since your conduct
Is such, even though you are really a brahmin,
So the excellent speech which Devakī's son
Has spoken will certainly come true—for you
Are one who has assumed the *kṣatriya dharma*.'*

Aśvatthāman replied:

18 'Together with you, brahmin, I shall live on
Among men.* May the words of this great lord
Become true—for he is the Supreme Being.'

Vaiśaṃpāyana continued:

19 Then Droṇa's son gave up his jewel to the mighty
Pāṇḍavas, and in the sight of them all
Dejectedly set off towards the forest.*

20 Now that their enemy had been defeated,
The Pāṇḍavas honoured Govinda, Kṛṣṇa-
Dvaipāyana, and the great sage Nārada.
21 Then taking with them that jewel, which had been born with
Droṇa's son, they hastened back to where Draupadī
Was concentrated in her death-fast, their horses,
22 Like the wind itself, bearing those tigerish men,
Along with Kṛṣṇa's people,* once more to camp.

23 Stepping from their chariots and rushing forward,
At the sight of afflicted Kṛṣṇā Draupadī,
The great warriors' suffering surpassed even hers.
24 Approaching that woman, who was so joyless,
So full of grief and sorrow, the Pāṇḍavas,
Along with Keśava, encircled her.
25 Then with the permission of the king, mighty
Bhīmasena gave her the divine jewel, and said:

26 'This jewel, my dear, is yours. The killer of your sons
Has been defeated. Cast off your grief and rise—
And remember the *kṣatriyas' dharma*.*
27 When Vāsudeva was setting out on his peace
Mission, modest, dark-eyed lady, you spoke
These very words to that slayer of Madhu:

28 ' "I have neither husbands, sons, nor brothers, and
Even you, Govinda, do not exist for me,
Since the king wants peace."*

29 'Remember you spoke those bitter words, according
With *kṣatriya dharma*, to the Supreme Being?

30 'Evil Duryodhana, who barred us from the throne,
Has been slain—I have drunk Duḥśāsana's blood* while
His heart was still beating.
31 No one can blame us—we have acquitted
Our debt to the foe,* and out of respect for his
Father, our teacher, and because he's a brahmin,*
Having defeated Droṇa's son, we have freed him.
32 His glory has been snuffed out, my queen, and only
His body remains; he has been deprived of this
Jewel, and made to lay his weapon on the earth.'

Draupadī replied:

33 'We are free of the entire debt, Bhārata,
And my superior's son is my superior.*
Now let the king* bind this jewel to his head.'

Vaiśaṃpāyana continued:

34 So at Draupadī's request, and thinking
Of it as a relic of the teacher,*
The king took that jewel and placed it on his head.
35 Then with that divine jewel of jewels upon his brow,
The great and mighty king seemed as beautiful and
Bright as a mountain crested by the rising moon.

36 So strong-minded Draupadī, though stricken with grief
For her sons, gave up her fast to the death.

Then Dharmarāja turned to great-armed Kṛṣṇa . . .

CHAPTER 17

Vaiśaṃpāyana continued:

1 After brooding on how the entire army
Had been massacred at night by just three warriors,
King Yudhiṣṭhira in his grief asked Kṛṣṇa:

2 'Kṛṣṇa, how were all my sons, those great warriors, killed,
By that unskilled, vile, and wicked son of Droṇa?
3 And how were Drupada's sons, so honed in weapons,
Bold fighters of a hundred thousand foes,
Slain by Droṇa's son?
4 How could he have killed Dhṛṣṭadyumna, greatest of
Warriors, before whom the great archer Droṇa
Himself could not appear?
5 Bull of a man, what unbalanced act was done
By the teacher's son that, single-handed,
He was able to destroy our entire camp?'

Vāsudeva replied:

6 'Certainly, Droṇa's son sought the protection
Of the imperishable god of gods,
Lord of lords, and in that way, single-handed,
He killed so many.
7 For gratified, Mahādeva may bestow
Immortality itself, and Giriśa
Can give the strength to knock down even Indra.
8 For I know Mahādeva as he is
In reality, and his various former deeds,
Bull of the Bharatas—
9 He is the beginning, the middle, and the end
Of beings: the entire universe is
Active, Bhārata, through his activity.*

10 'Desiring to create living beings, the all—
Pervading grandsire* saw the Original,*
And said to him:

"Emit beings without delay!"

11 'Harikeśa replied:

"So be it!"

And knowing
The defects of living beings,* that great
Ascetic plunged into the waters and
Practised austerity for a long time.

12 'But after waiting for him endlessly,
The grandsire, through a supreme act of will,
Created another creator* for
All living beings.
13 He, seeing Giriśa immersed in the water,
Said to his father:

"If there is no first-born
Other than me, I will create offspring."

14 The father replied:

"Besides you there is
No other first-born person. This motionless one
Is immersed in the water. Create without fear!"

15 'So he created many living beings—
The progenitors, of whom Dakṣa was the first,*
Who in turn made all this fourfold race of creatures.*
16 But once all these hungry creatures were fully
Created, they immediately turned on their
Creator, Prajāpati,* wanting to eat him.
17 Being devoured, he ran to the grandsire for help—

'"Lord, protect me from these—grant them subsistence!"

18 'Then Brahmā assigned food to them—herbs and all kinds
Of vegetables, and the weaker creatures
He gave to the stronger.
19 As they had come, so now those creatures, their food
Apportioned, went satisfied away: then
Pleasuring themselves in union with their own
Species, they reproduced.

20 'After the original collection of creatures
Had multiplied, to the world *guru*'s* great
Satisfaction, Śiva, the most excellent,
Rose up from the water and saw those beings.
21 Beholding the huge variety of creatures,
Who had, through their own energy, reproduced,
Lord Rudra was angry* and threw down his *liṅga*.*
22 And when he had cast it into the earth he stood
Still.
Then, in a soothing tone, imperishable
Brahmā addressed him:

23 '"Śarva, why did you stay in the water so long?
And why did you tear out your *liṅga* and
Cast it into the earth?"

24 'Then the universal *guru*,* whose fury
Had been kindled, replied to that other *guru*:*

'"Since these creatures have been created by
Another, what should I do with this *liṅga*?
25 Grandsire, through my austerities I have made food*
For these my creatures. And just like the creatures
That feed on them, these herbs shall be perpetually
Renewed."

26 With these words, the great ascetic Bhava,
Dejected and very angry, went away
To the foot of the Muñjavat mountain*
To practise his austerities alone.'

CHAPTER 18

Vāsudeva continued:

1 'After their age* had elapsed, the gods prepared
To make a sacrifice, wanting to give an
Offering in line with Vedic injunction.
2 Insouciantly, they assigned the shares proper to
The sacrifice, the gods entitled to a share,
And the material worthy of sacrifice.*
3 But ignorant of the reality of
Rudra, the gods failed to assign a share to the
Divine Sthāṇu, O king.*
4 With no share assigned to him by the celestials,
Rudra-Śiva, covered in a deer skin,*
Desiring his portion, to that end swiftly
Created a bow.

5 'There is the world-sacrifice,* the sacrifice
Of rites,* the eternal domestic sacrifice,*
And the fivefold sacrifice,* whose fifth part
Is the sacrifice to be offered to men.
6 Kapardin, desiring his sacrificial share,
Produced, through a world-sacrifice, a bow
With a hundred and twenty thumb-breadth span.
7 That bow's string was the *vaṣaṭ mantra*,* and
The four parts of the sacrifice* were in its strength.

8 'Enraged, Mahādeva grasped that weapon,
And came to the place where the gods had assembled.
9 Seeing the imperishable celibate armed
With his bow, goddess Earth quaked, and the mountains
shook.
10 The wind dropped, fire though fed did not burn, in heaven
Terrified clusters of stars spun from their orbits.
11 The sun was eclipsed, the moon's halo went out;
From point to point the sky brimmed with darkness.

12 Stupefied, the gods were thrown from their purpose—
The sacrifice would not manifest for them,
The Vedas* tottered.*

13 'Then with an arrow Rudra pierced that sacrifice
Through the heart—at which, turning into a deer,
The sacrifice fled, together with the fire.*
14 Pursued in that form to the firmament
By Rudra, the sacrifice, on reaching
High heaven, flared up.

15 'And after the sacrifice had fled away,
The gods had no idea what was happening,
And once the gods had lost their understanding
Everything toppled into confusion.
16 Then, with the curved end of his bow, three-eyed
Śiva,* in a fury, broke Savitṛ's* arms,
Blinded Bhaga, and knocked out Pūṣan's teeth.
17 At this, the gods and the limbs of the sacrifice
Fled away together, some shaking as though
In the throes of death.

18 'But blue-throated Rudra,* who had put all the gods
To flight, laughed, and with the curved end of his bow
Stopped them in their tracks.
19 Then the gods cried out, the bowstring broke, and the bow
Immediately lost tension and straightened out.
20 Then the gods, together with the sacrifice,
Sought the protection of the bowless god of gods.

'And the god was kind.

21 'Soothed, the lord cast his rage into the ocean,
Where, becoming fire, it incessantly
Evaporates the sea.
22 Then he restored Bhaga's eyes, Savitṛ's arms,
And Pūṣan's teeth, together with the sacrifice,
23 So the world returned to its natural state; and as
His share, the gods gave Śiva all the oblations.

24 'When he was angry everything was out of joint;
But when he was pleased all became sound again.
That potent god was pleased with Droṇa's son, my king,*
25 And because of that, those great warriors, your sons,
Were all killed, and many other heroes too—
The Pāñcālas together with their followers.

26 'Don't dwell on it—what couldn't be done by Droṇa's son
Alone was achieved through Mahādeva's favour.

'Now do what you must.'

APPENDIX

THE *MAHĀBHĀRATA*: A BOOK-BY-BOOK SUMMARY OF THE PRINCIPAL EPISODES

This summary is necessarily highly condensed, and does nothing more than trace the events of the main story to give the *Sauptika-parvan* a narrative context.

The *Mahābhārata* tells the story of the descendants of Bharata, also known as the Kauravas,[1] Kurus (Kuru being another ancestor in the same line of descent), or the Lunar Dynasty. The setting for the epic is thus the 'land of the Kurus' (*kurukṣetra*) in what is now north-west India, roughly between the (upper) Ganges and Yamunā (Jumna) rivers.[2]

Book 1: The Beginning (*Ādiparvan*)[3]

The epic begins with various lists of contents and summaries, human and divine dramatis personae, legends concerning the author, Kṛṣṇa Dvaipāyana Vyāsa, and a number of narrative framing stories dealing with the first legendary recitals of the poem (see Introduction, 'Narration and Narrators'). Two elements in this rather halting start are worth noting: first, the outer layer is a Brahminical and sacrificial one; second, the very first recital is to King Janamejaya, the son of Parikṣit, and therefore the only descendant of the Pāṇḍava heroes of the poem, and of the Lunar Dynasty itself. (Janamejaya is, in fact, the great-grandson of Arjuna and Subhadrā, Kṛṣṇa Vāsudeva's sister.)

[1] The two contending parties in the narrative are both Kauravas (they are cousins), but the name is usually reserved for the 'bad' group, the others being known as the Pāṇḍavas (see below).

[2] The 'sites' of the major cities of the *Mahābhārata*—Hāstinapura, Indraprastha (in modern Delhi), and Mathurā—have been 'identified' and excavated. There is, however, no evidence that any of the events depicted in the *Mahābhārata* have a historical basis. John Smith states the position concisely: 'At an indeterminate point in the remote past, in the North-West of India, there may have been a dynastic struggle between people calling themselves Kauravas and Pāṇḍavas; or there may not. We have no way of knowing.' Smith, 'Old Indian: The Two Sanskrit Epics', 51.

[3] In this context, the Sanskrit word *parvan* means 'The Book of...', e.g. *Ādi-parvan*: 'The Book of the Beginning'.

The early history of the Lunar Dynasty is established, amid a series of miraculous births. The main narrative starts with the descent, or incarnation in human form, of Viṣṇu and other gods to relieve the burden of the goddess Earth, who is being afflicted by the *asuras* (anti-gods or 'demons'); they too take the form of various human incarnations. However, the direct causes of the conflict that becomes the *Mahābhārata* war (which culminates in the relief of the Earth) only become apparent in the events following the birth of Bhīṣma (*Mahābhārata* 1. 90. 50). Bhīṣma is the legitimate heir to the Kuru or Lunar Dynasty, born of King Śāṃtanu and the goddess Gaṅgā. Śāṃtanu later, however, wants to marry Satyavatī (who has already given birth to Kṛṣṇa Dvaipāyana Vyāsa by another man); but her father will only consent if Bhīṣma renounces the succession for himself and his descendants. This he is happy to do; moreover, he takes a vow to become a celibate ascetic, ensuring that he will remain sonless. As thanks, Śāṃtanu grants Bhīṣma the ability to die only when he wills it. Śāṃtanu and Satyavatī marry and have two sons, Citrāṇgada and Vicitravīrya, who reign successively after Śāṃtanu's death, before both dying childless. To assure the survival of the dynasty, Bhīṣma and Satyavatī arrange for her illegitimate brahmin son Kṛṣṇa Dvaipāyana Vyāsa to father children on Vicitravīrya's widows Ambikā and Ambālikā. Although the widows agree to this, they are so frightened by the physical appearance of their partner that Ambikā shuts her eyes during intercourse, and Ambālikā turns pale. As a result, the elder son, Dhṛtarāṣṭra, is born blind, and the younger, Pāṇḍu, as his name indicates, sickly pale. (A third son, Vidura, is born of Kṛṣṇa Dvaipāyana Vyāsa and a low-class servant girl, who has been substituted in a bed trick by the reluctant Ambikā.)

Neither a blind man, nor a bastard of mixed blood, is thought fit to be king of the Kurus; only the marginally tainted Pāṇḍu is considered worthy of the throne. Pāṇḍu has two wives, Kuntī (the senior) and Mādrī (the junior); after a series of wars, he directs his kingdom, not from his capital, Hāstinapura, but from the neighbouring forests, via messengers. While in the forest, he mortally wounds an ascetic who has taken the form of a deer and is in the act of mating with a doe. The ascetic curses Pāṇḍu to die the moment he makes love to a woman, thus causing a new crisis for the succession, since he has not yet had any sons. This time it is overcome by Kuntī, who has at her disposal a mantra (a formula or magic spell) through which she can invoke any deity and conceive by him a child. Pāṇḍu orders her to make use of it, and invoking the gods Dharma, Vāyu (the Wind), and Indra, she gives birth, at yearly intervals, to three sons: Yudhiṣṭhira, Bhīma, and Arjuna. Kuntī then allows her co-wife Mādrī to use the mantra; invoking the divine Aśvin twins, she gives birth a year later to twin boys, Nakula and Sahadeva. These five together are known, somewhat inaccurately, as 'the Pāṇḍavas' ('the sons of Pāṇḍu'); their divine parentage is, in fact, part of the sequence of interventions through which the gods plan to rescue Earth from the anti-gods.

Meanwhile, the blind Dhṛtarāṣṭra has married the princess Gāndhārī, who, in inauspicious circumstances, bears him a hundred sons and one daughter, known collectively as 'the Kauravas' ('descendants of Kuru'). The eldest of these, Duryodhana, is born after Yudhiṣṭhira, the eldest Pāṇḍava, although apparently conceived before him (Gāndhārī bears her extraordinary foetus for two years). The text at this point (1. 107. 9 f.) refers to Dhṛtarāṣṭra as the father of the Kauravas, but elsewhere in the *Mahābhārata* (first at 1. 61. 80 f.) Duryodhana is described as being born on earth from a portion of the anti-god (*asura*) Kali (Discord), and the other ninety-nine sons as creatures of the demonic *rākṣasas*. It is clear from the beginning, therefore, that while the Pāṇḍavas, who are partial incarnations of gods, represent cosmic and social order (*dharma*), the Kauravas, partial incarnations of anti-gods, represent the opposite: disorder veering into chaos (*adharma*).

Finally unable to control his desire for Mādrī, Pāṇḍu dies, and Dhṛtarāṣṭra effectively becomes king during the minority of Yudhiṣṭhira. Yudhiṣṭhira should eventually come to the throne, but Duryodhana plots to prevent this, manipulating his perpetually weak father, and setting potentially fatal traps for the Pāṇḍavas, which are foiled through the help of their uncle Vidura. Meanwhile, under the general tutelage of Bhīṣma, the two groups of cousins are educated together, at Hāstinapura. Specific training in arms and the martial skills is given by two brahmins, Kṛpa and Droṇa. Droṇa grew up with Drupada, who succeeded to the neighbouring throne of Pāñcāla, but they subsequently fell out, at which point Droṇa came to Hāstinapura and was engaged as a teacher for the cousins, the Vṛṣṇis, and Karṇa (see below). Droṇa has a son, Aśvatthāman, who also studies weaponry with his father. The third Pāṇḍava brother, Arjuna, becomes Droṇa's favourite, excelling all others in his skill as an archer. As a reward for his prowess, Droṇa gives Arjuna the invincible and world-destroying *brahmaśiras* weapon.

Various alliances are formed in this period, including that of Duryodhana and Karṇa, who, unknown to himself and everyone else except Kuntī, is actually the Pāṇḍavas' older half-brother, the result of an early use of Kuntī's mantra to invoke the sun god Sūrya. As a fee for his teaching, Droṇa demands that his Kuru pupils make an attack upon Drupada, king of Pāñcāla. Drupada is captured, and subsequently released to reign over half his previous kingdom, but now bears a grudge against Droṇa. At Duryodhana's urging, Dhṛtarāṣṭra puts pressure on the Pāṇḍavas and Kuntī to go and live in a specially built house in the city of Vāraṇāvata. This lacquer house is literally a fire trap, but Bhīma rescues the Pāṇḍavas and carries them to safety in the forest, where various adventures ensue as they travel around disguised as brahmin ascetics. There they hear that Drupada, seeking revenge on Droṇa, has, through a special sacrifice, acquired a powerful son, Dhṛṣṭadyumna, and a daughter, Kṛṣṇā (Draupadī). Dhṛṣṭadyumna becomes Droṇa's pupil.

Still disguised as brahmins, the Pāṇḍavas travel to Drupada's city where a contest for Draupadī's hand in marriage is being held. It is at this marriage that Kṛṣṇa Vāsudeva, his brother Balarāma, and other Vṛṣṇis first become involved in the affairs of the Pāṇḍavas. (Kṛṣṇa is the son of Vasudeva, Kuntī's brother, and so the Pāṇḍavas' cousin; he is also an incarnation of the god Viṣṇu.) All the Pāṇḍavas fall in love with Draupadī, but it is Arjuna who wins the contest, and so Draupadī's hand in marriage. When a fight breaks out because the *kṣatriyas* (warrior class) think Drupada has given his daughter to a brahmin, Kṛṣṇa recognizes the Pāṇḍavas. Returning to the forest with his bride, Arjuna calls out to his mother: 'See what we have found!' Thinking he is simply referring to alms, she replies without looking: 'Share it together!' As a result of this, and of the need for Yudhiṣṭhira as the eldest to marry first, Draupadī becomes the wife of all five brothers. Once their identity is clear, King Drupada welcomes the Pāṇḍavas to his court, and allies himself with them against Dhṛtarāṣṭra and his followers. The latter are not sure how to react, and argue among themselves, but eventually Dhṛtarāṣṭra agrees that he is responsible to the Pāṇḍavas as well, and sends Vidura to invite them back. They return to Hāstinapura where Dhṛtarāṣṭra offers them the Khāṇḍava territory (half the kingdom) in settlement. They accept and found their own capital there, Indraprastha, ruled over by Yudhiṣṭhira. From here Arjuna insists on going into exile in the forest for twelve months (years, according to the Critical Edition) in expiation for a forced breach of etiquette. He has various adventures, and during a tour of pilgrimage sites meets up with Kṛṣṇa again, who entertains him in his own house. Arjuna falls in love with Kṛṣṇa's sister Subhadrā, and, at Kṛṣṇa's prompting, carries her off to Indraprastha. The Vṛṣṇis, Bhojas, and Andhakas are incensed and want to wage war, but Kṛṣṇa persuades them otherwise, and effects an alliance between the Vṛṣṇis and the Pāṇḍavas. Arjuna marries Subhadrā and they have a son, Abhimanyu, who is educated in the arts of war by his father. Meanwhile, over a period of five years, Draupadī has a son by each of her five husbands (known collectively as the Draupadeyas). Arjuna and Kṛṣṇa (who has stayed on with the Pāṇḍavas after his sister's wedding) are summoned by the fire god to deliver the Khāṇḍava forest and its denizens to him. During the conflagration they shoot down the fleeing creatures. This episode perhaps reflects the need of the Pāṇḍavas to clear a space for their kingdom.

Book 2: The Assembly Hall (*Sabhāparvan*)

The architect Maya, who was rescued by Arjuna from the Khāṇḍava fire, reciprocates by building a great assembly hall or palace for the Pāṇḍavas. Prompted by Kṛṣṇa, and preceded by various ritually required conquests made by his brothers, Yudhiṣṭhira performs a *rājasūya* sacrifice (a royal consecration), thus laying claim to universal sovereignty. During the ceremony, Kṛṣṇa's divinity is extolled by Bhīṣma. The Kauravas have been invited to attend the ceremony as guests; Duryodhana lodges in the palace and becomes deeply depressed by, and envious of, Yudhiṣṭhira's wealth. On his return to Hāstinapura he persuades the reluctant Dhṛtarāṣṭra to agree to a dicing match between Śakuni (Duryodhana's maternal uncle) and Yudhiṣṭhira, to win the latter's wealth and power. (A dicing match may have been the ritually required postscript to a royal consecration, and normally a formality.) Yudhiṣṭhira feels obliged to accept the challenge, and the Pāṇḍavas travel to

Hāstinapura for the match. Vidura attempts to stop the proceedings, but to no avail. Śakuni dices on Duryodhana's behalf, and through his trickery defeats Yudhiṣṭhira at every throw, winning from the Pāṇḍava his army, his wealth, his city, his country, his brothers, and then himself. There is one throw left, and Śakuni suggests that Yudhiṣṭhira stake Draupadī. He does so and loses again. Exultant, Duryodhana sends an usher to fetch Draupadī to the hall. Draupadī asks if Yudhiṣṭhira lost himself before losing her (i.e. was she his to stake?), a riddle that divides opinion in the assembly. Angrily, Duryodhana sends his brother Duḥśāsana to fetch Draupadī. He drags her by the hair into the hall, wearing only a single garment and in the middle of her menstrual period. Karṇa enjoins Duḥśāsana to strip Draupadī naked, but miraculously new clothes keep descending and covering her.[4] Bhīma vows to drink Duḥśāsana's blood. Duryodhana exposes his thigh to Draupadī, and Bhīma vows to break it in battle. Scandalized by Duryodhana's behaviour, Dhṛtarāṣṭra grants Draupadī a boon and she secures the freedom of the Pāṇḍava brothers.

The Pāṇḍavas set out to return to their capital, Indraprastha. Dhṛtarāṣṭra, however, gives in to Duryodhana's demand that there should be another throw of the dice. Yudhiṣṭhira returns, and it is agreed that the losers this time should be exiled to the forest for twelve years, and spend a thirteenth year incognito in a populated place, if they are to regain their kingdom. Yudhiṣṭhira loses again. The Pāṇḍavas and Draupadī take to the forest amid various dire prophecies. (Bhīma predicts he will kill Duryodhana, Arjuna will kill Karṇa, and Sahadeva Śakuni.) Draupadī's treatment becomes the general inspiration for Pāṇḍava acts of vengeance in the war to come.

Book 3: The Forest (*Vanaparvan*)

This is the longest book of the *Mahābhārata*, but it contains much non-narrative material, swelling out the Pāṇḍavas' twelve years of exile in the forest with various supernatural adventures, stories, and teachings. (It contains the famous episode of Nala and Damayantī, familiar to generations of western Sanskrit students, and the equally

[4] According to some versions, but not the Critical Edition, this is as a result of a prayer to Kṛṣṇa. Kṛṣṇa's absence is both notable and, in terms of the dramatic development, necessary during this dicing episode—see Hiltebeitel, *The Ritual of Battle*, ch. 4.

well-known story of the devoted wife Sāvitrī, and her encounter with Death.) A significant episode is Arjuna's solo journey to Indra's heaven to obtain weapons, which includes his period of asceticism in the mountains, and his meeting with the god Śiva, from whom he also gains arms. Kṛṣṇa visits the Pāṇḍavas in the forest, and Vyāsa foils Duryodhana's plan to assassinate them. Jayadratha, the king of Sindh, and brother-in-law of Duryodhana, abducts Draupadī, is caught by Bhīma and Arjuna, but spared. Later he allies himself and his army with the Kauravas. After a riddling test, which Yudhiṣṭhira passes, the god Dharma guarantees the Pāṇḍavas the ability to remain incognito during the thirteenth year of their exile.

Book 4: King Virāṭa (*Virāṭaparvan*)

The Pāṇḍavas spend their thirteenth year of exile in disguise (Arjuna posing as a eunuch) in the service of King Virāṭa of the Matsyas. (According to some, this last year in exile represents a *dīkṣā* or consecration in which they prepare themselves for the sacrifice of battle to follow.[5]) Bhīma kills one of the king's generals, Kīcaka, who has attempted to seduce Draupadī. The Pāṇḍavas save the king from a double invasion, the second, in the form of a cattle raid, the work of the Kauravas.[6] At the end of the year, the Pāṇḍavas reveal their identity and settle in Virāṭa's city of Upaplavya. Virāṭa offers his daughter Uttarā in marriage to Arjuna; he accepts her, but for his son Abhimanyu, who has been staying with his uncle, Kṛṣṇa. Kṛṣṇa arrives with Abhimanyu and the Vṛṣṇis, and the wedding is held, sealing the alliance between the Matsyas and the Pāṇḍavas. (Abhimanyu and Uttarā are the parents-to-be of Parikṣit.)

Book 5: Preparations (*Udyogaparvan*)

Yudhiṣṭhira seeks the return of his half of the kingdom. Both sides begin preparing for war, the Pāṇḍavas raising seven armies, the Kauravas eleven. From this point on, Kṛṣṇa becomes a principal character in the poem in his role as protector of the Pāṇḍavas and their cause, although ostensibly acting as a neutral ambassador in

[5] See Alf Hiltebeitel's entry on the 'Mahābhārata' in *The Encyclopedia of Religions*.
[6] Dumézil sees this as a rehearsal of the war to come in Books 6 to 9: see *Mythe et épopée*, i. 38.

negotiations between the antagonistic parties. In fact, an alliance has been sought with him by both Arjuna and Duryodhana, but offered the choice between Kṛṣṇa himself as a non-combatant charioteer and adviser, and thousands of Kṛṣṇa's troops, Arjuna chooses the former, and Duryodhana happily accepts the latter. Kṛṣṇa's brother Balarāma remains neutral, but Kṛtavarman, a friend of Kṛṣṇa's, allies himself with the Kauravas.

Before setting out on his peace mission to Hāstinapura, Kṛṣṇa is reminded by Draupadī of her humiliation at the hands of the Kauravas, and she demands war. He promises the death of her enemies. Although the Pāṇḍavas have fulfilled the terms of their exile, and despite the wish of Dhṛtarāṣṭra and other Kaurava supporters for an agreement and peace, Duryodhana remains intransigent, and refuses to restore any of the kingdom to Yudhiṣṭhira. Kṛṣṇa reveals to Karṇa the latter's true parentage, but he refuses to change sides, even to be recognized as the rightful king, for Duryodhana has been his patron. War, just but disastrous, is now inevitable. The reluctant 'grandfather', Bhīṣma, is made commander of the Kaurava troops by Duryodhana. Karṇa falls out with him and refuses to fight until he is dead. Bhīṣma, for his part, refuses to fight Śikhaṇḍin, one of the Pāṇḍava army, who was born to King Drupada as a girl, but has since been changed into a man. (In fact, in her previous life as Ambā, a woman, Bhīṣma was responsible for her rejection by her chosen husband, and so he/she now pursues him with implacable hatred.)

On the Pāṇḍava side, Yudhiṣṭhira appoints Dhṛṣṭadyumna as commander. The two armies set up camp and prepare to fight at Kurukṣetra, 'the field of the Kurus', an ancient sacrificial area.

Book 6: Bhīṣma (*Bhīṣmaparvan*)

Before the battle (which will last for eighteen days) begins, Arjuna, stationed between the two armies in his chariot driven by Kṛṣṇa, is suddenly overcome by disabling scruples at the prospect of killing his kinsmen and teachers. This is the famous *Bhagavadgītā* section of the *Mahābhārata*, which, according to Madeleine Biardeau, expresses the entire 'philosophy' of the epic.[7] Caught in the dilemma of either fighting a just and duty-bound war that will, nevertheless,

[7] Péterfalvi and Biardeau, *Le Mahābhārata*, ii. 21.

have disastrous consequences, or renouncing his duty and withdrawing from the battle, with equally bad consequences for himself, Arjuna is immobilized. Kṛṣṇa, however, teaches him that it is his duty as a *kṣatriya* to fight without further motivation, without desire for the results of his actions. Indeed such desire would be deluded, for Kṛṣṇa himself, as God, is the only real actor: therefore it is to God alone that the results of actions accrue, and the ostensible actor is merely his instrument. The solution to the problem of action (*karma*) and its results is, therefore, to act in a spirit of devotion (*bhakti*), offering the fruits of all one's actions to God, since they are his anyway. In a great theophany (which is also an image of the end of a world age), Kṛṣṇa allows Arjuna to see him in his overwhelming, universal form, as Time, the destroyer of the universe, mangling the warriors on both sides between his jaws. The *Bhagavadgītā* section ends with Kṛṣṇa's guarantee to Arjuna (and to devotees generally) that he will be released from all evils because he is dear to him. Arjuna takes up his bow ready to fight.

Yudhiṣṭhira, ever mindful of *dharma* (what is right), pays respect to his teachers and elders, who are obliged, by the wealth of the Kurus, to fight against him; but along with permission to fight them he also asks them to tell him how they may be killed. Bhīṣma tells him that his time of death has not yet come, and he should ask him later. Droṇa reveals that he can only be killed if he lays down his weapons voluntarily, and this he will do if he hears something very disagreeable from a man of truth. Kṛpa tells him he is incapable of being slain. Śalya renews a promise to weaken Karṇa's energy in the battle. Dhṛtarāṣṭra's youngest son, Yuyutsu, born, in addition to the hundred, from a servant (*śūdra*) woman, joins the Pāṇḍavas.

The first ten days of the battle are now fought with the Kauravas under the command of Bhīṣma. The ebb and flow is recorded in great detail, usually in the form of duels between key characters; but fighting takes place only in daylight, and in the intervals the adversaries visit each other's camps. On the eve of the tenth day the Pāṇḍavas again visit Bhīṣma to ask how they can kill him. He advises Arjuna to fight him from behind the human shield of the man-woman Śikhaṇḍin, against whom he has sworn not to defend himself; he thereby wills his own death. On the tenth day of battle, the Pāṇḍavas, with Śikhaṇḍin at their head, consequently shoot down Bhīṣma in the prescribed fashion. Although mortally wounded, he postpones his death, and remains suspended above the earth, on a 'bed' made of the arrows that have pierced him, to witness the outcome of the battle. Karṇa is now free to take part in the conflict.

Book 7: Droṇa (*Droṇaparvan*)

At Duryodhana's request, Droṇa now takes command of the Kaurava army. On the thirteenth day, Arjuna's son Abhimanyu is killed in a cowardly fashion, after help from the rest of the Pāṇḍava army has been cut off by Jayadratha. With the aid of Śiva, and a trick of Kṛṣṇa's, Arjuna fulfils his vow to slay Jayadratha before sunset on the next day. Ghaṭotkaca, a gigantic *rākṣasa* (demon) son of Bhīma, causes havoc among the Kauravas, but is eventually slain by Karṇa with a magic missile (one that he will not now be able to use against Arjuna). On the fifteenth day of battle, Droṇa is causing great carnage among the Pāṇḍavas and their allies (the Pāñcālas, Somakas, Sṛñjayas, etc.). Kṛṣṇa urges the Pāṇḍavas to lie to Droṇa and tell him that his son Aśvatthāman has been slain in battle. Bhīma kills an elephant called 'Aśvatthāman', and calls out that Aśvatthāman has been slain. Droṇa does not believe him, and goes on slaughtering with his extraordinary weapons. Eventually, he asks Yudhiṣṭhira, a man of truth, if the report is true. Kṛṣṇa urges the latter to save his army with an untruth. Yudhiṣṭhira confirms that Aśvatthāman is dead, adding the word 'elephant' beneath his breath. Yudhiṣṭhira's chariot, which had previously floated just above the earth, immediately falls to the ground. Droṇa meanwhile becomes dejected, lays his weapons aside, and assuming a yogic posture enters heaven (*brahmaloka*). Dhṛṣṭadyumna, at Bhīma's urging, cuts off Droṇa's head. His son Aśvatthāman is filled with rage, and vows to destroy the Pāñcālas and the Pāṇḍavas for this unrighteous act, using his father's magic weapons. After some destruction, however, this threat is neutralized.

Book 8: Karṇa (*Karṇaparvan*)

Karṇa is now made commander of the Kaurava armies. The slaughter continues. Bhīma kills Duḥśāsana, and, in fulfilment of his vow to Draupadī, cuts open the Kaurava's breast and drinks his blood in sight of Duryodhana and Karṇa. Arjuna and Karṇa engage in a lengthy single combat. Eventually, Karṇa's chariot wheel becomes stuck in the earth and he unsuccessfully tries to free it. He appeals to Arjuna to follow the rules of fair combat and the warrior's code (*kṣatriya dharma*), and hold off until he has extricated himself. Kṛṣṇa mocks him: where was his *dharma* on all those occasions when the Kauravas flouted it in their treatment of the Pāṇḍavas? Urged on by Kṛṣṇa, Arjuna strikes off Karṇa's head before he can remount his chariot. His energy leaves his body and enters the sun (his father). Duryodhana is in despair, but decides to make a last stand.

Book 9: Śalya (*Śalyaparvan*)

Śalya is made the Kaurava commander. It is now the eighteenth day of the war, but the battle continues as relentlessly as before. Yudhiṣṭhira kills Śalya. The demoralized Kaurava army is steadily destroyed; as predicted by Bhīma, Sahadeva kills Śakuni. Of the one hundred sons of Dhṛtarāṣṭra, only Duryodhana remains alive. Fleeing on foot, and bearing a mace, he magically enters the waters of a lake. Aśvatthāman, Kṛpa, and Kṛtavarman are the only other surviving Kaurava combatants. Taking Saṃjaya, who knows the whereabouts of Duryodhana, with them, they flee to the Kuru camp. The Pāṇḍavas search for Duryodhana without success, and retire to rest. Aśvatthāman, Kṛpa, and Kṛtavarman approach the lake and implore Duryodhana to fight with them against Yudhiṣṭhira. He agrees to do so after a night's rest; but Aśvatthāman swears that he will destroy all the Somakas and Pāñcālas before the sun rises. Some hunters alert the Pāṇḍavas to Duryodhana's whereabouts. Hearing their enemies approaching, Aśvatthāman and the others take their leave of Duryodhana and flee away by a circuitous route, eventually resting under a great tree.

Duryodhana, meanwhile, has caused the lake to freeze over above him. Yudhiṣṭhira taunts Duryodhana, and then lures him out by promising he can remain king if he can defeat just one of the Pāṇḍavas in single combat. He emerges to fight Bhīma with his mace. Kṛṣṇa tells Arjuna that Yudhiṣṭhira's promise is foolish, because Bhīma will never defeat Duryodhana in a fair fight. But for Arjuna's benefit, he recalls Bhīma's vow to Draupadī to break Duryodhana's thighs. Arjuna signals to Bhīma by striking his own left thigh, and his brother (in a move that contravenes the rules for this kind of combat, which forbid striking below the navel) hurls his mace at Duryodhana, fracturing his thighs. The stricken Duryodhana charges Kṛṣṇa with being behind all the contraventions of *dharma* by which the Pāṇḍavas have won the war. Kṛṣṇa reminds him that all the Kaurava misfortunes stem from Duryodhana's own evil actions, which have now come to full fruition. Duryodhana asserts that his end is glorious and in accord with *kṣatriya dharma*; celestial flowers fall on him. Kṛṣṇa however insists that unfair means were necessary for the good to triumph.

The Pāṇḍavas and their followers proceed to the deserted Kaurava camp, which is full of booty. Yudhiṣṭhira attributes the Pāṇḍava victory to Kṛṣṇa's power. Kṛṣṇa suggests that the five Pāṇḍava brothers and his kinsman Sātyaki should spend the night outside the camp on the banks of the Oghavatī river, 'for the sake of acting auspiciously'. All the others remain in the occupied camp. The Pāṇḍava brothers then send Kṛṣṇa to Hāstinapura to comfort Dhṛtarāṣṭra and Gāndhārī for the death of their sons. While there, Kṛṣṇa tells Dhṛtarāṣṭra and Gāndhārī that it is Aśvatthāman's intention to kill the Pāṇḍavas in the night; they ask him to protect the Pāṇḍavas, and he leaves abruptly. When he returns, he tells the Pāṇḍavas what happened at the Kuru court, but makes no effort to foil Aśvatthāman.

Meanwhile, Duryodhana lies on the field with his thighs broken. Hearing what has happened from messengers, Aśvatthāman, Kṛpa, and Kṛtavarman hurry back to him. Aśvatthāman laments the reversal of fortune that leaves such a great king in the dust. Duryodhana sees himself as a victim of the universal destruction which is coming to pass. But he reiterates that he has nothing to regret because he has not deviated from his *kṣatriya dharma*. Aśvatthāman asks his permission to kill, by any means possible, all the Pāñcālas in the sight of Vāsudeva (Kṛṣṇa). Replying that when a brahmin lives according to the *kṣatriya dharma* he has the right to fight, especially if the king commands, Duryodhana instructs Kṛpa to consecrate Aśvatthāman as the final commander of the Kaurava army. The three warriors then leave the dying Duryodhana for the night, and quit the battlefield.

Book 10: The Massacre at Night (*Sauptikaparvan*)

Fleeing the jubilant Pāṇḍavas, Aśvatthāman, Kṛpa, and Kṛtavarman take refuge in a forest. While the others sleep, Aśvatthāman sees a ferocious owl slaughtering some crows, and is inspired by this to make a night attack on his sleeping enemies. Undeterred by Kṛpa's arguments against this plan, he sets out for the camp; Kṛpa and Kṛtavarman follow him. At the camp's gate Aśvatthāman is confronted by a gigantic spirit, which he attacks, but to no avail. Fearlessly, he offers himself as a sacrifice to Śiva. Śiva tells him that, although he has protected the Pāñcālas until now, their time has now expired. He gives Aśvatthāman a sword and enters his body. Thus possessed, and attended by a demonic troop, Aśvatthāman enters the camp, leaving Kṛpa and Kṛtavarman to kill anyone who attempts to escape.

Inside the camp, Aśvatthāman roams around killing the sleepers and those rising from sleep in an orgy of slaughter. He shows no mercy to Dhṛṣṭadyumna, and kills Śikhaṇḍin and the Draupadeyas (Draupadī's five sons). Before long he has slaughtered the entire host of Pāñcālas and Pāṇḍavas (apart from Dhṛṣṭadyumna's charioteer, who escapes to break the news). Demonic *rākṣasas* and *piśācas* feast on the flesh of the warriors. Meanwhile, Kṛpa and Kṛtavarman set fire to the camp. Aśvatthāman issues out at dawn, and the three of them return to where Duryodhana is lying, surrounded by carnivorous animals. He revives for long enough to hear of their success, then dies and ascends to heaven.

Yudhiṣṭhira is told that his army has been destroyed. He sends to Upaplavya for Draupadī and the other women. Draupadī begins a fast to the death, which she will only end if Aśvatthāman is found and killed. Acting on her words, Bhīma sets out in pursuit. Kṛṣṇa warns Yudhiṣṭhira that Aśvatthāman has the all-exterminating *brahmaśiras* weapon, and that Bhīma is in great danger. The Pāṇḍavas and Kṛṣṇa catch up with him just as he discovers Aśvatthāman with Kṛṣṇa Dvaipāyana (Vyāsa) and other sages on the banks of the Ganges. Cornered, Aśvatthāman makes an arrow from a blade of grass or stalk, and charges it with the *brahmaśiras* weapon. He hurls it for the destruction of the Pāṇḍavas. At Kṛṣṇa's urging, Arjuna releases the equally powerful weapon which had been given him by Droṇa to neutralize Aśvatthāman's. Universal destruction is threatened. The sages Nārada and Vyāsa intervene. Arjuna withdraws his weapon, but Aśvatthāman does not have the requisite purity to do likewise. Instead, he diverts the lethal effect into the wombs of the Pāṇḍava women, thus making them barren. This seems to be the end of the Pāṇḍava line, but Kṛṣṇa promises to revivify the foetus that Abhimanyu's widow Uttarā bears in her womb: he predicts that she will give birth to a son, Parikṣit, who will rule the Kurus for sixty years.[8] Aśvatthāman, on the other hand, is condemned to wander the earth in misery for 3,000 years. Surrendering the jewel he wears on his head to the Pāṇḍavas, he sets off towards the forest, allowed to live because he is a brahmin and their teacher's son.

The Pāṇḍavas return to Draupadī with the jewel and the news of Aśvatthāman's defeat. Draupadī gives up her death-fast, and instructs Yudhiṣṭhira to wear the jewel. Yudhiṣṭhira then asks Kṛṣṇa how it was possible for one man to have destroyed the whole Pāṇḍava camp. Kṛṣṇa explains that it was not Aśvatthāman who was really responsible, but Śiva, and points up the connection with a retelling of the story of Śiva's destruction of Dakṣa's sacrifice.

Book 11: The Women (*Strīparvan*)

Dhṛtarāṣṭra is consoled by Vidura and Vyāsa, and then sets out with Gāndhārī and the Kuru women to visit the field of battle and perform the proper rites for the dead. The Pāṇḍavas and Kṛṣṇa come to meet them. Gāndhārī, and the women of both sides, mourn the dead. After various recriminations, the Pāṇḍavas are reconciled with Dhṛtarāṣṭra and Gāndhārī, but the latter curses Kṛṣṇa for having failed to prevent the slaughter, predicting the end of the Vṛṣṇis and his own death. Kṛṣṇa blames Gāndhārī, who, as Duryodhana's mother, was responsible for the slaughter. The bodies of the dead are burned, and various funeral rites are performed on the banks of the Ganges. Kuntī discloses Karṇa's true parentage to her surviving sons, who grieve for their elder brother.

Book 12: The Peace (*Śāntiparvan*)

Yudhiṣṭhira wishes to renounce the kingdom; his brothers, Kṛṣṇa, and Vyāsa persuade him that his duty is to rule. Vyāsa recommends a horse sacrifice as expiation. Yudhiṣṭhira relents and proceeds to Hāstinapura to be crowned. Bhīṣma is discovered still lying on his bed of arrows on the banks of the Oghavatī river, and still at the

[8] See the summary of Book 14, below.

point of death. Kṛṣṇa asks him to instruct Yudhiṣṭhira before he dies. This he does at extraordinary length, discoursing on kingly duties, social order, morality, and every kind of cosmological, religious, and soteriological matter.

Book 13: The Teaching (*Anuśāsanaparvan*)

Bhīṣma's teaching to Yudhiṣṭhira, copiously illustrated with edifying stories, continues. This extraordinary anthology of Hindu thought and practice only comes to an end when Bhīṣma, who has been lying on his bed of arrows for fifty-eight nights, finally dies. At the end he instructs Dhṛtarāṣṭra to treat the Pāṇḍavas as his own sons, praises Kṛṣṇa as the supreme God, and asks his permission to die. His soul passes from his body through the crown of his head and ascends to heaven.

Book 14: The Horse Sacrifice (*Āśvamedhikaparvan*)

The Pāṇḍavas reconquer and pacify their kingdom. Vyāsa again urges Yudhiṣṭhira to perform the horse sacrifice. Uttarā gives birth to Parikṣit, but because of the *brahmaśiras* weapon he is stillborn. However, true to his word, Kṛṣṇa revives him. Yudhiṣṭhira decides to perform the horse sacrifice (*aśvamedha*); the horse is let loose, followed by Arjuna, who fights many great battles during its wanderings. Eventually, having wandered over the whole earth, the horse returns to Hāstinapura, and the sacrifice takes place on a gigantic scale, atoning for the Pāṇḍavas' destruction of their Kaurava cousins.

Book 15: The Stay in the Hermitage (*Āśramavāsikaparvan*)

With the help of Dhṛtarāṣṭra and Vidura, the Pāṇḍavas rule the kingdom. After fifteen years, Dhṛtarāṣṭra and Gāndhārī retire into the forest to practise asceticism; Kuntī, Vidura, and Saṃjaya accompany them. During a visit made to them by the Pāṇḍavas, Vidura (an incarnation of Dharma) uses his yogic power to abandon his own physical body and enter that of Yudhiṣṭhira, King Dharma himself. Vyāsa affords Dhṛtarāṣṭra and the others a paradisaical vision of the dead warriors, now in total harmony with each other. The Pāṇḍavas return to Hāstinapura. After three years' asceticism, Dhṛtarāṣṭra, Gāndhārī, and Kuntī meet their deaths in a forest fire, caused by Dhṛtarāṣṭra's own abandoned sacrificial fires. The Pāṇḍavas perform their funeral rites. Saṃjaya escapes the fire and leaves for the Himālayas.

Book 16: The Battle with Clubs (*Mausalaparvan*)

Thirty-six years after the great Bhārata battle, word comes to the Pāṇḍavas that Gāndhārī's curse has taken effect and that a quarrel has resulted in the self-destruction of Kṛṣṇa's Yādava people (the Vṛṣṇis, Andhakas, and Bhojas). A drunken brawl had broken out, reeds had been magically turned to clubs, and, incited by Kṛṣṇa, they had beaten each other to death. (Among the dead were Sātyaki and Kṛtavarman, the latter killed by the former.) Only Kṛṣṇa and his brother Balarāma had escaped. Their city, Dvārakā, had been engulfed by the ocean.

Balarāma soon dies, and after wandering for a while Kṛṣṇa decides the time has come to die himself. Taking up a yogic posture, he is mistaken for a deer by a hunter, who shoots him in the heel with an arrow. Kṛṣṇa ascends to heaven. Arjuna, who performs the funeral rites, is told by Vyāsa that, like Kṛṣṇa, the Pāṇḍavas have finished their work in the world, and it is time to depart.

Book 17: The Great Departure (*Mahāprasthānikaparvan*)

Deciding it is indeed time to leave the world, Yudhiṣṭhira installs his young nephew Parikṣit as king in Hāstinapura, with Kṛpa as his preceptor. Then the five Pāṇḍava brothers and Draupadī ritually renounce the world; as yogin ascetics, they set out on their journey accompanied by a dog. Crossing the Himālayas, they come to Mount Meru, the *axis mundi*, connecting earth to heaven. They begin the ascent, but one by one fall, until only Yudhiṣṭhira and the dog are left. The god Indra arrives in a chariot, and, telling Yudhiṣṭhira that his wife and brothers are already in heaven, enjoins him to mount the chariot and ascend himself. Yudhiṣṭhira wants to take the dog with him, but is told that there is no place in heaven for someone with a dog. He refuses to mount the chariot. The dog then reveals itself to be Dharma, his real father, who praises him. They ascend to heaven, where Yudhiṣṭhira asks to be reunited with his brothers and Draupadī.

Book 18: The Ascent to Heaven (*Svargārohaṇaparvan*)

Duryodhana, enthroned and radiating splendour, is the first person Yudhiṣṭhira sees in heaven. Indignantly, he asks for his brothers and Karṇa, vowing he will not remain in heaven if they are not to be found there. A messenger leads him to the region his brothers have reached. The path is black and stinking. He hears voices calling him; they belong to Karṇa and his brothers entreating him to stay with them, since he is the only comfort in their torment. Dumbfounded, Yudhiṣṭhira rails against the gods and Dharma, declaring he will stay in hell to comfort his relatives. Indra and the others appear and reveal that what he has experienced was an illusion: Yudhiṣṭhira had to see hell because he deceived Droṇa into thinking Aśvatthāman was dead. His brothers and Karṇa have in fact all been cleansed of their sins and now reside in a blissful region. Having bathed in the celestial river Gaṅgā, Yudhiṣṭhira leaves his human body and, assuming a heavenly form, reaches the heavenly regions where the Pāṇḍavas and Kauravas reside, free of all enmity and suffering. Those who are the sons of gods are seen with their fathers; those who are incarnations or part-incarnations of gods take on various divine forms in a variety of heavens.

The *Mahābhārata* ends by closing its various 'narrative boxes', and eulogizing its 'author', Vyāsa, and the text itself.

EXPLANATORY NOTES

For general notes on named individuals, see 'Proper Names and Epithets'.

Part I *The Sleepers*: the Sanskrit text of the *Sauptikaparvan* is divided into two sections, consisting of, respectively, *adhyāyas* (Chapters) 1–9, and 10–18. The first of these sections shares the name of the whole book (*Sauptika*), but to distinguish it from the latter in the English version I have used the alternative translation 'The Sleepers.' The second section, *Aiṣīka* ('The Arrow Made from Stalks'), takes its name from the way in which Aśvatthāman launches his weapon of mass destruction in Chapter 13.

CHAPTER 1

1. 1 *Those heroes*: Aśvatthāman (Droṇa's son), Kṛpa, and Kṛtavarman.

the warriors' camp: it is not clear whether the camp referred to is their (i.e. the Kaurava) camp, which has now been occupied by the jubilant Pāṇḍava armies (see summary of Book 9: 'Śalya'), or the Pāṇḍavas' own camp. It seems as though the three warriors stealthily approach their own camp, only to find it occupied, and so have to ride on. The camp where Aśvatthāman later perpetrates the massacre, however, is clearly the Pāṇḍavas' and Pāñcālas' home camp (see, for example, 3. 26, 10. 2–3, etc.), to which they must have returned for the night, and not the occupied Kaurava one. It is the latter, however, from which Kṛṣṇa has removed the Pāṇḍava brothers and Sātyaki to safety, which makes no sense if it is not the one to be attacked. This inconsistency, apparently unnoticed by previous commentators (although Madeleine Biardeau seems to assume it is the Kaurava camp throughout—Péterfalvi and Biardeau, *Le Mahābhārata* ii.284) may be due to the expansion of an earlier account of the destruction of the Pāñcālas—part perhaps of a cycle of specifically Pāñcāla tales—into one incorporating the destruction of the entire Pāṇḍava camp and end of the war.

1. 6 *their king*: Duryodhana, who is in fact lying in his death agony, but not yet dead—see *Sauptikaparvan* Ch.9.

1. 7 *My son*: Duryodhana.

1. 15 *The words of... Vidura*: Vidura, uncle to the Kurus and Pāṇḍavas alike, immediately recognized the danger to the Lunar Dynasty posed by Duryodhana and tried to persuade Dhṛtarāṣṭra to abandon him at birth (*Mahābhārata* 1. 107. 30). Throughout the narrative he attempts to promote peace by shielding the Pāṇḍavas from Duryodhana, and persistently warning that conflict will bring disaster for all. Here, Dhṛtarāṣṭra is probably referring to the warning Vidura gives during the fixed game of dice that Duryodhana's actions will result in

a terrible war (*Mahābhārata* 2. 56. 1), for which the latter derides him (*Mahābhārata* 2. 57. 1).

1. 23 *Their evening ritual*: Sanskrit *saṃdhyā*, literally 'juncture' of the three divisions of the day (morning, noon, and evening), at which male members of the three classes initiated into the Veda (known as 'the twice-born' classes—see note on 3. 19) perform a ritual (also known as *saṃdhyā*) consisting of recitation of Vedic mantras (especially the Gāyatrī), restraint of the breath, sipping and sprinkling water, and pouring libations of water to the sun (=the worshipper's chosen deity).

1. 34–5 *banyan*: i.e. the fig tree (*ficus indica),* the peculiarity of which is the secondary roots, or fibres, which reach down from its branches to the earth to form new stems. It has become a standard symbol in Indian religious discourse (see note on 1. 36, below).

1. 36 *crows . . . owl*: Indian popular literature contains many stories of battles between crows and owls—see, for instance, the *Pañcatantra* book III (trans. Patrick Olivelle). In India the owl is the classic bird of ill-omen, considered both ugly and evil, and associated with night and the forces of destruction. Jacques Scheuer points out that in this context the story of the massacre of the crows is more than just a fable from which Aśvatthāman draws a practical teaching, it is also a kind of allegory or image of the end of time. The fig tree symbolizes the world; the owl massacring the inhabitants of the fig tree (the crows) therefore prefigures both the extermination of the sleeping warriors and, at a cosmic level, the *pralaya* (see Introduction) which will bring about the end of the world and its population. See Scheuer, *Śiva dans le Mahābhārata*, 294, for full references and examples. He also points out the connection in many Vedic texts between the fig tree and *kurukṣetra* (the land of the Kurus, and where the battle takes place): each may be considered to be at the centre of the world.

1. 45 *I promised to destroy them*: see the summary of Book 9; cf. Book 7, where he promises to avenge the death of his father.

1. 47 *treatises on statecraft*: Sanskrit *arthaśāstra*, a category of literature dealing with the state, administration, government, and practical life in general. The model for this is the *Arthaśāstra* traditionally attributed to Kauṭilya (Cāṇakya) (fourth century BCE).

1. 48 *warrior's code*: see the section on '*Dharma*' in the Introduction; also see the note on 3. 19.

1. 50 *universal law*: Sanskrit *dharma*. See section on '*Dharma*' in the Introduction.

1. 51–2 *The enemy's army . . . as one*: Scheuer (*Śiva dans le Mahābhārata*, 295) suggests that these two stanzas are from some work of *nītiśāstra* (i.e. a work on political ethics), but in common with other commentators cannot identify the source. Such a proof-text is, of course, convenient for Aśvatthāman, since the warrior code (*kṣatriya dharma*) normally forbids one to attack at night or while one's enemies are asleep (as Kṛpa

reminds Aśvatthāman at 5. 9ff.; and see, for instance *The Laws of Manu* 7. 92). But there is little doubt that enraged revenge, rather than argument, will prevail in this case.

1. 53 *at night*: reading *niśi* against the Critical Edition's preferred *yudhi*, 'in battle'.

1. 54 *his... uncle and the Bhoja king*: i.e. Kṛpa and Kṛtavarman.

1. 58 *Vṛkodara*: Bhīma (Bhīmasena); the second of the five Pāṇḍava brothers.

CHAPTER 2

2. 2 *fate and human effort*: Sanskrit *daiva and karman*. See section on 'Fate' in the Introduction.

2. 14 *are seldom found*: reading *durdarśau* against the Critical Edition's preferred *durdaśau*, 'living in a bad state'.

CHAPTER 3

3. 1 *Great king*: Saṃjaya continues to address Dhṛtarāṣṭra.

3. 18 *Creator Prajāpati*: the progenitor and Vedic demiurge (sometimes equated with Brahmā), who appears in this role in the myth retold in *Sauptikaparvan* Ch.17.

estate: Sanskrit *varṇa* ('estate'; 'class'; widely, but inaccurately, 'caste'). According to Brahminical ideology, society is structured into a hierarchy of functionally complementary *varṇa* (listed at 3. 19), each of which has its own 'inherent duty' (*sva-dharma*). See the section on '*Dharma*' in the Introduction.

3. 19 *brahmin*: Sanskrit *brāhmaṇa*.

warriors and rulers: Sanskrit *kṣatriya*.

merchants and farmers: Sanskrit *vaiśya*.

labourer and serf: Sanskrit *śūdra*. The first three classes (brahmin, *kṣatriya*, and *vaiśya*) have 'twice-born' status, since individuals who belong to them are initiated into the ritual and social world (are 'born again') through a ceremony known as *upanayana*.

3. 21 *I was born... Kṣatriya duty*: *kṣatriya* duty, i.e. warrior duty—see note on 3. 19. Aśvatthāman's irregular position *vis-à-vis* his *sva-dharma* is discussed in the '*Dharma*' section of the Introduction. The suggestion here may be that the Creator has 'committed an error of distribution' (Scheuer's phrase—*Śiva dans le Mahābhārata*, 295—my translation). Nevertheless, it is not clear whether Aśvatthāman is a warrior through economic necessity (a case provided for in the treatises on *dharma*—see, for example, *The Laws of Manu* 10. 81), or because he was allotted that duty in spite of his parentage (see Scheuer's discussion, 296). In one way, of course, he is simply following in his father's equally irregular footsteps as a fighting brahmin, for it is precisely from his

father that he has learned to use the 'secret' or magical weapons he refers to at 3. 23. His maternal uncle, and interlocutor here, Kṛpa, is in a similar position: he too is a warrior-brahmin. Kṛtavarman is the only true warrior (*kṣatriya*) among the three surviving Kauravas.

3. 23 *the magic Bow*: one of the weapons given him by his father Droṇa.

Recite the mantra at the sacrifice: reciting a mantra (i.e. verses from the Veda) at the sacrifice is a typically brahmin activity, whereas waging war is, of course, the duty of the warrior. The literal meaning is 'one who speaks in a sacrifice', or even 'one who speaks in an assembly', but clearly a contrast between prescribed brahmin and prescribed warrior activities is intended.

3. 24 *tread the path . . . before me*: i.e. Duryodhana and his father Droṇa. The 'path' seems to be that of battle, but since Droṇa is already dead, and Duryodhana dying, the undercurrent seems to be a willingness to embrace death in arms, and so attain heaven.

3. 27 *Maghavat against the Dānavas*: Maghavat is an epithet of Indra, the king of the Vedic gods (*devas*). The reference is to his destruction of a group of *asuras* or 'anti-gods'.

3. 28 *whose lord Is Dhṛṣṭadyumna*: Dhṛṣṭadyumna commands not only the Pāñcāla army, but the entire force of the Pāṇḍavas and their allies.

3. 29 *bow Pināka*: the name of Rudra-Śiva's bow; all great weapons have their own names.

As wrathful Rudra . . . victims: Rudra is the Vedic name of Śiva. Aśvatthāman's apparent simile here becomes reality in what follows. The sacrificial aspect of at least part of the slaughter to come already starts to emerge with the use of the word *paśu* (=sacrificial animal, translated here as 'victim').

3. 31 *that debt I owe My father*: i.e. to revenge his death; see note on 16. 31.

3. 32 *king of Sindh*: Jayadratha, brother-in-law of Duryodhana, and king of the Sindhus. He has been killed by Arjuna in the battle (during the events depicted in Book 7: 'Droṇa').

3. 33 *tethered goat*: the Sanskrit word is again *paśu*, designating a sacrificial victim.

CHAPTER 4

4. 7 *god of war*: Sanskrit *pāvaki*= 'son of fire', a name of Skanda, sometimes thought to be the son of Śiva, sometimes, as his name suggests here, the son of Agni (fire and the god of fire).

4. 8 *king of heaven*: Indra.

4. 14 *asuras*: 'anti-gods'; adversaries of the *devas* and their leader Indra in Vedic mythology.

4. 15 *killer of the Dānavas*: see note on 3. 27 above.

4. 15 *Daitya army*: another group of *asuras*.

4. 16 *Indra*: in the Sanskrit he is referred to here by his epithet *vajrapāṇi*—'thunderbolt wielder'.

4. 24 *That special way . . . was slain*: this refers to the illegitimate killing of Droṇa. See the summary of Book 7: 'Droṇa'.

4. 27 *the king whose thigh's been shattered*: Duryodhana. His thigh was shattered by Bhīma in revenge for the insult he offered Draupadī by inviting her to sit on his thigh after the Pāṇḍavas had lost the game of dice (see summary of Book 2: 'The Assembly Hall'). As Charles Malamoud has pointed out, 'The narrative fabric of the Epic is . . . a network of tales of vengeance', and (as we see in Chapter 11 of this text) avenging Draupadī is 'Bhīma's speciality' (*Cooking the World: Ritual and Thought in Ancient India*, trans. David White (Delhi: Oxford University Press, 1996), 156–7).

4. 30 *them while Vāsudeva . . . for their protection*: 'them'—i.e. the Pāṇḍava and Pāñcāla armies. This seems to suggest that Aśvatthāman is aware that Kṛṣṇa (Vāsudeva) and Arjuna are absent from the camp, and that he therefore has an opportunity; certainly, he shows no surprise at their absence later. There is, however, no indication how he would know this in advance, and according to Scheuer, at least, he does not (*Śiva dans le Mahābhārata*, 302–3). Perhaps this is another indication that the destruction of the Pāñcālas was originally part of a separate narrative thread.

CHAPTER 5

5. 1 *the pursuit of worldly ends and dharma*: Sanskrit *artha* and *dharma*. Traditionally, *artha* (worldly ends and 'wealth'—5. 2) and *dharma* are two of the three legitimate ends of human endeavour; the other is *kāma* ('desire' or 'pleasure', i.e. erotic and aesthetic pleasures), with *mokṣa* ('liberation' from rebirth), which involves, at some level, renunciation from the others, added as a fourth. On *dharma*, see the Introduction ('*Dharma*').

5. 2 *Even though . . . soup's flavours*: this section appears only in some manuscripts, and in the Critical Edition is printed in the footnotes to its constituted text.

5. 10 *dishevelled hair*: this is the standard indication that a warrior is in flight, and so according to the normal rules of conduct should not be injured.

5. 16–21 *the limits . . . lords of the earth*: this passage lists some key instances of the Pāṇḍavas' violations of *dharma*: the death of the unarmed Droṇa (5. 17), of Karṇa at the hands of Arjuna (his is the Gāṇḍiva bow (5. 18)), of Bhīṣma, who, knowing Śikhaṇḍin to have been a woman who had exchanged his sex with a *yakṣa* (a nature spirit), declined to fight with him and, laying down his arms, was killed by Arjuna (5. 19), of Bhūriśravas at the hands of Yuyudhāna (Sātyaki), and of Duryodhana (5. 21), mortally wounded by Bhīma with an illegitimate strike. (Bhīṣma is actually still alive, but dying,

at this point. Sātyaki slew Bhūriśravas when the latter was sitting fasting to death (in *prāya*), after his arm had been lopped off by Arjuna (*Mahābhārata* 7. 143).) For further details see the summaries of Books 6–9; and for a discussion of what these violations of *dharma* mean, see the '*Dharma*' section of the Introduction.

5. 34 *the worlds . . . in war by arms*: Aśvatthāman plans here the sacrifice-like death of Dhṛṣṭadyumna, which he carries out in Chapter 8. The 'worlds' referred to are after-death places or states into which people may be reborn in accordance with their actions during the present life. There is a general belief that a warrior (*kṣatriya*) will attain a good world if, in accordance with his inherent duty, he dies in arms. According to *The Laws of Manu*, 'Kings who try to kill one another in battle and fight to their utmost ability, never averting their faces, go to heaven' (7. 89, trans. Doniger with Smith). (See Scheuer, *Śiva dans le Mahābhārata*, 311, for a list of references.) Because Dhṛṣṭadyumna has killed his teacher, who was also Aśvatthāman's father, Aśvatthāman refuses him the appropriate and liberating warrior's death. A similar consideration underlies Hamlet's refusal to kill Claudius while he is praying. In both cases, the emotion is so powerful that the revengers need to prolong the effects of their actions beyond the moment of death itself. Cf. 8. 19–20.

5. 36 *my king*: i.e. Dhṛtarāṣṭra.

5. 37 *sacrificial fires*: Sanskrit *havyavāhana*. See the Introduction, 'A universal sacrifice', for general comments.

ghee: clarified butter.

CHAPTER 6

6. 4–8 *It was draped . . . high flames*: the spirit is clearly (although not to Aśvatthāman) a terrible Rudraic form of Śiva: it wears the insignia of an ascetic, characteristic of Śiva—a tiger's skin, etc.—and, like Śiva, has a snake for its sacred thread (6. 4). Also like the god, it has a snake encircling its bicep (6. 5). (For a human being the sacred thread is a symbol of 'twice-born' status: i.e. that, as a member of one of the three upper classes (*varṇa*), he has been initiated into the ritual and social world through a ceremony known as *upanayana*.) As we learn later (7. 62), the camp has (at Kṛṣṇa's request) been under the protection of Śiva, and this spirit is a manifestation of his *māyā* or magical power. It is also intended to provide a test for Aśvatthāman (7. 62). As Jacques Scheuer has pointed out (*Śiva dans le Mahābhārata*, 305), the fact that this spirit is both terrible and protective is not contradictory: even the door-guardians of the most benevolent gods have a terrifying aspect (as the approach to any Indian temple bears witness).

6. 9 *Hṛṣīkeśas*: multiple terrible forms of Viṣṇu (Kṛṣṇa). This is explained by the fact that, as we have seen, Śiva at this point is protecting the camp for

Kṛṣṇa, another example of what Biardeau calls 'the rapport between the two great gods of *bhakti*' (Péterfalvi and Biardeau, *Le Mahābhārata*, ii. 272, my translation). For further remarks on this see 'A cosmic crisis' in the Introduction. According to Hiltebeitel, the dispelling of these Kṛṣṇa images by Aśvatthāman's homage to Śiva duplicates the absence of Kṛṣṇa from this key episode (*The Ritual of Battle*, 319).

6. 9 *a conch, a disc, and a mace*: insignia of Viṣṇu-Kṛṣṇa. Scheuer notes that a fourth emblem of Viṣṇu, the lotus, is missing from this list, perhaps because it is 'peaceful' as opposed to 'terrifying' (*Śiva dans le Mahābhārata*, 303 n. 17).

6. 11 *the mare's-mouth fire*: a submarine fire said to emerge from a cavity called 'mare's mouth' at the 'South Pole', and sometimes associated with Śiva (see '*vaḍabā*' in M. Monier-Williams, *A Sanskrit–English Dictionary* (Oxford: Oxford University Press, 1899), 915).

6. 13 *as an age . . . comes to an end*: for a discussion of this kind of imagery in the *Sauptikaparvan*, see 'A cosmic crisis' in the Introduction.

6. 15 *like a mongoose into A hole*: reading *bilaṃ nakulavad yayau* against the Critical Edition's preferred *vilayaṃ tūlavad yayau*, 'like cotton disappearing'.

6. 17 *Janārdanas*: terrible Viṣṇu-Kṛṣṇas (also one of the thousand names of Śiva, and for that reason used to indicate the 'Rudraic' form of Viṣṇu—Scheuer, *Śiva dans le Mahābhārata*, 305 n. 20). See note on 6. 9.

6. 20 *śāstra*: collections of precepts or rules governing behaviour, but perhaps here referring more loosely to authoritative sources rather than to 'law' books (*dharmaśāstra*) as such.

6. 30 *the fruit of my impure Intention*: i.e. it is karmic retribution for that intention.

6. 33 *Umā's lord*: i.e. Śiva, Umā being one of many names for the goddess who is his consort or wife.

Skull-garlanded Rudra: epithet of Śiva.

destroyer Of . . . Bhaga's sight: epithet of Śiva. See 18. 16, for one version of this well-known story.

6. 34 *trident-bearing mountain god*: the trident is Śiva's weapon, and many Śaiva ascetics also carry tridents in imitation of him. 'Mountain god' is a translation of Giriśa (lit. 'mountain-dwelling'), an epithet of Śiva.

CHAPTER 7

7. 2–5 *the destroyer . . . triple citadel*: for a translated version of this well-known myth of cosmic destruction (the triple citadel representing heaven, sky or atmosphere, and earth, and Śiva playing his usual role as destroyer), taken from Book 8 of the *Mahābhārata*, see O'Flaherty (trans.), *Hindu Myths*, 125–37.

7. 2–5 *Auspicious*: the literal meaning of the Sanskrit *śiva* is 'auspicious', a prophylactic euphemism.

Blue-throated: according to a version of the 'Churning of the Ocean' creation myth, when the gods and demons churn the ocean one of the liquids produced is poisonous, and threatens universal destruction. Śiva, however, swallows it to save the world, and in the process the poison sticks in his throat, or discolours it, hence he is referred to as 'blue-throated' or 'dark-necked'. For a version of this myth taken from the *Mahābhārata*, see O'Flaherty (trans.), *Hindu Myths*, 273–80.

the destroyer Of Dakṣa's sacrifice: reading *dakṣa* against the Critical Edition's preferred *kratham*, 'Kratha'. For the story of the destruction of Dakṣa's sacrifice see Ch. 18 above; also the Introduction ('A universal sacrifice').

Rudra, Śarva, Īśāna . . . three-eyed Hara: all epithets of Śiva. For a well-illustrated introduction to Śiva, his sons and attendants, etc., see ch. 3: 'Shiva' in T. Richard Blurton's *Hindu Art* (London: British Museum Press, 1992). Śiva is well-known to have a 'third eye' in his forehead; see note on 18. 16.

the cremation grounds . . . skull-topped pole: Śiva, as an ascetic, lives in the cremation gounds and is surrounded by the paraphernalia of death. Scheuer suggests that the whole Kuru field has in effect become an immense cremation ground, with Śiva-Aśvatthāman going to finish off his work of death by destroying the Pāñcāla camp (*Śiva dans le Mahābhārata*, 305).

7. 7 *Brahman*: (neuter) a multivalent term indicating, among other things, the supreme power principle underlying the cosmos and everything in it according to some *Upaniṣads* (a category of late Vedic text) and Advaita Vedānta (an influential school of Vedic exegesis, commonly associated with the great eighth-century teacher Śaṅkara); more popularly 'God'; sometimes personified as Brahmā (masculine); here subsumed in Śiva.

7. 9 *the bull*: Nandin, Śiva's 'vehicle' or mount; often seen at the entrance to Śiva temples.

7. 12 *all five of my elements*: the five gross elements (ether, air, fire, water, earth) of which human beings are thought, physically, to be composed, i.e. the *mahābhūtas*. The original Sanskrit is, however, ambiguous: *sarvabhūta*, could refer to the bodily elements, and so to Aśvatthāman himself (as translated), or it could refer to 'all beings'—i.e. a sacrifice of the entire world. An alternative translation would therefore be:

> . . . with a pure
> Oblation of the world in its entirety,
> I shall sacrifice to the god who is pure.

This latter reading of the nature of Aśvatthāman's sacrifice is favoured by, for instance, Scheuer (*Śiva dans le Mahābhārata*, 306), so stressing its connection with *pralaya*, the universal destruction at the end of a world age (on which, see the Introduction 'A cosmic crisis'). But it is probably more significant that groups of five are commonly associated with Śiva: he comes to be depicted as five-faced, he receives five offerings, etc.; moreover, one of his epithets is *bhūteśa*, 'lord of the elements'.

7. 14 *blazing fire . . . every point in space*: the sacrifice threatens to become the universal conflagration at the end of a world-age. See Introduction, 'A universal sacrifice'.

7. 15 *troops of creatures*: reading *mahāgaṇāḥ* against the Critical Edition's preferred *mahānanāḥ*, 'those with great mouths'.

7. 21 *my king*: i.e. Dhṛtarāṣṭra.

7. 27 *śataghnī disc*: lit. 'which kills one hundred at a time'; probably a mythical weapon.

Bhārata: =Dhṛtarāṣṭra.

bhuśuṇḍī weapon: unidentified weapon.

7. 31 *Their bodies . . .* : reading *-aṅgās te* against the Critical Edition's preferred *-aṅgāṃs te.*

7. 39 *fourfold host*: either gods, anti-gods, humans, and animals (plus hell-beings), or divine, human, animal, and vegetable 'beings'.

7. 40 *lord of the triple world*: I interpret this as referring to Śiva, so they are his 'lords' in so far as they are his servants, as English barons were the lords of the lord of the realm (the king). The Sanskrit, however, is ambiguous as to number, and others have taken it as plural ('The lords of the lords of the triple world'). The triple world is the universe, i.e. heaven, sky or atmosphere, and earth.

7. 41 *Eight kinds of superhuman power*: the power of making oneself as small as an atom (*aṇiman*), of assuming excessive lightness at will (*laghiman*), of increasing one's size at will (*mahiman*), of obtaining everything (*prāpti*), of irresistible fiat (*prākāmya*), of subduing to one's own will (*vaśitva*), of supremacy (*īśitva*), and of suppressing desire (*kāmāvasāyitva*).

7. 43 *soma*: a liquid produced by pressing a plant of the same name (which is also a god) in the sacrifice; when drunk by the brahmin celebrants it apparently produced ecstatic or visionary states, but its identity was 'lost' at an early date, and it was replaced in the ritual by non-intoxicating substitutes.

the ritual chant in twenty-four parts: following the suggestion in the notes to the Critical Edition and taking *caturviṃśātmakaṃ* as 'accompanied by the *caturviṃśa stoma*'—*stoma* designating a form of ritual chant. It may be, however, that the *caturviṃśātmakaṃ* refers to *types of soma*, as James W. Laine suggests (*Visions of God: Narratives of Theophany in the Mahābhārata* (Vienna: Publications of the De Nobili Research Library, XVI, 1989), 156 n. 47).

7. 44 *Vedic recitation*: i.e. with mantras from the Veda, a body of texts regarded as uncreated revelation in the Brahminical and mainstream

Hindu traditions. No orthoprax sacrifice is complete without such mantras.

7. 49 *the triple world*: see note on 7. 40.

7. 50 *Iguana skin*: used as protection against the bowstring.

7. 51 *bows were the fuel . . . the filters*: as Scheuer points out, this is obviously the oblation of a *kṣatriya* (*Śiva dans le Mahābhārata*, 307). Arrows are compared to the filters used for the *soma* because such filters were often made of sharp-pointed *kuśa* grass (ibid., 307 n. 22).

mantra . . . soma: see note on 7. 43.

7. 54 *Āṅgirasa clan*: descendants of Aṅgiras, an ancient sage mentioned in the *Ṛg Veda*, and regarded as the first sacrificer. He is especially associated with the sacrificial fire; his descendants were originally fire priests, and one of the chief Vedic priestly families, which is no doubt why Aśvatthāman connects himself with them in this context. It is, indeed, a real connection since his father Droṇa was considered to be an incarnation on earth of Bṛhaspati, the chaplain (*purohita*) of the gods and a descendant of Aṅgiras. Given that Aśvatthāman is a brahmin by birth who follows the *kṣatriya dharma*, it is perhaps an interesting inversion that some descendants of Aṅgiras were *kṣatriyas* by birth and brahmins by 'profession', being descended from Aṅgiras's union with the wife of a childless *kṣatriya* (see the entry on 'Aṅgiras' in Margaret and James Stutley, *A Dictionary of Hinduism* (London: Routledge & Kegan Paul, 1977)).

7. 59 *In person*: i.e. this is the moment Śiva manifests himself to Aśvatthāman.

7. 61 *worshipped by Kṛṣṇa*: see Notes on 6. 4–8. and 6. 9. The complementarity of Kṛṣṇa and Śiva is discussed in the Introduction ('A cosmic crisis').

7. 63 *Time*: Sanskrit *kāla*, an epithet of Śiva himself; see the Introduction ('A cosmic crisis') for further remarks on this.

7. 64 *entered his body*: Jacques Scheuer argues that the Sanskrit here should be taken to mean that Śiva enters into Aśvatthāman's body *which was his* (i.e. Śiva's), stressing their already well-established connection: as Aśvatthāman is a possession of Śiva's, so he is possessed by him (*Śiva dans le Mahābhārata*, 308 n. 24). The Sanskrit verb *ā-viś*, used here, usually designates the possession of a man by a spirit or demon, which 'enters' into him. According to Scheuer, for a god to enter into such a relationship of possession is perhaps unique in the *Mahābhārata*, and simply serves to stress the violent and irresistible character of the action of Rudra-Śiva at the time of final cosmic destruction (ibid., 308–9). In contrast, Arjuna (especially in the *Bhagavadgītā*) is portrayed as Kṛṣṇa's devotee; the man goes to the god, not *vice versa*. Similarly, in the relationship between Arjuna and Śiva there is no question of possession. Hiltebeitel remarks that this possession simply doubles Aśvatthāman's identification with Śiva, since he is a partial incarnation of him anyway (*The Ritual of Battle*, 319).

7. 66 *rākṣasas*: nocturnal shape-shifting demons.

CHAPTER 8

8. 8 *The two of you Must ensure... I have decided that it must be so*: I have translated an extra line here, given in some manuscripts but not printed in the main text of the Critical Edition; as a consequence I have also read *vām* ('The two of you') against the Critical Edition's preferred *me* (i.e. Aśvatthāman himself).

8. 18 *one foot on his chest*: Hiltebeitel suggests that this trampling of Dhṛṣṭadyumna is crudely symbolic of 'putting out a fire' (*The Ritual of Battle*, 324). Dhṛṣṭadyumna is in fact an incarnation of the auspicious portion of Agni, the god of fire; he is also Aśvatthāman-Śiva's 'share' of the 'sacrifice of battle', and 'when a combatant slays his "share," some quality which both opponents possess is enhanced in the victor at the expense of the vanquished. In slaying the incarnation of Agni, Aśvatthāman... eliminates the "auspicious Agni" and takes on the character of "the fire at the end of the yuga"' [see 8. 137], (ibid. 323). The general point is interesting but the fire-extinguishing symbolism doubtful, since the Pāñcāla Uttamaujas (who is *not* an incarnation of Agni) is put to death in precisely the same way (see 8. 33).

like a sacrificial beast: Aśvatthāman is thus both victim of the sacrifice (to Śiva) and a 'sacrificer' of others. Generally, Dhṛṣṭadyumna and his companions can be seen as victims of the cosmic sacrifice which is the end of the world (see Scheuer, *Śiva dans le Mahābhārata*, 312, and the Introduction).

8. 19 *the worlds of those whose deeds were good*: the 'worlds' referred to here and in 8. 20 are after-death places or states into which people may be reborn in accordance with their actions during the present life. See the note on 5. 34.

8. 22 *that hero's dying cries*: in a normal sacrifice animals should be strangled silently. As Hiltebeitel remarks, the noise here and in the following slaughter 'seems to be one of several indications that the *Sauptikaparvan* tells of a sacrifice gone out of control' (*The Ritual of Battle*, 321 n. 57).

8. 27 *Wives*: reading the variant *sarvāḥ* against the Critical Edition's preferred *sarve*, and so attributing this grief to the wives not the warriors.

8. 30 *rākṣasa*: a nocturnal shape-shifting demon.

8. 31 *with the Rudra Weapon*: i.e. apparently with the sword that Śiva has given him (although the verb conveys crushing rather than cutting), in contrast to the animal-like executions of Dhṛṣṭadyumna and others. Hiltebeitel and Scheuer make a distinction between the sacrificial killings and the symbolic mutilations with the sword which follow, Scheuer linking the sword to the weapon carried by ferocious forms of the Goddess (Durgā-Kālī) (*Śiva dans le Mahābhārata*, 312). It seems to me, however, that the imagery used throughout this passage (whatever the means of slaughter) is never very far from suggesting a sacrifice.

8. 32 *Uttamaujas*: a Pāñcāla, and therefore, because Drupada is his king, a sworn enemy of both Droṇa and Aśvatthāman; brother to Yudhāmanyu.

8. 37 *sword like a sacrificial knife*: the Sanskrit word can mean both 'sword' and 'sacrificial knife'; in the context, both meanings are probably intended to resonate, hence the use of a simile in the translation. Cf. note on 8. 31.

8. 43 *foe-tormentor's*: reading *-karśinaḥ* against the Critical Edition's preferred *-karśanāḥ*.

8. 44 *Draupadī's sons*: i.e. her five sons by the five Pāṇḍava brothers: Prativindhya (by Yudhiṣṭhira), Sutasoma (by Bhīma), Śrutakīrti (by Arjuna), Śatānīka (by Nakula), and Śrutakarman (by Sahadeva), known collectively as the 'Draupadeyas'. Alf Hiltebeitel (*The Ritual of Battle*, 324–6) has pointed out that their mutilations at the hands of Aśvatthāman in the following passage appear, in some instances at least, to be symbolically related to qualities associated with their fathers: hence, the son of mighty, 'long-armed' Bhīma loses his arm (8. 52), the son of beautiful Nakula loses his head (8. 54), the son of eloquent Sahadeva has his mouth disfigured (8. 56). More than just the apparent extinction of the dynasty (Uttarā's pregnancy will not be revealed until Chapter 16), the mutilation and death of the Draupadeyas symbolizes 'the fact that the ideal image of sovereignty which the Pāṇḍavas represent... cannot be revived' (ibid., 325).

the Somaka remnant: name of a people either allied to or synonymous with the Pāñcālas.

8. 46 *Śikhaṇḍin and the Prabhadrakas*: on Śikhaṇḍin see the summary of Books 5 and 6. The Prabhadrakas are a group of Pāñcālas allied to him.

8. 54 *twice-born*: see note on 3. 19.

8. 60 *split him in two*: appropriately, since he is half-male half-female (see summary of Book 5).

8. 64–5 *chanting*: reading *gāyamānām* against the Critical Edition's *smayamānām* ('smiling').

8. 64–7 *the Night of all-destroying Time*: Sanskrit *kālarātrī*, a personification of Death. The term is used in a similar way in a number of other places in the *Mahābhārata* (see the entry in S. Sørensen, *An Index to the Names in the Mahābhārata* (1904; Delhi: Motilal Banarsidass, 1963)).

With the great warriors, divested of their arms: I have translated an extra line here, given in some manuscripts but not printed in the main text of the Critical Edition.

there appeared... baleful goddess: this sudden appearance in the narrative of a terrible goddess (or the Goddess in her terrible form—the obvious comparison is with Durgā or Kālī) is regarded by most commentators as either an 'intrusion' (Hiltebeitel, *The Ritual of Battle*, 326) or an inserted variation on the theme of cosmic destruction

(Scheuer, *Śiva dans le Mahābhārata*, 316 ff.). Whatever its provenance, it seems to me to have great poetic force.

8. 68 *Bhairava*: a terrible form of Śiva.

8. 74 *Sṛñjaya hordes*: another name for the Pāñcālas or their allies.

8. 78 *offered them to the Night of Time*: see note on 8. 64–5. It is indeed a great sacrifice of, and to, Death.

8. 87 *O bullish man, O best of Bharatas*: Dhṛtarāṣṭra.

8. 94 *By Time the Destroyer*: as attested in some manuscripts, reading *kālena* against the Critical Edition's preferred *lokena*.

8. 103 *in three places they fired the camp*: see Introduction, 'A universal sacrifice'.

8. 108 *trunks stood up*: i.e. the weight of the fallen, acting like a see-saw, forced the dead bodies upwards.

8. 114 *yakṣas*: ubiquitous shape-shifting nature spirits, particularly associated with all kinds of vegetation.

8. 115–16 *sons of Pṛthā*: i.e. Yudhiṣṭhira, Bhīma, and Arjuna, the Pāṇḍavas who are the sons of Kuntī (Pṛthā), and who have been withdrawn from the camp by Kṛṣṇa.

8. 117 *gandharva*: one of a class of celestial musicians.

8. 118 *he would never kill the sleeping*: compare this with Aśvatthāman's speech at 1. 47–52.

8. 122 *Paśupati*: 'lord of animals' or 'lord of sacrificial victims'—i.e. Śiva.

8. 124 *Yama's realm*: 'the house of Death' of 8. 125, Yama being the lord, or god, of Death.

8. 127 *piśācas*: flesh-eating, shape-shifting demons.

8. 137 *like the fire . . . to ash*: see note on 8. 18, and the Introduction ('A cosmic crisis').

8. 143 *us*: i.e the Kauravas (Saṃjaya is addressing Dhṛtarāṣṭra).

8. 151 *our king*: i.e. Duryodhana.

CHAPTER 9

9. 2 *your son, my lord*: Saṃjaya is still addressing Dhṛtarāṣṭra.

9. 7 *like a sacrificial altar . . . three fires*: the sacrificial simile persists, but here the significance seems to be restricted to Duryodhana: he too has finally run out of substitutes (enemies) and become a victim-offering in the sacrifice of battle (see Introduction, 'A universal sacrifice').

9. 13 *gold from the river Jambū*: gold, known as *jāmbūnada*, obtained at a spot where a river, which flows from the fruit of the rose-apple tree at the centre of the mythical continent of Jambūdvīpa (which contains India), comes to rest. It is said to be used for celestial ornaments, and to look

like the complexion of cochineal insects (see the entry on Jambū in Sørensen's *An Index to the Names in the Mahābhārata*, 349).

9. 17 *Brahmins*: reading *dvijāḥ* ('twice-born') against the Critical Edition's preferred *nṛpāḥ* ('kings'); although this epithet ('twice-born') can refer to any member of the three higher classes (see note on 3. 19), it is virtually synonymous with 'brahmin'.

Now it is carnivores who wait for meat: I have translated one of the variant readings for this line; the Critical Edition has: 'Alas! He lies stricken today—see the whirligig of Time.'

9. 19 *Saṃkarṣaṇa*: one of the names of Balarāma, elder brother of Kṛṣṇa. He taught both Bhīma and Duryodhana, and takes no part in the war (*Mahābhārata* 5. 154. 30f.).

9. 22 *struck you down through fraud*: equally matched with Bhīma in a mace fight, Duryodhana was only brought low by a strike below the belt; Bhīma then trampled on his head in front of Yudhiṣṭhira and the others. For an outline of the episode, see the summary of Book 9: 'Śalya'.

9. 30 *dharma*: see Introduction, '*Dharma*'.

9. 37 *the abundant fees from . . . sacrifices*: a reminder that Aśvatthāman is essentially a brahmin. As king, Duryodhana would have been the major patron of sacrifices, and therefore responsible for the payment of fees (without which no sacrifice was complete) to the brahmin celebrants.

9. 43 *our teacher*: Aśvatthāman's father Droṇa.

9. 44–5 *Bhūriśravas*: see note on 5. 16–21 on the death of Bhūriśravas.

9. 55 *heaven*: in spite of all his evil deeds, Duryodhana, as a warrior killed in active combat, can be confident of a place in heaven (he has acted in full accord with his *sva-dharma*)—see note on 5. 34; and, to Yudhiṣṭhira's discomfort, heaven is where Duryodhana is found at the end of the epic—see summary of Book 18. For a further discussion of this, and its wider implications, see the Introduction ('*Dharma*').

His soul . . . his foes: I have translated three extra lines here, given in some manuscripts but not printed in the main text of the Critical Edition.

9. 56 *they each . . . chariots*: Chapter 10 (in the Critical Edition, Chapter 11 in Ganguli's translation) of the following book (Book 11: 'The Women') recounts how, just after this, the three warriors encounter Dhṛtarāṣṭra and Gāndhārī, who have left Hāstinapura to visit the field of battle, and tell them what has happened. In the text as constituted this is redundant, since Saṃjaya has already informed Dhṛtarāṣṭra (see note on 9. 57–9), but it does provide an account, not otherwise found, of how the three separate on the banks of the Ganges, Kṛpa going to Hāstinapura, Kṛtavarman to his own kingdom, and Aśvatthāman to refuge with Vyāsa (where we meet him again in Chapter 13 of the *Sauptikaparvan*).

9. 57 *In this way . . . my king*: I have translated two extra lines here, given in some manuscripts but not printed in the main text of the Critical Edition. If these lines are included, it is tempting to read the epithet 'Blameless one' (9. 58) as irony, but perhaps it is simply an affirmation that the king is not ultimately responsible for that policy?

9. 57–9 *So I . . . lost in thought*: i.e. Saṃjaya came to Dhṛtarāṣṭra in Hāstinapura. This raises (for the literal-minded, at least) the question of where, exactly, he has been. The spiritual vision granted him by Vyāsa at the beginning of the *Bhīṣmaparvan* (6. 2) is apparently not some kind of remote vision or clairvoyance, since it includes the promise that weapons will not harm him and he will come out of the battle alive. Indeed, he is frequently involved in his own narrative, at one point having to be rescued by Vyāsa from death at the hands of Sātyaki, and borne away to the Kuru camp on Kṛpa's chariot (*Śalyaparvan* 9. 29). There, as elsewhere, his presence is necessary to convey vital information between participants in the battle, and so facilitate the next dramatic development. Much of the time, however, like the Chorus in Shakespeare's *Henry V*, he is 'present' but unnoticed. (Modern readers might do well, in general, to view the *Mahābhārata* through the lens of theatrical rather than cinematic convention—a point marvellously well made by Peter Brook's version.) It is also essential to realize that Saṃjaya's narration to Dhṛtarāṣṭra is always in the past tense: i.e. the events he describes are not 'live', they have already taken place. Indeed, Dhṛtarāṣṭra, like the audience, usually knows the main happenings in advance, and is merely pressing Saṃjaya for the details. As early as the beginning of Book 9, (*Śalyaparvan* 1), Saṃjaya arrives at Hāstinapura with the news of the night massacre and all the events up to and including Duryodhana's death. And it is there (*Śalyaparvan* 3) that he begins the detailed narration to Dhṛtarāṣṭra (who has recovered from his initial shock) of these and the preceding events—a narrative which ends at precisely this point, midway through the *Sauptikaparvan*. As already noticed, Saṃjaya has in fact been the major narrator since the beginning of Book 6, the *Bhīṣmaparvan*. He has, however, occasionally been 'interrupted' by the next narrator up in this Russian doll of a narrative, Vaiśaṃpāyana, who now takes over with the withdrawal of Saṃjaya's divine sight. These narrative layers or recitations probably reflect at some level the stages by which the epic developed or evolved. Ruth Katz, for instance, proposes the following pattern: 'The early period of oral composition is represented by Samjaya's reporting to Dhrtarashtra. The period of late transmission is embodied in Ugrashravas's recitation to Shaunaka. Vaishampayana's recitation to Janamejaya is, thus, left to represent the intermediate stage of epic development, the period of collection and reworking' (*Arjuna in the Mahabharata*, 13). This may be over-simplistic, but at least presents a working hypothesis.

Part II *The Arrow Made from Stalks*: see note on Part I: 'The Sleepers', above.

CHAPTER 10

10. 2–3 *heedless*: this word (Sanskrit *pramatta*) and the related one translated as 'negligence' (*pramāda*) at 10. 15 f. provide the refrain for the lament which concludes this chapter (see 10. 17–23.). 'Negligence' here is closer to the English 'dereliction of duty' than simple 'carelessness', and has something of the stigma of a moral defect (although this is not so clearly the case in the epic as it is in Jain religious texts, for instance). Functionally, it bears some similarity to the *hubris* resulting in *nemesis* of Greek tragedy: catastrophe follows it. Madeleine Biardeau remarks how its opposite (*apramatta*—being 'vigilant', 'undistracted', 'heedful'—10. 14) begins as a *yogin* quality, but is transferred to the warrior in the *Mahābhārata*, where it becomes part of the technical vocabulary of the war, and of royalty (Péterfalvi and Biardeau, *Le Mahābhārata*, i. 125).

Gautama's son Kṛpa: Kṛpa is the seer (*ṛṣi*) Gotama's grandson, and son of Śaradvat Gautama (Gotama's son).

10. 14 *we have sinfully slain our kinsmen*: this seems to refer to the Pāṇḍava dead, who have died for the sake of their Pāñcāla allies ('these seeming conquerors'); it might, however, refer to the Kauravas who, unlike the Pāñcālas, are at least blood relatives of the Pāṇḍavas.

10. 20–1 *homa*: the act of making a sacrificial oblation by offering something (often ghee) into the fire; widely, any sacrifice.

10. 24 *Kṛṣṇā*: Draupadī (Drupada's daughter); wife of the five Pāṇḍava brothers.

CHAPTER 11

11 *Janamejaya*: see Introduction, 'Narration and Narrators'.

11. 5 *Upaplavya*: the city in King Virāṭa's kingdom where the Pāṇḍavas settled after their exile (see summary of Book 4: 'Virāṭa').

11. 9 *the Pāṇḍava*: namely Yudhiṣṭhira.

11. 10 *obtained through offering your sons*: the 'sacrifice of battle' metaphor is never far from the surface.

the kṣatriya rule: cf. 11. 12, *kṣatriya dharma*; see Introduction ('*Dharma*').

11. 11 *Subhadrā*: Kṛṣṇa's sister and Arjuna's second wife, Abhimanyu being their son. His death in battle, combined with the slaughter of the Draupadeyas, apparently extinguishes the line of succession. The revelation of Abhimanyu's unborn son will come in Chapter 16.

11. 10–15 *How fortunate . . . I shall do this*: there is something paradoxical about Draupadī's (Kṛṣṇā's) bitter words here. It is this same craving

for revenge—now directed towards Aśvatthāman—which has caused her throughout the narrative to urge her husbands, children, and brothers to wage war to regain the kingdom. Biardeau points to the connection here between the princess and the goddess Earth: the latter calls on the gods to restore *dharma*, but that very restoration involves, inevitably, the death of her human 'children' (Péterfalvi and Biardeau, *Le Mahābhārata*, ii. 294).

11. 20 *a jewel*: It is not clear from the Sanskrit whether the jewel is embedded *in* Aśvatthāman's head, or simply worn on it. This is the first time this jewel has been mentioned in the epic. Aśvatthāman's own description of it (15. 28 f.) stresses its wide-ranging protective properties. Biardeau sees him as abandoning both his Brahminic power and his (questionable) ability as a warrior with the jewel ('Études de mythologie hindoue (IV)', 213). When Yudhiṣṭhira later places it on his head (16. 34), he does so as a 'relic' of Droṇa. It may therefore concentrate something of brahmin power and reinforce the link between king and brahmins (Péterfalvi and Biardeau, *Le Mahābhārata*, ii. 294). Scheuer, on the other hand, suggests that it may be a kind of talisman, symbolizing Aśvatthāman's pretension to the throne (*Śiva dans le Mahābhārata*, 323 n. 44), but this seems unlikely. More suggestive is Shulman's comment that 'The congenital fore-head ornament links Aśvatthāman with the serpent (said to carry a precious stone on his hood) and with Rudra-Śiva, with his third eye' (*The King and the Clown*, 134 n. 82). In terms of the narrative, the jewel is a useful device to satisfy Draupadī's desire for revenge without actually killing Aśvatthāman, and in that sense it brings the cycle of revenge to a close.

11. 22 *As Maghavat killed the asura Śambara*: by throwing him off a mountain (Maghavat is Indra).

11. 23 *the saviour of the sons of Pṛthā*: i.e the Pāṇḍavas, saved from the fire in the lacquer house at Vāraṇāvata by Bhīma (see summary of Book 1: 'The Beginning').

the rākṣasa Hiḍimba: while they are in the forest, disguised as brahmin ascetics (see summary of Book 1: 'The Beginning'), the Pāṇḍavas are threatened by a cannibal demon, Hiḍimba. Bhīma kills him in a wrestling match, then marries his sister. Their son Ghaṭotkaca appears during the war to fight for the Pāṇḍavas (see the summary of Book 7: 'Droṇa').

11. 24 *molested . . . in Virāṭa's city*: Kīcaka is one of King Virāṭa's generals, who attempts to seduce Draupadī during the Pāṇḍavas' thirteenth year in exile, and is killed by Bhīma for his pains (see the summary of Book 4: 'King Virāṭa').

like Maghavat His wife Paulomī: Maghavat (Indra) rescued Paulomī (Śacī) from her father, the demon Puloman, killing him and making her his wife.

11. 29 *tigerish man*: i.e. Janamejaya.

CHAPTER 12

12. 4 *brahmaśiras weapon*: 'the (fifth) head of Brahmā' weapon; its name, and the fact that it comes from Droṇa, show it to be a brahmin weapon; moreover, it is thought to contain all the destructive powers of the brahmins (and by extension, of *brahman*, the power underlying the sacrifice and all other things). It is appropriate, therefore, that this weapon of universal destruction should be armed at the moment when the world order (and age) is in the balance (see Péterfalvi and Biardeau, *Le Mahābhārata*, i. 125–6). There are a number of powerful magical weapons in the *Mahābhārata*, notably the Śiva-affiliated *pāśupata* weapon, sometimes viewed as identical with the *brahmaśiras* (see Katz, *Arjuna in the Mahabharata*, 253, and note on 12. 26).

12. 5 *Dhanaṃjaya*: Droṇa originally gave the weapon to his pupil Arjuna (Dhanaṃjaya) after he proved capable of saving his teacher from a crocodile (*Mahābhārata* 1. 123. 68 ff.; see summary of Book 1: 'The Beginning'). Although not a brahmin, Arjuna is much better equipped to handle this prototypically Brahminical weapon than a brahmin by birth (Aśvatthāman). Arjuna's skill stems from his *yogin*-like training and his devotion to his teacher: he is the perfect warrior who puts his power at the service of *dharma* and the universe (see Péterfalvi and Biardeau, *Le Mahābhārāta*, i. 125–6; Biardeau,'Études de mythologie hindoue (IV)', 252). It is for this reason that Droṇa is entirely confident in Arjuna's ability to handle the *brahmaśiras* for good (essentially as a controlled and defensive weapon). Rightly, as it turns out, he has no such confidence in his own son Aśvatthāman, but nevertheless gives him the weapon with a health-warning attached (12. 8). (He has given a very similar warning to Arjuna, but allows its use in battle against a superhuman foe—see *Mahābhārata*, 1. 123. 75 ff.) According to Biardeau, by passing the *brahmaśiras* weapon on to Arjuna, the brahmin conveys something of his sacrificial or sacerdotal power to the *kṣatriya*, thus indicating that the proper activity of the warrior-prince is the sacrifice of war—the war conceived as a sacrifice, but also as a yogic act, done for the benefit of the universe and without concern for oneself. Thus the idea of sacrifice is changed, and in this 'universe of *bhakti*' (devotion) the warrior finds his salvation through the sacrifice of battle—essentially the teaching of the *Bhagavadgītā* (see Biardeau, 'Études de mythologie hindoue (IV)', 252–3).

12. 13–14 *gandharvas*: a class of celestial musicians.

Agastya: Droṇa's teacher's teacher. This appears to be the only place in the epic where Droṇa is said to have obtained the *brahmaśiras* weapon from him. Elsewhere, the transmission is said to be from another sage, Rāma Jāmadagnya, to Droṇa (see entry on 'Brahmāstra' in Sørensen's *An Index to the Names in the Mahābhārata*, 166— *Mahābhārata* 1. 121. 15 f.), although in the Critical Edition, at least, the specific identity of the weapon there is less clear.

12. 13–14 *in me*: the weapon needs a vehicle or medium (see 13. 17), and seems to be carried internally in the form of a spell (mantra), the speaking of which releases its power (see 13. 18–19).

12. 15 *discus*: Sanskrit *cakra*; Viṣṇu-Kṛṣṇa's favourite weapon, and one of his classical attributes, along with the mace or club (*gadā*) (see 12. 18), the conch shell, and the lotus. The discus, as a weapon of war, is a steel or iron disc, with a hole at the centre and a sharpened edge, like a thick-rimmed letter 'O'—a kind of lethal frisbee. Kṛṣṇa's is clearly much more ornate than this (see the description at 12. 20). Like other divine weapons, it is sometimes personified and worshipped in its own right. The solar symbolism is obvious, but, beyond that, the discus here, according to Scheuer, is an emblem of royal power and a symbol of domination over Time. He reads the incident generally as an illustration of Aśvatthāman's ambition, and a warning of the danger he represents to Bhīma (*Śiva dans le Mahābhārata*, 321).

12. 17 *dānavas*: a group of anti-gods (*asuras*).

12. 18 *my bow, my spear, my discus, and my mace*: see note on 12. 15.

12. 21 '*Take the discus!*': I interpret this as part of a skirmish in which Kṛṣṇa assumes an attitude of 'Here it is—if you want it, come and get it', and throws the discus down, or towards Aśvatthāman, who then tries to pick it up, without success.

12. 25 *the most excellent of apes*: Hanumān, the monkey general, who is depicted on Arjuna's banner. In the epic *Rāmāyaṇa*, he is portrayed as Rāma's greatest devotee. Rāma (not to be confused with the *Mahābhārata*'s Balarāma) is an incarnation of the great god Viṣṇu, and so Hanumān becomes particularly associated with Vaiṣṇava (Viṣṇu) worship, and also a popular deity in his own right, celebrated for his great physical strength.

12. 26 *succumbing... appeased Śaṃkara*: Śaṃkara is Śiva, and this refers to Arjuna's wrestling match with the god, disguised as a mountain man, when Arjuna was acquiring divine weapons during the Pāṇḍavas' exile (see summary of Book 3: 'The Forest', and *Mahābhārata* 3. 39–41). The god prevails, of course, but is pleased with Arjuna and grants him his request for the *pāśupata/brahmaśiras* weapon (although Arjuna apparently has it already from Droṇa—see notes on 12. 4 and 12. 5).

blue-throated lord of Umā: see note on 7. 2–5. Umā is another name of Śiva's wife.

12. 25–8 *He who... have made of me*: this passage refers to Arjuna.

12. 29–30 *Sanatkumāra... a son for Rukmiṇī*: here a well-known Śaiva myth about the peculiar circumstances surrounding the birth of Kumāra (also known as Sanatkumāra and Skanda) seems to have been assimilated to Kṛṣṇa's mythology. Kumāra was conceived when Śiva, who was deep in ascetic meditation, finally had his attention attracted by his wife Pārvatī, who had herself been practising asceticism for that pre-

cise purpose. Once aroused, Śiva discharges his semen, from which Kumāra is born directly, without female participation.

12. 36–7 *dānavas*: see note on 12. 17.

12. 40 *brahmaśiras weapon*: see note on 12. 4.

CHAPTER 13

13. 4 *the enemy of snakes*: the stories of the bird deity Vainateya's (Garuḍa's) attacks on snakes reflect a long-standing mythological antagonism between the two types of creature, possibly derived from a rivalry between ancient animal cults, but also quite consonant with their natural enmity. They are said to represent the basic oppositions of sun and darkness, fire and water (Garuḍa being an embodiment of the sun).

13. 13 *seers*: *ṛṣis*. The setting is a brahmin one, at what appears to be Vyāsa's *āśrama* or hermitage on the banks of the holy Ganges. It is possible that Aśvatthāman is claiming some kind of right of sanctuary here (Scheuer, *Śiva dans le Mahābhārata*, 321); if so, he is not successful.

Kṛṣṇa Dvaipāyana Vyāsa: a great seer, and the 'author' of the *Mahābhārata*—see summary of the principal episodes (Book 1, etc.) and the Introduction.

13. 14 *in a garment of kuśa grass... with ghee*: *kuśa* (*dharba*) is a species of sacred grass, widely used in the sacrifice (to cover the sacrificial area etc.), which has purificatory and other powers; ghee (clarified butter) is likewise an essential sacrificial component. Aśvatthāman has therefore been transformed into a pure brahmin, and is behaving either as a celebrant (a role apparently not foreign to him—see note on 9. 37) or as a patron of the sacrifice (*yajamāna*) (see note on 13. 18). According to Biardeau, the scene is described in this way to produce the impression of a display of brahmin power, both good (the *ṛṣis*) and bad (Aśvatthāman) (Biardeau, 'Études de mythologie hindoue (IV)', 212).

13. 17 *stalks*: cf. 13. 19–20; 15. 31 The *brahmaśiras* weapon is launched in an arrow made of stalks (*iṣīkā*) (see note on 12. 13–14), an event from which this subsection (Chapters 10–18) of the *Sauptikaparvan* takes its name of *Aiṣīkaparvan*. As Scheuer remarks, the frailty of the stalk of grass contrasts with the potency of the mantra that makes the weapon capable of destroying the universe (*Śiva dans le Mahābhārata*, 322 n. 42). But more specifically, by using a stalk of grass, Aśvatthāman employs the standard sacrificial procedure of substituting grass for the 'real' victim (himself) in the cataclysmic sacrifice of destruction upon which he is engaged.

13. 18 *For the annihilation Of the Pāṇḍavas*: this is the deadly mantra that arms the weapon. The sacrificial metaphor seems to be still active here: every sacrifice requires a *saṃkalpa*, or statement of purpose, and this is Aśvatthāman's. Compare this with Arjuna's (defensive or neutralizing)

mantra at 14. 6. For a discussion of the possible parallels between this contest of *brahmaśiras* weapons and various versions of the destruction of Dakṣa's sacrifice (although not the one treated in Chapter 18 of the *Sauptikaparvan*), see Hiltebeitel, *The Ritual of Battle*, 327–9.

13. 19 *My tigerish king*: i.e. Janamejaya.

13. 20 *All three worlds . . . all-destroying Time*: the threat of universal destruction resumes—Yama, as the god of Death, consumes the universe at the end of time—the *pralaya* is imminent. What is there still to burn after the firing of the Pāṇḍava camp? Still everything, according to Biardeau (Péterfalvi and Biardeau, *Le Mahāhārata*, ii. 295): i.e. the necessary men and women for life to start again on earth, represented here by the Pāṇḍavas. In Biardeau's characterization (cf. 13. 14), Aśvatthāman is 'a fire-lighter ready to light a fire, but a fire that the dust will make sooty' (ibid. 294, my translation).

CHAPTER 14

14. 2 *that celestial weapon Droṇa taught you*: see note on 12. 5.

14. 4 *Stepped from the chariot*: according to Biardeau, Kṛṣṇa delegates his power as an *avatāra* to Arjuna at this point (although he will intervene directly himself later), noting that Arjuna has literally 'descended' (Sanskrit *avatārat*) from his chariot ('Études de mythologie hindoue (IV)', 212f.).

14. 5 *blessed first The teacher's son*: i.e. Aśvatthāman—probably *because* he is his teacher's son. But perhaps more widely indicative of the spirit of detachment with which Arjuna acts in conformity with his *dharma* (as prescribed and exemplified by Kṛṣṇa in the *Bhagavadgītā*).

14. 7 *like the fire at the end of a world age*: the fire-storm at the end of a *yuga*—see Introduction, 'A cosmic crisis'.

14. 11 *showed themselves*: reading *-sthitau* against the Critical Edition's preferred *sthite*, giving the sense that the seers showed themselves, not the weapons.

14. 12 *Nārada . . . and Vyāsa*: Nārada—a divine *ṛṣi*, associated with the celestial musicians (*gandharvas*), and acting as a link between heaven and earth. For Vyāsa see note on 13. 13. The latter's arrival is redundant, since he is already on the scene; Nārada too may be one of the seers mentioned at 13. 13.

14. 13–15 *energy . . . power*: these translate the same Sanskrit word, *tejas*, which is a kind of fiery energy, but also the vital spirit in both warriors and ascetics.

14. 15 *dānavas*: see note on 12. 17.

the triple world: i.e. the inhabited universe of heaven, sky or atmosphere, and earth.

14. 16 *Then why . . . a great evil*: I have translated an extra line here, given in some manuscripts but not printed in the main text of the Critical Edition.

CHAPTER 15

15. 7 *brahmic-energy*: Sanskrit *brahma-tejas*. See notes on 12. 4 and 14. 13–15.

the vow of celibate Asceticism: Sanskrit *brahmacarya*—a vow of celibacy taken by ascetics and Vedic students. Arjuna practised extraordinary asceticism during his quest for weapons (*Mahābhārata* 3. 39. 10f.), culminating in his wrestling match with Śiva and his acquisition of the *pāśupata/brahmaśiras* weapon (see note on 12. 26). It is this version of the acquisition of the weapon (rather than the one connected with Droṇa) that is stressed here (12. 9). Cf. 15. 21, where Arjuna is said to have acquired the weapon from Droṇa.

15. 10 *the vow Of truth*: sometimes referred to as 'the act of truth', based on the belief, widespread in ancient India, that a person with the right qualities or qualifications could utilize the inherent power of truth to attain their ends (see Katz, *Arjuna in the Mahabharata*, 152 n. 18, for references).

15. 14 *dharma was violated*: see note on 5. 16–21 and '*Dharma*' section of the Introduction.

15. 19 *brahmaśiras weapon*: see note on 12. 4 above.

15. 21 *Brahmic-weapon*: Sanskrit *brahma-astra*; the *brahmaśiras* weapon—see note on 12. 4.

Duties as a warrior: *kṣatriya dharma*.

15. 25 *You*: is the inclusion of Aśvatthāman himself in the list of what should be protected a psychologically astute move by Vyāsa—the equivalent of trying to persuade the criminal to drop his gun for his own good?

15. 26 *a sinful act*: Sanskrit *adharma*. In what sense Yudhiṣṭhira would win through such an act is not clear; the general suggestion seems to be that Arjuna's weapon has been withdrawn for the good of *dharma*.

15. 27 *jewel*: see note on 11. 20.

15. 29 *nāgas*: subterranean serpents, sometimes depicted as men, or as half-man, half-snake.

rākṣasas: see note on 8. 30.

15. 31 *Here is the jewel, and here am I*: Scheuer stresses the almost organic relation between the jewel and Aśvatthāman (*Śiva dans le Mahābhārata*, 323 n. 44). In the light of that reading, another possible translation of this line would be: 'This is the jewel, and it is me!'

15. 31 *into The wombs of the Pāṇḍava women*: i.e. they will be made barren.

and I am . . . great sage: I have translated three extra lines here, given in some manuscripts but not printed in the main text of the Critical Edition.

CHAPTER 16

16. 2 *Arjuna's daughter-in-law*: Uttarā, the wife of Abhimanyu; see summary of Book 4: 'King Virāṭa'.

16. 3 *Parikṣit*: see Introduction, especially 'Fate' and 'A cosmic crisis'. Briefly, Madeleine Biardeau's reading of this whole episode in terms of the Purāṇic *pralaya* myth is that it passes from the fire to the flood to the re-creation. Between the night massacre and the resurrection of Parikṣit (in Book 14 of the *Mahābhārata*), there is this 'magic murder' ('meurtre magique') of an embryo in a woman's womb. From one perspective, the waters of the deluge, in which the residue of the conflagration disappears, are like a fertile womb which will give birth to the universe again. Conversely, it is possible to think of Uttarā's womb as the symbolic equivalent of the ocean of the deluge. (Uttarā is the daughter of the king of the Matsyas—lit. 'the Fishes'.) The rains of the Purāṇic myth would be fatal if they persisted for too long, destroying the residue committed to the ocean. But the rains are dispersed by a violent wind. Viṣṇu, become Brahmā, desiring to create, transforms himself into Vāyu (the god of the wind). This echoes the transfer of the jewel from Aśvatthāman to Bhīma (the son of Vāyu): the destructive power of Śiva-Aśvatthāman, of the fire and deluge itself, is henceforward checked for the benefit of a new beginning for life, initiated by Kṛṣṇa-Viṣṇu. This new life takes the form of the infant Parikṣit (grandson of the perfect devotee, Arjuna) to whom, at the end of the age, Kṛṣṇa delegates his powers on earth. According to Biardeau the entire purpose of the epic is thus brought to light in this scenario: the king is the emanation of God, and more particularly of his *avatāra*. (It should be remembered that Janamejaya, currently being addressed at the narrative level by Vaiśampāyana, is Parikṣit's son.) See Biardeau, 'Études de mythologie hindoue (IV)', 213–14.

16. 13 *Vedic study*: part of the required education of all twice-born males, undertaken during a period of studentship which begins with their *upanayana* (see note on 6. 4–8.). For details, see Doniger with Smith (trans.), *The Laws of Manu*, ch. 2.

Kṛpa: the very same Kṛpa who has helped Aśvatthāman destroy the Pāṇḍava camp.

16. 14 *kṣatriya dharma*: see section on '*Dharma*' in the Introduction.

16. 15 *Although . . . live again*: I have translated an extra line here, given in some manuscripts but not printed in the main text of the Critical Edition. As previously mentioned, the actual revival of Parikṣit takes

place in Book 14: 'The Horse Sacrifice'. A convenient translation of the relevant passage (*Mahābhārata* 14. 69. 1–11) is provided by Katz (*Arjuna in the Mahabharata*, 256).

16. 16–17 *really a brahmin... assumed the kṣatriya dharma:* see section on '*Dharma*' in the Introduction, and note on 3. 21.

16. 18 *with you... Among men*: I have translated with the sense of 'We two shall be the survivors in the human world for a long time', since this is no more than turns out to be the case: Vyāsa is still alive when Parikṣit's son Janamejaya is king. However, it also seems that Aśvatthāman, although condemned to be a wanderer, has some special affinity with Vyāsa, the 'author' of the *Mahābhārata*, a relationship perhaps reflected in the legend that Aśvatthāman is said to be there whenever the *Mahābhārata* is recited (Shulman, *The King and the Clown*, 135 n. 84). This line could certainly also be translated: 'Of all men, it is with you, brahmin, that I shall live.' See, for instance, Scheuer on the affinity between Śiva (and so Aśvatthāman) and Vyāsa (*Śiva dans le Mahābhārata*, 325 n. 46); and Péterfalvi's trans., *Le Mahābhārata*, ii. 292. For a western audience, Aśvatthāman's fate inevitably brings to mind that of the biblical Cain, or the medieval 'wandering Jew', Ahasuerus.

16. 19 *the forest*: the forest here indicating everywhere and everything that lies beyond the socially ordered world of the village or city. It was to the forest that the Pāṇḍavas went in their long period of exile; it is also to the forest that holy men and ascetics go to practise their vows. Significantly, Rudra-Śiva is the ascetic *par excellence*, and also, from Vedic times, 'the outsider', a solitary, unpredictable figure at the margins of the sacrificial world. Aśvatthāman's fate conforms, therefore, to his generally Śiva-like character in the *Sauptikaparvan*, and to that of renouncers (*saṃnyāsins*) in general (see Dumézil, *Mythe et épopée*, i. 218; Hiltebeitel, *The Ritual of Battle*, 330–1) . There is a significant difference, of course: Aśvatthāman's behaviour is not a matter of free choice, it is forced upon him by Kṛṣṇa. Furthermore, he will acquire nothing from his exile: his actions in the world mean that he will not go to heaven (*Mahābhārata* 13. 6. 33). (For a discussion of an interesting ritual passage in the *Śatapatha Brāhmaṇa* which may 'provide a ground plan' for some of these themes and others, see Hiltebeitel, *The Ritual of Battle*, 331–2.)

16. 22 *Kṛṣṇa's people*: Sanskrit: *dāśārhāḥ* (plural) in all manuscripts, although the context suggests it should be singular here, 'one who merits devotion', i.e. Kṛṣṇa himself, since there has been no previous mention of his people in this passage.

16. 26 *kṣatriya dharma*: see '*Dharma*' in the Introduction.

16. 27–8 *When Vāsudeva... wants peace*: see summary of Book 5: 'Preparations'. This is a précis of Draupadī's impassioned speech to Kṛṣṇa at *Mahābhārata* 5. 80. 1–45. Yudhiṣṭhira and the other Pāṇḍava brothers

have agreed that Kṛṣṇa should try to make peace with the Kauravas before it is too late. Draupadī reminds Kṛṣṇa of her humiliation at the dicing match, and the thirteen years of exile during which she has hidden her rage, waiting for revenge; and it is only revenge that will satisfy her now.

16. 30 *Duḥśāsana's blood*: see summary of Book 8: 'Karṇa'; cf. summary of Book 2: 'The Assembly Hall'.

16. 31 *debt to the foe*: cf. 16. 33: 'the entire debt'; apparently 'debt' in the sense of revenge, as demanded by Draupadī (see notes to 11. 10–15 and 11. 20), yet the precise sense in which this complex concept is used here is not clear. Although the 'debt' at one level is to Draupadī and those killed by the Kauravas, the Sanskrit word *ṛṇa* ('debt') may also mean a 'fault' (that is punished). In other words, Bhīma is saying, 'we have corrected the faults of our enemies by punishment'. For a discussion of this concept, although not in relation to the *Mahābhārata*, see Malamoud, 'The Theology of Debt in Brahminism', in *Cooking the World*, 92–108, and 291 nn. 8 and 11. The general argument of this passage, however, is clearly that the cycle of revenge is at an end, in the sense that 'we are all level now'.

because he's a brahmin: in the words of *The Laws of Manu*: '[The king] should never kill a priest [brahmin], even one who persists in every sort of evil; he should banish such a man from the kingdom' (8. 380, trans. Doniger with Smith).

16. 33 *my superior's son is my superior*: namely Droṇa, the teacher (Sanskrit *guru*) of the Pāṇḍavas, and his son (Aśvatthāman). On the respect owed to one's *guru*, see *The Laws of Manu* 2. 194f., and 2. 207, where it is said that one should always treat one's *guru's* son like one's *guru* when he is also a teacher (which only partly fits the case here).

the king: Yudhiṣṭhira.

16. 34 *the teacher*: Droṇa; see note on 11. 20.

CHAPTER 17

The accounts of Śiva's 'former deeds' which follow here and in the next chapter (18) provide what Hiltebeitel calls keys to, or reflections of, the preceding narrative. While this may be true of the myth of Dakṣa's sacrifice, retold in Chapter 18, the myth told here about the *liṅga* seems to be little more than a preamble to what follows. The editor of the Critical Edition, H. D. Velankar, finds it 'rather extraneous' (*Mahābhārata*, Critical Edition, introduction, p. xxix), a judgement with which Hiltebeitel, for one, agrees (*The Ritual of Battle*, 313 n. 44). However, in some versions the two myths are run together, in that Śiva emerges from the waters to discover Dakṣa making a sacrifice attended by the creation which has taken place in the meantime, and from which Śiva himself would have been excluded. This sparks his destructive anger. See O'Flaherty (trans. and ed.), *Hindu Myths*, 123–5, for a version like this, taken from the *Varāha Purāṇa*. For an account of the version given here, in the light of others, and a general analysis of the myth, see Stella Kramrisch, *The Presence of Śiva* (Princeton: Princeton University Press, 1981), 127–33.

17. 1–9 *After brooding... activity*: cf. 8. 144–7. Comparing these two passages, the complementary relationship between Kṛṣṇa and Śiva becomes clear. As Hiltebeitel expresses it: 'In reciting the former deeds of Mahādeva [Śiva], Krishna was responding to the same question from Yudhiṣṭhira as was asked of Saṃjaya by Dhṛtarāṣṭra. Where the Kuru king learned that Asvatthāman could succeed only by Krishna's absence, the Pāṇḍava king learned that he could succeed only by Śiva's presence' (*The Ritual of Battle*, 334).

17. 10 *the all-Pervading grandsire*: Brahmā.

the Original: Śiva.

The defects of living beings: Śiva foresees possible defects in the living beings he intends to create: they will need food and be subject to death. His austerities in the waters seem to be an attempt to rectify this. (On this, and the rest of the story, see the note on 17. 11 in the Critical Edition, p. 112.)

17. 12 *another creator*: i.e. Prajāpati, the secondary creator or demiurge, sometimes (but not here) an epithet of Brahmā—see 17. 16.

17. 15 *The progenitors, of whom Dakṣa was the first*: strangely Dakṣa appears by name here, but not in the retelling of the myth most commonly associated with him in Chapter 18. Dakṣa, as we see, is a son of Prajāpati, and therefore of Brahmā; he is a kind of secondary creator (or son of the secondary creator) and seer, present in each age, and particularly associated with the power of the sacrifice.

fourfold race of creatures: probably, divine, human, animal, and vegetable beings; but if referring to animals alone, then village, whole-hoofed, small, and jungle animals. See Brian K. Smith, *Classifying the Universe: The Ancient Indian Varṇa System and the Origins of Caste* (New York: Oxford University Press, 1994), ch. 8: 'Classifying Fauna', on the various ways animals were classified in ancient India.

17. 16 *Prajāpati*: see note on 17. 12.

17. 20 *world guru*: Brahmā; cf. the 'universal *guru*' of 17. 24, who is Śiva.

17. 21 *Lord Rudra was angry*: Śiva was angry because he emerged from his austerities to discover his task had been assigned to another, who had undertaken it without removing the defects he had foreseen.

liṅga: Śiva's phallus, here representing his generative power.

17. 24 *universal guru*: Śiva.

other guru: Brahmā.

17. 25 *I have made food...*: according to the note on 17. 11 in the Critical Edition (p. 112), Brahmā's solution to the food problem is only

temporary, yet 'propagation of the race and supply of food to its members must be automatic'. Śiva has come up with such a permanent solution with his *liṅga* and the herbs, and, despite his anger, he leaves them behind when he goes away to the mountains. The note concludes that 'We have to understand, though this is not actually stated, that with the help of these, Pitāmaha [Brahmā] secured uninterrupted creation and maintenance of creatures in the world.' In other words, without the herbs, living beings would have died. For a more detailed analysis, see Kramrisch, *The Presence of Śiva*, 127–33.

17. 26 *Muñjavat mountain*: a mythical peak in the Himālayas, where Śiva is constantly engaged in asceticism.

CHAPTER 18

For general remarks on the relation of the myth retold in this chapter to the *Sauptikaparvan* as a whole, see the Introduction ('A universal sacrifice'). Alf Hiltebeitel has made a detailed, fourteen-point comparison between the events of the *Sauptikaparvan* and the fully developed version of Śiva's destruction of the sacrifice of the gods (known elsewhere as 'Dakṣa's sacrifice') (*The Ritual of Battle*, 312–35). This in turn has been critically analysed by Jacques Scheuer (*Śiva dans le Mahābhārata*, 333–9); see also James W. Laine's summary of Hiltebeitel (*Visions of God*: 121–6). Two longer versions of the myth of Dakṣa's sacrifice, one of them taken from the *Mahābhārata* itself (Book 12), can be conveniently found in O'Flaherty (trans. and ed.), *Hindu Myths*, 118–25, which also contains a list of further references (pp. 324–5). For a general analysis of the myth, with some reference to the *Sauptikaparvan* version, see Kramrisch, *The Presence of Śiva*, 322–40.

18. 1 *their age*: Sanskrit *devayuga*; i.e. either the first age of the world, the *kṛta-yuga*, or the end of a full cycle of four ages (see Introduction, 'A cosmic crisis'). According to Hiltebeitel, through placing this myth at the end of a *yuga*, the poets of the *Sauptikaparvan* make the connection between the sacrificial ideology of the *Brāhmaṇas* (with which he believes the *Sauptikaparvan*, through its connection to the myth, to be permeated) and the eschatological character of the epic crisis (*The Ritual of Battle*, 334 f.).

18. 2 *they assigned the shares . . . worthy of sacrifice*: see Brian K. Smith, *Reflections on Resemblance, Ritual, and Religion* (New York: Oxford University Press, 1989), 74: 'The construction of a sacrifice, an ideally continuous and complete entity made out of the joining of discrete parts (rites, performers, implements, offerings, etc.), is a reconstruction of the universe itself in the sense that one supposedly reproduces—in a different form—the other.'

18. 3 *O king*: refers to Yudhiṣṭhira.

18. 4 *covered in a deer skin*: i.e. wearing the insignia of a celibate Vedic student (cf. 6. 4), but also carrying a bow. As Kramrisch remarks, no

wonder the other gods failed to know him in reality (*The Presence of Śiva*, 329).

18. 5 *the world-sacrifice*: this seems to refer to Śiva's destruction of the world at the end of an age, continuing the *pralayic* theme. Cf. *Mahābhārata* 12. 8. 36 in which (in the context of Yudhiṣṭhira's *aśvamedha*) Rudra offers himself in a universal sacrifice (*sarva-medha*) into which he pours all creatures and then himself (cited by Kramrisch, *The Presence of Śiva*, 61; cf. Scheuer, *Śiva dans le Mahābhārata*, 354).

the sacrifice Of rites: Sanskrit *kriyā-yajña; kriyā* itself is a general term for sacrifice, but here seems to refer specifically to the complex of *śrauta* or 'solemn' sacrifices, as opposed to the smaller-scale, but more widely performed, domestic sacrifice.

the eternal domestic sacrifice: Sanskrit *gṛha [gṛhya]*. For details see Smith, *Reflections on Resemblance, Ritual, and Religion*, 143–54.

the fivefold sacrifice: the text here is uncertain and difficult to interpret (this verse is missing from some manuscripts altogether). Ganguli, using a text which differs from that preferred by the Critical Edition, begins his translation of this: 'the sacrifice consisting in the gratification derived by man from his enjoyment of the five elemental substances and their compounds' (*The Mahabharata of Krishna-Dwaipayana Vyasa*, 12 vols. (1884–9; repr. New Delhi: Munshiram Manoharlal, 1970), vii: *Sauptika Parva*, 40). While it is true that *pañcabhūta* often refers to the five elements (earth, air, water, fire, and space/ether—see note on 7. 12), the context suggests that the reference is more likely to be to the five 'great sacrifices' (*mahāyajña*). Despite the name, these are in fact extremely simple and condensed forms of Vedic ritualism; as Brian Smith puts it, 'they represent a minimalistic form of Vedic ritual as a whole for householders with limited means' (*Reflections on Resemblance, Ritual, and Religion*, 197), and are supposed to be offered every day. Following the account in *The Laws of Manu*, the *mahāyajñas* are as follows: 'The study (of the Veda) is the sacrifice to ultimate reality [*brahman*], and the refreshing libation is the sacrifice to the ancestors [*pitṛ*]; the offering into the fire is for the gods [*deva*], the propitiatory offering of portions of food is for the disembodied spirits [*bhūta*], and the revering of guests is the sacrifice to men [*nṛ*] (3. 70, trans. Doniger with Smith, Sanskrit added by me from J. L. Shastri (ed.), *Manusmṛti, with the Sanskrit Commentary of Kullūka Bhaṭṭa* (Delhi: Motilal Banarsidass, 1983)). The 'sacrifice to men' translates the same compound (*nṛ-yajña*) which occurs in the *Sauptikaparvan* (translated here as 'the sacrifice to be offered to men'), and it is indeed the fifth *mahāyajña* in Manu's list.

18. 7 *the vaṣaṭ mantra*: an exclamation uttered by the *hotṛ* priest at the end of the sacrificial verse; on hearing it the *adhvaryu* priest casts the oblation offered to the deity into the fire. The *hotṛ* and the *adhvaryu* are both principals in the solemn (*śrauta*) sacrifice.

18. 7 *The four parts of the sacrifice*: literally, 'limbs' of the sacrifice—a standard metaphor for any part, instrument, or means of a sacrifice. These may be the four types of sacrifice listed at 18. 5. Ganguli, however, translates 'The four parts, of which a Sacrifice consists', although it is not clear what these are in this context (*The Mahabharata of Krishna-Dwaipayana Vyasa*, vii. 40). Moreover, since the limbs are said to flee, together with the gods, at 18. 17, when the sacrifice itself, in the shape of a deer, has already fled away (18. 13–15), this may be referring to means or instruments rather than the sacrifice itself. Alternatively, it may be a reference to a standard division of the sacrifice into four types: *nitya* (indispensable or obligatory), *naimittika* (occasional or calendrical), *kāmya* (optional), and *prayaścitta* (expiatory or purificatory).

18. 12 *The Vedas*: on the Vedas see the Introduction, 'The significance of the *Mahābhārata* in Indian religious culture', esp. n. 4.

18. 9–12 *goddess Earth quaked . . . Vedas tottered*: according to Hiltebeitel (*The Ritual of Battle*, 334 f.) this passage is an expression of the eschatological potential of the myth, i.e. an image of the (near-) end of the world.

18. 13 *the fire*: i.e. the fire god Agni, who is embodied in the sacrificial fire.

18. 16 *three-eyed Śiva*: Śiva is well-known to have a third eye in the centre of his forehead which acts as a channel for the internal heat he has acquired through asceticism. While it is regarded as a 'spiritual' eye, it also represents Śiva's power to incinerate the universe.

Savitṛ: the 'vivifier', an epithet of the sun. Bhaga and Pūṣan are also solar deities. Various explanations are given for their particular mutilations: for example, in fuller versions of the myth than that given here, Pūṣan is said to have shown his teeth in laughter when Śiva was cursed by Dakṣa–see Kramrisch, *The Presence of Śiva*, 322–40. The general idea, of course, is that the universe has been thrown into chaos and is on the edge of destruction.

18. 18 *blue-throated Rudra*: see note on 7. 2–5.

18. 24 *my king*: Yudhiṣṭhira.

PROPER NAMES AND EPITHETS

The purpose of this list is the purely practical one of indicating which character is being referred to at any particular moment. No attempt has been made to provide literal renditions into English of the names or epithets of the characters (e.g. Kṛṣṇā, 'Black'; Dhanaṃjaya, 'Wealth Winner', etc.). An invaluable guide, in this and other respects, for any prolonged study of the *Mahābhārata* is S. Sørensen's *An Index to the Names in the Mahābhārata* (see Select Bibliography). I have also made use of the very helpful but not exhaustive 'Répertoire des noms propres' in Péterfalvi and Biardeau's *Le Mahābhārata*, vol. ii.

As Ruth Katz has pointed out in connection with Arjuna, most of these names are typical oral epithets, i.e. formulas used to fill out the metre in lines of verse, rather than attempts to convey a meaning particularly appropriate to that context (*Arjuna in the Mahabharata*, 277). Nevertheless, all epithets do have meanings related to the characters' personalities, and therefore they sometimes provide a key to the interpretation of particular passages, as Dumézil and others have stressed. (Biardeau, for instance, provides what she calls 'a tentative interpretation' of the patronymics of the protagonists in 'Études de mythologie hindoue (IV)', 259 ff.) Where an epithet has seemed significant in the *Sauptikaparvan*, I have translated its meaning as part of the text.

Abhimanyu Arjuna and Subhadrā's son; husband of Uttarā and father of Parikṣit

Agastya Droṇa's teacher's teacher

Ajamīḍha royal ancestor of the Kurus and Pāṇḍavas alike

Ajamīḍha's scion Yudhiṣṭhira

Andhaka one of the peoples surrounding Kṛṣṇa; cf. Vṛṣṇis

Āṅgirasa clan descendants of the sage Aṅgiras; see note on 7. 54

Arjuna third of the five Pāṇḍava brothers; =Dhanaṃjaya=Pārtha Dhanaṃjaya; see Appendix

Aśvatthāman Droṇa's son; =Bhāradvāja; see Appendix, Introduction, and Explanatory Notes

Aśvin twins twin gods associated with the sun, agriculture, and healing; fathers of the Pāṇḍava twins Nakula and Sahadeva, by Mādrī

Bāhlika (usually spelt *Bāhlīka*) younger brother of Śāntanu, and so Bhīṣma's uncle; father of Somadatta, and so grandfather of Bhūriśravas

Balāhaka one of Kṛṣṇa's chariot horses

Balarāma Kṛṣṇa's elder brother; =Rāma=Saṃkarṣaṇa

Bhaga a Vedic solar deity; see note on 18. 16
Bhāgirathī river the sacred Gaṅgā or Ganges, Gaṅgā being the daughter of Bhagīratha
Bhairava Śiva
Bhāradvāja Aśvatthāman (Bharadvāja's heir)
Bharadvāja's heir Aśvatthāman, the grandson of Bharadvāja
Bharata prototypical ruler; forerunner of Indian culture; see Introduction ('The origins, composition, and transmission of the Sanskrit *Mahābhārata*')
Bhārata Dhṛtarāṣṭra 1. 32; Yudhiṣṭhira 7. 27, 10. 5, 12. 2, 12. 11, 17. 9; Arjuna 14. 3; Bhīma 16. 33
Bhāratas the descendants of Bharata, i.e. the Kurus and the Pāṇḍavas 12. 13–14
Bharatas (best of) Dhṛtarāṣṭra 8. 87, 9. 18
Bharatas (bull of the) Yudhiṣṭhira 12. 3, 12. 16, 17. 8; Janamejaya 13. 10
Bharatas (father of the) Vyāsa 14. 12
Bhava Rudra-Śiva
Bhīma second of the five Pāṇḍava brothers; = Bhīmasena = Vṛkodara; see Appendix
Bhīmasena Bhīma
Bhīṣma forefather of the Lunar (Kuru) Dynasty; =Gaṅgā's son= Śāṃtanu's son; see Appendix
Bhoja a group of the Yādava people associated with Kṛṣṇa
Bhoja king Kṛtavarman
Bhūriśravas a Kuru; son of Somadatta; see note on 5. 16–21.
Brahmā creator god
Brahman the Absolute; see note on 7. 7
Daitya one of a group of anti-gods (*asuras*)
Dakṣa a secondary creator and seer; see note on 17. 15
Dānavas a group of anti-gods (*asuras*)
Dāśārha Kṛṣṇa
Devakī mother of Kṛṣṇa
Devakī's son Kṛṣṇa
Dhanaṃjaya Arjuna
Dharma the personification of *dharma*; a god, and Yudhiṣṭhira's father; see the Introduction ('*Dharma*')
Dharmarāja Yudhiṣṭhira
Dhṛṣṭadyumna prince then king of the Pāñcālas; son of Drupada and brother of Draupadī; see Appendix
Dhṛtarāṣṭra the blind Kuru king; father of the hundred Kauravas; see Appendix
Dhṛtarāṣṭra (son of) Duryodhana 15. 14

Dhṛtarāṣṭra (sons of) the Kauravas
Draupadī Drupada's daughter; wife of the five Pāṇḍava brothers; = Kṛṣṇā; see Appendix
Draupadī (sons of) Draupadī's sons by the five Pāṇḍava brothers; see note on 8. 44
Droṇa brahmin-warrior; teacher of the Kauravas and Pāṇḍavas alike; father of Aśvatthāman; see Appendix
Droṇa's son Aśvatthāman
Drupada king of the Pāñcālas; sworn enemy of Droṇa; =Yājñasena; see Appendix
Drupada's sons Dhṛṣṭadyumna, Śikhaṇḍin, and others
Duḥśāsana brother of Duryodhana; see Appendix
Duryodhana eldest son of Dhṛtarāṣṭra, and king of the Kauravas; see Appendix
Dvaipāyana Vyāsa
Dvāraka the capital of the Vṛṣṇis, Kṛṣṇa's people
Gada Kṛṣṇa's younger brother
Gāndhārī wife of Dhṛtarāṣṭra and mother of the Kauravas; see Appendix
Gāṇḍīva bow Arjuna's bow
Gaṇeśa elephant-headed son of Śiva; leader—'lord of'—of his wild retinue (*gaṇa*)
Gaṅgā the Ganges river; a goddess; mother of Bhīṣma
Gaṅgā's son Bhīṣma
Garuḍa a bird deity; Viṣṇu-Kṛṣṇa's 'vehicle' or mount, portrayed on his banner; usually depicted with wings or talons and a beaked human face; =Vainateya
Gaurī Pārvatī, Śiva's wife
Gautama Śaradvat Gautama; Gotama's son; Kṛpa's father
Gautama's son Kṛpa
Giriśa Śiva
Gotama a seer (*ṛṣi*); father of Śaradvat, and grandfather of Kṛpa
Govinda Kṛṣṇa
Hanumān the monkey general; depicted on Arjuna's banner; see note on 12. 25
Hara Śiva
Hārdikya Kṛtavarman (son of Hṛdika)
Harikeśa Śiva
Hiḍimba a cannibal demon; see note on 11. 23
Himavat 'snow-clad'—the Himālaya mountain range
Hṛṣīkeśa Kṛṣṇa
Indra king of the Vedic gods (*devas*); father of Arjuna; =Maghavat=Śakra=Śatakratu=Vajrapāṇi=Vāsava

Īśāna Śiva
Īśvara Śiva
Jambū a mythical river; see note on 9. 13
Janamejaya son of Parikṣit; direct descendant of the Pāṇḍavas; the *Mahābhārata* is recited to him by Vaiśaṃpāyana; see Appendix (summary of Book 1) and Introduction ('Narration and Narrators')
Janārdana Kṛṣṇa
Jayadratha brother-in-law of Duryodhana, and king of Sindh; = Saindhava
Kāmboja name of a (semi-barbarous) people in Kuru camp; Kṛṣṇa's horses originate from their country
Kapardin Śiva
Karṇa ally of Duryodhana; the Pāṇḍavas' older half-brother; see Appendix
Kauravas descendants of Kuru; usually designating the sons of Dhṛtarāṣṭra and their followers; see Appendix
Keśava Kṛṣṇa
Kīcaka one of King Virāṭa's generals; see note on 11. 24
king of heaven Indra
king of the Pāñcālas Drupada
king of Sindh Jayadratha
Kṛpa a brahmin warrior; son of Śaradvat Gautama, and maternal uncle of Aśvatthāman; teacher of Parikṣit; =Śāradvat; see Appendix
Kṛṣṇa *avatāra* of the god Viṣṇu; =Dāśārha=Devakī's son=Govinda=Hṛṣīkeśa=Janārdana=Madhu (slayer of)=Keśava=Sātvatas (best of the)=Vārṣṇeya=Vāsudeva=Vṛṣṇis (bull of the)=Yadu bull=Yadus (foremost of the); see Appendix and Introduction
Kṛṣṇā Draupadī
Kṛṣṇa Dvaipāyana Vyāsa Vyāsa
Kṛtavarman warrior son of Hṛdika; a Bhoja friend of Kṛṣṇa, but in the Kaurava camp; =Hārdikya=Bhoja king=Sātvata (the); see Appendix
Kubera lord of riches; leader of the *yakṣas* and *rākṣasas*
Kumāra Skanda, the six-headed son of Śiva
Kuntī wife of Pāṇḍu, and mother of the three eldest Pāṇḍava brothers; = Pṛthā; see summary of the principal episodes
Kuntī's son Arjuna 8. 17; Yudhiṣṭhira 10. 7; Bhīma 13. 15
Kuru king of the Lunar Dynasty; common ancestor of the Kauravas and Pāṇḍavas
Kuru king Duryodhana 9. 41; Yudhiṣṭhira 10. 26
Kurus descendants of Kuru; the Kauravas and Pāṇḍavas; sometimes just the sons of Dhṛtarāṣṭra and their followers; see Appendix
Kurus (best of the) Yudhiṣṭhira

Kuru's race (son of) Dhṛtarāṣṭra
Madhu an anti-god (*asura*) killed by Kṛṣṇa
Madhu (slayer of) Kṛṣṇa
Mādrī Pāṇḍu's second wife, and mother (by the Aśvins) of the twins Nakula and Sahadeva
Mādrī (sons of) Nakula and Sahadeva
Maghavat Indra
Mahādeva Śiva
Maheśvara Śiva
Maruts storm gods, forming Indra's entourage
Maruts (lord of the) Indra
Matsyas followers of King Virāṭa who fought on the Pāṇḍava side; see Appendix
Maya a non-Āryan architect responsible for building the Pāṇḍavas' palace
Meghapuṣpa one of Kṛṣṇa's chariot horses
Muñjavat a mythical mountain in the Himālaya range
Nakula one of the Pāṇḍava twins; son of Mādrī and the Aśvins
Nandin the bull; Śiva's 'vehicle' or mount
Nārada a divine seer (*ṛṣi*)
Pāñcāla king Dhṛṣṭadyumna 10. 27
Pāñcālas people of King Drupada; allied to the Pāṇḍavas by their marriage to Draupadī; sworn enemies of Droṇa (and Aśvatthāman); see Appendix
Pāñcālas (king of the) Drupada 10. 24
Pāṇḍava Yudhiṣṭhira 11. 9, 11. 17; Arjuna 14. 2, 14. 4, 15. 6
Pāṇḍavas the five sons of Pāṇḍu; their followers and relatives; see Appendix
Pāṇḍava twins Nakula and Sahadeva
Pāṇḍu heir to the Lunar Dynasty; brother of Dhṛtarāṣṭra; 'father' of the Pāṇḍavas; husband of Kuntī and Mādrī; see Appendix, Introduction, and Explanatory Notes
Pāṇḍu's son Yudhiṣṭhira
Pāṇḍu's sons the Pāṇḍavas
Parikṣit grandson of Arjuna; son of Abhimanyu and Uttarā; see Appendix, Introduction, and Explanatory Notes
Pārtha Yudhiṣṭhira 11. 11, 11. 13; Bhīma 11. 25; Arjuna 12. 28
Pārtha Dhanaṃjaya Arjuna
Pārthas the three Pāṇḍava sons of Pṛthā (Kuntī)
Pārvatī wife of Śiva
Paśupati Śiva

Paulomī a goddess (also known as Śacī) personifying divine power; daughter of Puloman, and wife of Indra (Maghavat); see note on 11. 24
Pāvaki son of Agni; or son of Śiva=Skanda=Kumāra; see note on 4. 7
Pināka Rudra's bow
Prabhadrakas a group of Pāñcālas allied to Śikhaṇḍin
Pradyumna Kṛṣṇa's son by Rukmiṇī; =Sanatkumāra
Prajāpati the secondary creator or demiurge; sometimes an epithet of Brahmā
Prativindhya son of Yudhiṣṭhira and Draupadī; see note on 8. 44
Pṛthā Kuntī
Pṛthā (sons of) the three eldest Pāṇḍava brothers
Pūṣan a Vedic solar deity; see note on 18. 16
Rāma (of Yadu's race) Balarāma, the elder brother of Kṛṣṇa (not to be confused with the divine hero of the epic *Rāmāyaṇa*)
Rudra Śiva
Rukmiṇī wife of Kṛṣṇa, and mother of Pradyumna
Saindhava Jayadratha, the king of Sindh
Sainya one of Kṛṣṇa's chariot horses
Śakra Indra
Sāmba son of Kṛṣṇa and Jāmbavatī
Śambara an anti-god (*asura*); see note on 11. 22
Saṃjaya Dhṛtarāṣṭra's driver, who narrates the battle to the blind king—see Appendix, Introduction ('Narration and Narrators'), and note on 9. 57–9
Śaṃkara Śiva
Saṃkarṣaṇa =Balarāma=Rāma
Śāṃtanu Bhīṣma's father; see Appendix (summary of Book 1)
Śāṃtanu's son Bhīṣma
Sanatkumāra Pradyumna, Kṛṣṇa's son by Rukmiṇī
Śaradvat =Gautama; son of Gotama, and father of Kṛpa
Śāradvat ='son of Śaradvat'=Kṛpa
Śaradvat (son of) Kṛpa
Śārṅga name of Kṛṣṇa's bow
Śarva Śiva
Śatakratu Indra
Śātānīka son of Nakula and Draupadī; see note on 8. 44
Sātvata (the) Kṛtavarman 9. 6
Sātvatas a people belonging to Kṛṣṇa; =Yādavas
Sātvatas (best of the) Kṛṣṇa 16. 5
Sātyaki kinsman of Kṛṣṇa; a Vṛṣṇi allied to the Pāṇḍavas; =Yuyudhāna
Savitṛ the sun god; see note on 18. 16

Śikhaṇḍin the son of Drupada, originally born female; see Appendix (summaries of Books 5 and 6)

Sindh(u) region around the Indus river

Śiva one of the two great Hindu gods (cf. Viṣṇu); God;=Bhairava=Bhava=Giriśa=Hara=Harikeśa=Īśāna=Īśvara=Kapardin=Mahādeva=Maheśvara=Paśupati=Rudra=Śaṃkara=Śarva=Sthāṇu; see Appendix and Introduction

Skanda son of Śiva; =Kumāra=Pāvaki

Somadatta Bāhlika's son, and Bhūriśravas's father

Somakas sometimes referring to the Pāñcālas, and sometimes to allies of the Pāñcālas

Sṛñjaya(s) sometimes referring to the Pāñcālas as a whole, and sometimes to a subgroup, or to their allies

Śrutakarman son of Sahadeva and Draupadī; see note on 8. 44

Śrutakīrti son of Arjuna and Draupadī; see note on 8. 44

Sthāṇu Śiva

Subhadrā Kṛṣṇa's sister and Arjuna's second wife; mother of Abhimanyu

Sugrīva one of Kṛṣṇa's chariot horses

Sūrya sun god; father of Karṇa

Sutasoma son of Bhīma and Draupadī; see note on 8. 44

Umā name of a goddess, wife of Śiva

Upaplavya the city in King Virāṭa's kingdom where the Pāṇḍavas settled after their exile

Uttamaujas a Pāñcāla; brother of Yudhāmanyu

Uttarā daughter of Virāṭa, wife of Abhimanyu (Arjuna's son), and mother of Parikṣit

Vainateya Garuḍa

Vaiśaṃpāyana Vyāsa's pupil who recites the *Mahābhārata* to Janamejaya; see Introduction ('Narration and Narrators')

Vajrapāṇi Indra

Vāraṇāvata name of a city; see note on 11. 23 and Appendix (summary of Book 1)

Vārṣṇeya Kṛṣṇa

Vāsava Indra

Vāsudeva Kṛṣṇa

Veda(s) revelation; see Introduction ('The significance of the *Mahābhārata* in Indian religious culture')

Vidura uncle of both sets of cousins (the Kurus and the Pāṇḍavas); see note on 1. 15, and Appendix

Virāṭa king of the Matsyas, whose force is allied to the Pāṇḍavas; see Appendix (summary of Book 4)

Virāṭa's daughter Uttarā
Viṣṇu one of the two great Hindu gods (cf. Śiva); God; =Kṛṣṇa; see Appendix and Introduction
Viśvakarman architect of the gods; his earthly counterpart is Maya
Vṛkodara Bhīma
Vṛṣṇis people belonging to the Yādavas; Kṛṣṇa's 'race', and under his protection
Vṛṣṇis (bull of the) Kṛṣṇa
Vyāsa the 'author' of the epic, and a great seer who himself intervenes crucially in the action; =Dvaipāyana=Kṛṣṇa Dvaipāyana Vyāsa; see Appendix and Introduction
Yādavas 'descendants of Yadu'; Kṛṣṇa's tribe or 'race'
Yadu the ancestor of the Yādavas and Vṛṣṇis
Yadu bull Kṛṣṇa
Yadus (foremost of the) Kṛṣṇa
Yājñasena Drupada
Yama god of death
Yudhāmanyu a Pāñcāla; brother of Uttamaujas
Yudhiṣṭhira first of the five Pāṇḍava brothers; =Dharmarāja= Ajamīḍha's scion; see Appendix
Yuyudhāna Sātyaki

MORE ABOUT **OXFORD WORLD'S CLASSICS**

American Literature
British and Irish Literature
Children's Literature
Classics and Ancient Literature
Colonial Literature
Eastern Literature
European Literature
History
Medieval Literature
Oxford English Drama
Poetry
Philosophy
Politics
Religion
The Oxford Shakespeare